"Let it go, Krysty. He's out. Let it go and get out yourself."

The tall woman, her fiery hair in a tight knot at her nape, stepped back, allowing the branch to slip from her shoulders. It rolled a little, then fell, completely free of the main trunk of the fallen spruce. It landed with a terrifying crash on the very spot where Dean's head had been, narrowly missing Krysty's own legs.

Ryan had been kneeling by his son, but he stood and started to move to support Krysty. He was too slow as she crumpled like a dead leaf, toppling to the ground on her back, her eyes wide open and staring blankly at the sky.

"She's chilled herself," Trader whispered with an almost superstitious awe.

Ryan crouched at her side, holding her hand, chafing her wrist. "Happens when she calls on the Gaia power. Always happens. She'll be fine in a minute or two."

Mildred put a hand on Ryan's shoulder and eased him to one side. "Need to examine her properly."

"She's fine, Mildred."

Krysty hadn't moved, her face like ivory, her eyes blank and lifeless. A thread of brilliantly crimson blood inched from her nose and mouth.

Mildred checked for a pulse, then looked up at Ryan, her face bleak. "I'm sorry," she said quietly.

Also available in the Deathlands saga:

JAMES AXLER

DEATH LANDS®

Genesis Echo

A GOLD EAGLE BOOK FROM
W☯RLDWIDE®

TORONTO • NEW YORK • LONDON
AMSTERDAM • PARIS • SYDNEY • HAMBURG
STOCKHOLM • ATHENS • TOKYO • MILAN
MADRID • WARSAW • BUDAPEST • AUCKLAND

Like the wonderful Meat Loaf says,
I'd do anything for love.
And all my love is for Liz.
It always has been and it always will be.

First edition March 1995

ISBN 0-373-62525-1

GENESIS ECHO

Printed in U.S.A.

There is a belief that somewhere in the world everyone has an identical double. If I ever meet up with mine I'd ask him how he copes with being so irresistibly charming and sexually attractive to all women. No, listen, that's a joke, right? If I really bumped into my double then I'd figure that I was either mad or dead. Probably dead.

—*Heads I Win, Tails You Lose*,
by Lucky Giordano, priv. pub.,
NY, 1982

Prologue

The Volvo stood in the lee of a high bluff that protected it from the worst of the midday heat, the metal ticking and clicking as it cooled a little.

"By evening?" Ryan Cawdor asked.

"Should be," J. B. Dix replied, lying flat on his back, fedora shading his eyes, his glasses folded neatly and stuck in the top pocket of his jacket.

Trader had been complaining of some stomach pains earlier in the morning, but that might have had something to do with the fact that he'd eaten a very large bowl of fiery chili beans at ten o'clock, at the kindly invitation of a pair of Navaho sheepherders.

Abe was under the land wag, working away with a length of baling wire to fix a loose part of the exhaust system that had been rattling for the past thirty miles.

"How's your guts coming along, Trader?" the little gunner called.

"Gettin' better, thanks, Lee. Damn it! I mean, Abe. Yeah, gettin' better after I emptied myself out in that ditch an hour back. But a clean bed, some sleep and home cooking wouldn't be a bad idea."

"Be there by evening," the Armorer repeated.

"Looking forward to it," Ryan agreed. "Lost touch with how long we've been away."

"Long enough." J.B. flapped a persistent hornet from his face.

Trader was picking at his lip, where the sun had started a small sore. "You men sure changed since you rode with me. All this talk of goin' back. Getting to a fixed place. Wantin' to stop the moving."

Ryan nodded slowly. "It's true. All those years with the war wags, we were always moving, weren't we? One day the Lantic, then a few days later in the bayous. Week later chilling stickies in the Shens, then a firefight with the baron of some pesthole ville in the Darks."

"Damn right!" Trader whistled between his teeth. "That was the life all right. Never a dull moment. Living on the edge. Fighting over the edge. Running, always running hard, crossing the borderline. We should get back to that. Get us all back to the real basics of life."

"Nobody's stopping you, Trader." J.B. looked at the older man. "We heard you were living and we wanted to check that out. Now we know. You want to go back to that life, then we'll wish you all the best. But it's not for us anymore."

"Mean you got soft, Armorer?" He turned to Abe. "What do you say, gunner?"

"I say that I'll sort of go with what other folks decide," Abe said quietly.

"Well, I guess I'll meet up with all these good folks at the spread yonder." Trader sniffed. "Then I'll decide what we'll be doing after."

"No." Ryan stood. "You decide what *you'll* be doing, Trader. We'll do the same for ourselves. I reckon we ought to get this land wag on the highway if we're going to get back by dusk. Let's move it."

"IT LOOKS REAL PRETTY, Doc."

They stood together, looking at the way the setting sun was throwing their shadows ten yards beyond their feet. There had been a brief rainfall, the bank of dark cloud moving low over the desert, turning the rutted dust to mud in a heavy downpour, lasting no more than ten minutes. Now the land smelled clean and good, purged of the heat of the day.

Somewhere, far behind them in the foothills, they both heard a coyote howling.

"Another quarter hour and we'll be relishing some soup and fresh-baked break, Sukie. With some of the best souls in the whole world."

"I'm getting real antsy and nervous, Doc."

"Nervous, my sweet bird of youth?"

"Suppose they don't like me? I don't think I'll fit in with all of them. Them knowing you and about the time trawling and all that stuff."

"What difference does that make?" Doc Tanner had found himself stumbling over the explanation of his bizarre past, and he had grave doubts that the woman had really understood much of it, though she'd made a valiant effort.

"Old friends, Doc. And me bein' new and not their kind of caliber."

"Horsefeathers, madam! That is absolute tosh and complete balderdash!"

She pulled a face. "Sorry, Doc. But you and me have been getting on real well, haven't we?"

"Not even a house on fire could hardly have got on better than we," he offered gallantly, wrinkling his forehead at the sudden thought that there had been something not quite right with the sentence.

"Sure." She grabbed him by the arm. "I just wish it was you and me, Doc, together."

"Well, we shall have to wait and see what the future has to offer, Sukie. For now, we should step it out and get on to the house before dark." He looked around, hesitating and staring into the distance behind them. "Are my rheumy old eyes faltering, or can I make something moving out across the sands of the desert that are red with the blood of the square that broke and... I am so sorry, my dear. There goes my tripping tongue and my disconnected brain yet again."

She turned to shade her eyes and look westward, toward the vivid coppery glow of the setting sun. "Yeah, there could be something. About ten miles off, though. Can't tell which way it's moving, Doc. Best we get to the house, I guess."

"Indeed, I cannot but agree with that. One small thing puzzles me, you know."

"What?"

"We have been in the clearest sight of the ranch for an hour or more, yet nobody has noticed us and come out to greet us." Judas tossed his head and tugged at the reins. "Yes, quite right," Doc said with a smile. "We should indeed stop the talking and commence the walking. There will be a perfectly reasonable explanation, I am quite sure."

RYAN WAS AT THE WHEEL, applying the brakes and going through the gearbox. He brought the land wag to a halt and peered out through the windshield.

"There she is," he said. "Little gray home in the west, like Mildred called it."

The sun was low on the horizon behind them. Visible in a slight dip in the land, about three miles along the narrow sandy trail, was the white house.

J.B. was in the cab with him. "I'd have thought someone would have been on lookout and spotted us coming a ways back. Though I guess that rainstorm must have laid a lot of the dust. But, even so..."

"There'll be a good reason," Ryan said.

THEY HAD STOPPED about a dozen feet from the front door, which stood slightly ajar.

"Hello!" Doc called, his right hand creeping down to cover the butt of the Le Mat.

"Trouble, you figure?" Sukie asked.

"I fear that it is beginning to appear a distinct possibility. Perhaps you should wait here, my dear, and I shall reconnoiter."

"I'll come with you."

"Best you wait here."

"There's no sign of life, Doc. How about I go around the back?"

He considered the suggestion. "Perhaps you could go and keep a watch out, there. But I beg you not to go into the house until I have ascertained that it is safe."

"Sure thing."

He waited until the woman had walked around the side, then stepped up onto the creaking porch. Doc had often heard Ryan and Krysty speak about how they got a sort of a "feeling" that something was wrong.

"Well, I confess that I have that feeling," he said quietly to himself.

The light evening breeze was moving the half-open door very gently to and fro, the hinges creaking with the faintest whisper of sound. The sun was now close to set, and the hall inside was as dark as pitch.

"Hello," he said again, "is there anybody there? said the traveler. No, I believe that there isn't."

The house was silent. Doc stood in the entrance and hesitated for a few moments, hearing the crunching sound of Sukie's boot heels as she walked around the building toward the back door.

THE LAND WAG WAS less than a quarter of a mile away, and Ryan had again brought the vehicle to a halt. The sun was so far down on the western horizon behind them that the truck was sitting in a bowl of deepest shadow.

"I thought I saw someone goin' in the front door," Trader called.

"Who?"

"Come on, Ryan. How do I know who it was? Just looked like someone."

"Go ahead on foot," J.B. suggested. "This one's got a bad feel to it."

Ryan reached out and switched off the ignition. In the stillness they all heard the far-off howling of a lone coyote among the foothills.

SUKIE WAS STANDING a few paces from the kitchen door when it opened and Doc walked out.

"Made me jump," she said. "Anyone there?"

"I only walked straight through, but I called a couple of times. I did not look in any of the other rooms. Can't be anyone there. They would have answered me. I thought that there was the smell of..."

"What? Danger?"

"No." He holstered the big Le Mat. "Perhaps it was my imagination. You saw nothing? There wasn't a note left anywhere around?"

She answered him very quickly. "Note! Why should there be a note, Doc? If I'd found a note, I'd have given it to you, wouldn't I?"

"Yes, yes. Take it easy, my dear. You almost acted as if I had been accusing you of—"

"Well, there wasn't no note, all right? Means that we're here on our own."

The voice came from just behind them, making them both start. "Not alone. Hi, Doc."

Doc spun, eyes widening at the sight of his friend. "Greetings, my dear Ryan. The best of greetings. How are you, and did you find your old companion? There is something amiss here, is there not?"

"Time for all that later. How long you been here?"

"Five minutes. No longer. Is John Barrymore Dix with you? Abe and the Trader?"

"Covering the front of the house. All fine. Got a wag out front, as well. Was there a note? And who's this woman?"

"This is no woman, this is my... my friend. Susan Smith, known by the diminutive of 'Sukie.' And this is my truest friend, Ryan Cawdor, my dear."

She had been staring at the tall, powerfully built man with a horrified fascination, unable to keep from looking at the black patch over his left eye. And the dull gleam of the automatic blaster held in his right hand. "Hi, there," she said. "Doc's sure talked a bundle about you and the others."

"Yeah." He turned from her. "A note, Doc. Was there a note? They could've gone away for some good reason. If they did, then they'd likely have left us a note. On the front or, more likely, on the back door. Sure there was nothing?"

"I saw nothing. Nor did Sukie."

"Right, I didn't see nothing, Mr. Cawdor."

He ignored her, looking toward the main barn and the corral. "Livestock's gone as well. We checked for tracks, but that bout of heavy rain's washed everything away."

They all heard steps and moved toward them. J.B. appeared around one side of the building, raising a hand in greeting to Doc. Trader and Abe walked around the nearer wall of the house, both holding blasters.

The introductions took only a handful of seconds.

"It's Indians," Trader said vehemently, gesturing toward the shadowy outline of the mountains with the barrel of the Armalite.

"No bullets, no fire, no broken windows, no blood." J.B. ticked the points off on his fingers. "I don't see it as a firefight or an armed raid, Trader."

"Gone out hunting," Abe suggested. "Mebbe following deer and didn't notice the time passing. Could be they'll all return in the next hour or so."

Ryan considered the idea for a moment. "Possible, Abe. Guess that's the best one yet. But they wouldn't have left all of the doors open like this. It's unthinkable, isn't it? Must fine-comb the place. Soon as possible. First, though, we'll just have to bring the land wag up to the house. Get it parked safely out back. Abe, you can do that."

"Sure." He vanished at a quick trot around the side of the building.

Ryan continued. "All the rest of us can move inside and get some lamps lit and take us a room-by-room look around. Doc, you and..."

"Sukie." Both her fists were clenched tight in the pockets of her divided skirt.

He nodded to her. "Right. You two best go and wait in your room, Doc. Rest of us can search carefully."

"I would prefer it if you ceased treating us like a pair of country clodhoppers. We can search for clues, as well, Ryan. We are not totally stupid, you know."

"All right. Time's passing and the darkness is coming down on top of us."

The house was looming over them like a gaunt, ghostly sepulcher, the windows shadowed, blank eyes staring down at the small group.

He turned for a moment back to the stranger among them. "Sure about there not being any sort of message for us?"

"I said so."

"It is more than a remote possibility that Krysty or one of the others could have placed a letter for us, explaining precisely where they are, within the house, Ryan, my old friend." Doc moved a pace to stand next to the woman and placed a protective arm around her shoulders.

"Sure. Sorry, Doc. Sorry, Sukie."

"We will go into my room and keep out of your way, Ryan," Doc said.

"Fine." He watched them vanish into the kitchen.

J.B. was about to lead the way inside the house when he stopped, his eyes caught by something. He peered down at the lapel of his own jacket, breathing out, "Dark night!"

"How's that?" Ryan said.

"Rad counters," the Armorer replied. "Just look at your rad counter."

Ryan did so, angling it to catch the last fading rays of the setting sun. For a moment a rich crimson light confused him and he moved the little counter again, tilting it to make sure what he was seeing.

"It's right around into the red. That means we're all standing in one of the biggest radiation hot spots that I ever saw."

"Mine shows the same," Trader added. "Can't all've malfunctioned at the same time. Not even shading in the orange. It's way off the top of the danger scale."

For a few moments the three friends stood still, looking at each other, trying to work out what freakish combination of circumstances could have brought what the Apaches called "the silent death" to this secure, isolated place.

Chapter One

Ryan looked around. "Fireblast!" he said. "It's getting real dark."

At that moment they all heard the sound of a woman, from inside the building, screaming in blind terror.

J.B. was fastest, pushing open the kitchen door and running into the hall. Ryan was right at his heels, with Trader coming in a close third. They bumped into Doc in the shadowed hall, his arm around the woman he'd recently met during his trek in the mountains. She was sobbing uncontrollably, breath heaving, tears glistening on her cheek.

Ryan had his Smith & Wesson M-4000 12-gauge scattergun at the hip, cocked and ready. "What?" he said.

Doc was trembling, fighting for control over himself, while simultaneously seeking to comfort the almost-hysterical woman. "Two corpses in... No, it'll be all right, my dear, it will... I mean a dead woman and a man knocking on heaven's door... Come outside, Sukie, and away from it."

Now that they were inside the house, they could all taste the smell, a smell as familiar to each man as his own sweat. It was sour and bitter, flat and sharp, greasy and tart, all at the same time—the unmistakable taint of all-corrupting death.

"Where, Doc?" Ryan called.

"My room, I fear...." His voice faded as he hurried the woman out through the front door, where they could all hear the sound of the big Volvo land wag, driven by Abe, drawing to a halt.

"Get a lamp going." Ryan snapped out the command. "Got to have some light."

There were just enough remnants of the day left for them to see the two figures lying on each of the twin beds in Doc's room. It was even possible to make out that one of them was male and the other female.

But there wasn't nearly enough illumination to see who they might be.

Ryan's heart leapt in his chest at the thought that the woman might be his own beloved Krysty Wroth. J. B. Dix, the Armorer of the group, had the same fear that she might be his love, Mildred Wyeth, the black woman doctor, cryonically frozen way back in December of the year 2000, and brought to life again nearly a century later into the whirling madness of the postholocaust world that men called Deathlands.

Trader was fumbling around on one of the side tables. "Can't find the self-lights," he snapped. "One of you must know where they are. Your house."

In fact the house more or less belonged to Jak Lauren, the teenage friend of J.B. and Ryan. He had ridden with the others for some time, then split from them to marry and start a family on a spread in New Mexico. Tragedy had destroyed his happiness, and now he had been living at this ranch, with Ryan's eleven-year-old son, Dean, and Mildred, Krysty and Doc.

J.B. turned and picked his way past Trader, back into the kitchen. Ryan drew nearer the beds, stooping low, almost gagging at the terrible stench. Doc's instant summary looked like it had been accurate enough. The man was still alive, though his breathing would hardly have fluttered a moth's wing.

The woman was undeniably dead.

"Not Krysty or Mildred," Ryan called, reassuring his partner as he came in with the self-lights. "Just about enough for me to see that."

"And the man's not Jak or Dean. Too big for the boy, and Jak's white hair would blaze out in a privy at midnight. If it's not them, then who? Dark night? Ah, got it."

A sharp scratch was followed by a flicker of yellow flame, brightening as the wick of the oil lamp caught. J.B. clamped the gleaming glass chimney over it, adjusting the brass wheel to bring a steady light. He had pushed his fedora back from his high forehead, and his spectacles glittered.

"Hold it high," Ryan said.

Trader coughed. "I never did too good with sickies. Knife or a bullet wound and I don't flinch. You two know that well enough from all the long years you rode with me in the war wags."

· "Sure," Ryan replied, only listening with half his attention. "It's not a problem. You go check on Doc and the woman. See what they can tell us."

Trader had clapped his hand to his mouth and nose. He walked quickly from the room, bumping into the edge of the open door in his haste to get out.

"Can't blame the old man," J.B. stated, holding the oil lamp at shoulder level. "Seen better sights, and I guess we've smelled better smells."

"Woman's been gone for around a day. Two days at the outside. Eyes are milky, starting to dissolve. Belly's swelled with gas." He lifted the bone-thin wrist. "Gone through stiff. Starting to relax again."

The Armorer whistled, trying to breathe through his mouth. "Look at those sores around her lips. And the state of her hair. Ties in with the way our rad counters went off the scale outside the back there."

The scream and the discovery inside the house had temporarily driven that from Ryan's mind. Just as Doc and his friend had gone in, it had been J.B. who had noticed the miniature radiation counters, dating from the predark days. He and Ryan wore one on their lapels, and they were normally colored green, meaning that the ambient levels were completely safe.

Yellow meant some light radiation, orange was an indication that you were moving up the scale toward danger, and red was precisely that danger, imminent, all around, showing you were in a serious hot spot.

J.B. moved the lamp and looked down at the man. He was showing all the signs of radiation poisoning, His lips were tugged back off his loose teeth, showing bleeding gums. Like the woman, his hair was almost gone, patches of black blood showing across the peeling scalp, and his mouth was crusted with running sores.

"In a coma," Ryan said, pushing the man gently, then harder, but getting no response. He touched the pulse point at the angle of the man's throat, counting to himself. "Slow. Very slow. Breathing right down to the flat line, as well."

"Look." J.B. pointed to a small blaster on the table by the side of the man's bed.

"Over-and-under derringer."

"Yeah. Built like the .41-caliber Remington. Probably a European replica. Real rare gun if it was genuine. I recall Jak saying he had one of them somewhere around the place." J.B. picked it up, sniffing at it first, then checking the action. "Not fired. Got both bullets in it."

"Why?"

The Armorer looked at the dying stranger, lying in the tangled, fouled sheets. "My only guess could be that it was left here by his side for him to take the easy trail west. Mebbe got too sick to do anything with it."

"But who..." Ryan shook his head. "I can't work out what the fuck's been going down here."

"Two strangers, rad sick. Don't know why. Doc knows nothing, but he's been away, hasn't he? Said he'd just gotten back with that woman." He raised his eyebrows at Ryan.

"Don't ask me. Could be just friends. Could be a whole lot more than friends. Rain's beaten down any tracks that there might've been."

The Armorer moved back toward the door. "Listen, we have a double problem here."

"How's that?"

"First is to get the hell out of here. With the rad counters screaming red, we could get bone-fried if we hang around for a couple more hours."

"And the second thing?"

"Is to find what's happened to Mildred, Jak, Krysty and Dean."

THEY GATHERED on the back porch.

It was full dark, and Ryan and J.B. brought out a couple of oil lamps, setting them on the sills of the kitchen window where they immediately attacked a circling horde of small midges and bright-winged moths.

Sukie Smith sat on the stoop, head bowed, Doc's arm around her shoulders. She hadn't spoken, twice retching and bringing up strings of bile, golden bright in the lamplight. Her hands remained in the pockets of her skirt.

Doc was trying to comfort her, but she seemed to be oblivious to his words. Finally he looked up at Ryan. "This makes no sense at all to this poor addled old pate."

"Nor to me, Doc. You say everything was fine when you left on this sort of hunting trip."

"What's a sort of hunting trip, for Christ's sake?" Trader said.

"I merely wished to 'get me head together' as the saying has it. Find out where I was going. The usual classic odyssey of self-exploration."

"I don't rightly remember the old fuck talking like he'd swallowed all the long words ever made. Can't he just speak short and simple?"

Doc half bowed in Trader's direction. "I shall endeavor to gear my conversation toward your level, though I fear that the descent might be too great."

"Don't smart-mouth me, old man, or you'll find you walk with your asshole draggin' in the dirt."

"Leave it," Ryan said wearily. "Doc, you're triple sure that nothing was wrong? Not a clue of a problem? And no sign of these strangers?"

"No sign at all. I'm certain everything was hunky-dory. Their only small concern was that of caring friends for me and for my little expedition."

"And you saw nobody leaving the spread?"

"Nobody. I think there was a fire, somewhere around here, a brace of days ago, but I'm not certain."

"We should check the barns," J.B. suggested. "Could be clues there. Or a note."

"No." Ryan shook his head again. "The signs are that they left in good order. Mebbe because of the rad sickness. But I know..." He punched his fist into his other hand. "I *know* that Krysty would've left me a note."

"Where?" Trader asked.

"Table inside, but there isn't one there. By the front door or the back door. Checked them both and there's nothing. Doc and Sukie would've spotted them easily. There was enough light for it back then."

They all sat in silence. Trader walked into the house, and they heard his heels clicking on the oilcloth of the hall. He opened the front door, and there was a stillness. Then the door closed and he came back again. Taking the lamp, he held it close to the kitchen door, running his fingers over the scarred wood. The only person who showed any particular interest in what he was doing was Sukie Smith.

"The poor wretch in the bedroom could not tell us anything of what happened?" Doc asked.

Abe laughed. "That stupe bastard only got one thing to say and that's 'Goodbye,' ain't it?"

Trader turned back and replaced the lamp, moving to stand in front of Doc and the woman. "Which one of you came around to the rear of the house?" he asked with a gentle quietness.

Ryan sensed the implicit threat and started to stand, hand going to the butt of the SIG-Sauer.

"I did," Sukie replied, her voice shaking like an aspen in a hurricane. "And there was no note."

Trader slapped her hard across the face, knocking her to her knees in the dirt. "You're a fuckin' lyin' bitch!" he yelled.

Chapter Two

Doc Tanner wasn't essentially a man of violent and furious action. But he was up and across the porch and had swung a good solid haymaker at Trader's jaw before anyone could try to stop him.

Trader parried it without much difficulty, though he was taken aback at the speed of the old man's response. "Just hold off," he grunted.

"You damned dog!"

"What was that for, Trader?" Abe asked.

Neither Ryan nor J.B. had moved. They'd ridden enough miles with Trader to know that he wasn't a man to do something like that without having a good reason—or at least *thinking* that he had a good reason.

Doc stood in front of Trader, his fists clenched, eyes wide with anger. "You dare to strike down a defenseless woman like that?"

"I'm all right," Sukie muttered. She was on her hands and knees, head down, a line of blood, black in the lamplight, trickling from either her nose or her mouth.

Doc was blind with anger. He looked around and saw his ebony sword stick lying by the bench seat. He snatched it up, twisted the silver lion's-head hilt and withdrew the slender rapier. "I'll cut your damned throat open," he snarled.

Trader held the Armalite in his left hand, offering no threat with it. "Back off, Doc."

"Back off! How dare you?"

"Just let me ask the woman a question. One question. If she gives me the truth straight off, then we'll all know just what has been going on around here." He paused. "And if she lies again, then I'll keep beating her until she decides to show some sense."

Doc took a shuffling step closer to Trader, the point of the sword weaving like the tongue of a snake. "And you consider that enough explanation, do you?"

"Yeah."

"Ryan?" Doc turned to his friends. "You go to the ends of the earth to bring back this . . . this person and stand by as he insults my friend."

"Let him ask the question, Doc," Ryan said. "Then we'll all know what's happening."

Sukie had struggled into a fetal crouch. "Give me a hand up, Doc?"

He offered his left hand and pulled her upright, brushing dirt from her back and shoulders. He looked at the blood that came from a cut at the corner of her mouth. "Are you all right after that brutish attack?"

"Been better, Doc. Then again, I guess I also been a lot worse."

"What's this important question, Trader?" J.B. stared at his former leader. "You sure already?"

"Yeah. I'm sure already. Question's simple. What did you do with the note you found?"

"Upon my soul! This is intolerable, Trader. Susan has already told you there was no note back here."

"She lied."

"How do—"

Trader was losing his temper. "Let her give me the answer, Doc. Let her look me direct in the eye and tell me that she didn't find some kind of message out here. Better yet, as it seems like she's your woman, you ask her, Doc. See if she can tell her lie to you."

"Sukie?" Doubt rode over the word. "Tell him the truth. Tell us all."

Her voice sounded flat and full. "I got a letter."

"How did you know, Trader?" Ryan asked. "You were looking at the door, real careful."

"Four small window tacks. One got a little bitty piece of ragged paper caught under it, like something had been ripped away. The nails weren't old or rusted, and it looked to me like the bit of paper was new."

Doc wasn't listening to the explanation. He stared at the woman, his mouth sagging, his whole body drooping. "You got the letter, Sukie? Then, why did..."

"I saw it. Tore it down and stuck it straight into my pocket, Doc."

"You read it?" Ryan asked.

"No, sir, I haven't. There hasn't been a moment when I was able to do that."

"Why, Sukie?" Doc queried. "I find it impossible to come up with a satisfactory explanation."

"Easy. Liked you, Doc. You were kind to a lone woman. A woman wounded at that. You talked about your friends and how great they all were."

"I still do not really—"

"Seemed like they'd gone. If you didn't know why, then you couldn't go after them. Then there'd be just you and me. What I wanted. That was what raced through my brain. Then Ryan and these other men came and it was too late. Caught in the teeth of my own stupe lie."

Doc turned away, shaking his head. "This is, I admit, a severe disappointment, madam."

"Doc, I..." But he had stepped away from the porch, out of the circle of frail light from the oil lamps, and walked slowly into the darkness.

"Best that you give me the letter," Ryan said quietly. "Right now."

THE WRITING WAS undeniably Krysty Wroth's—the neat, clipped letters, with a forceful lean forward. The note was written in dark blue ink on unlined handmade paper, with crinkled deckle edges, and dated the day before.

Hi, lover. You read this and you're home. So, welcome back. Or, it might more likely be Doc. Either way, you see we're gone. You read this and you might not yet have gone into the house. There'll be at least one corpse, a woman, whose name is Raelene Warren. Dead of untreatable rad sickness. Husband is Ronny Warren. Too sick to move. Mildred offered to put him beyond pain, but he refused. Seems he's in some kind of Christian-linked sect that doesn't believe in that stuff. So Jak left the over-and-under. He might still be this side of the black river. Might not.

They came a day or so ago with a wag that's out in the barn with two dying horses. We guessed it was advanced rad cancer, and the cause is what

they called their "treasure," in the wag. Kind of
sick, Ryan. (Or Doc.) It's a nuke missile, rotted
and rusted and split from here back to sky dark,
leaking a trail from the old silo where they found
it. Dean reminds me that if it's Ryan or J.B.
reading this that you'll mebbe have spotted your
rad counters are going crazy.

Anyway, this place is poisoned. Too late to
move the wag and the missile. Jak said we should
go right away from here, and Mildred and I agree
with him. So does Dean. We've already been exposed for too long as it is. We're packing and
traveling light with saddle and pack animals,
some supplies and blasters and stuff. We're
heading south and west, into the hills.

Jak says to go eight miles south, past the old
bauxite working. Trail west goes up, partly on a
blacktop. Becomes a dirt road and forks. Take
left fork, and it'll bring you out higher up, by the
remains of a predark earth dam. Good water and
pasture. We'll go straight there and wait a week
before moving. If we move, we'll leave a message
there. Doc, you might be along sooner. See you
all soon, we hope. No time to bury the body.
Sorry. Now get away as quick as you can. That's
become a place of death and will be for a long
while. Lots of love from us all, Krysty.

Ryan finished reading the note, then carefully
folded the two pages and tucked them into a pocket.
"Well, least we know the worst," he said.

"And the worst could be worse," J.B. agreed.

"I'm sorry," Sukie said quietly. "If I'd have read it myself, then I wouldn't have kept it hid."

Doc walked back into the light. "I heard what Krysty said. The longer that we remain here, the worse are our chances of getting away free from sickness."

"She say it was a nuke out in the barn?" Trader asked. "Might just go take me a look."

"I'll come with you," J.B. said. "Probably it isn't as badly damaged as they reckon."

Abe grinned, tugging at one end of his mustache. "Could trade it to some baron, someplace?"

"Probably what those two strangers were thinking," Ryan said. "Got them death."

"We should go, Doc," the woman whispered, taking a hesitant step toward the old man.

He looked past her, staring at the door of the house, with the four tiny metal rails. "We will go, madam. We will go and rejoin my friends."

"How about me?"

"Leave her to go her own way," Trader snapped. "Never trust her again."

"No." Ryan gave Sukie Smith one of his smiles, as rare as July snow. "Everyone can make a mistake. Krysty taught me that. You want to come along?"

"If Doc will—"

"By the three Kennedys! While we stand here like Nantucket fishwives, the radiation is seeping into our eyes, hair, gums, blood and bones. Of course you are welcome to accompany us, Sukie."

Trader spit in the dirt, inches from her boots. "Damned if I understand this nicely-nicely shit! Comin' to look at this nuke, J.B., and you, Abe?"

"Sure," the Armorer replied, taking an oil lamp off the wall. "Then we move out. Best leave any food. It'll be tainted. Water in the well should be all right. Stock up on spare ammo, and then get out."

"I'll check on the dying man," Ryan said. "Doc, get what you want from your room."

"Can I help?" Sukie asked.

"Gas in the land wag. Fill her up. Probably be enough. Should be women's clothes in the house. Get what you want. We won't ever be back here."

J.B. LED TRADER and Abe back to the house in less than ten minutes.

"Krysty was ace on the line," the Armorer said. "Damaged, all right. Sooner we all get away from here, the better it'll be."

"The wag's fueled," Sukie announced. "But it took all the spare gas from the cans."

Ryan nodded. "Fine. Fifteen minutes for anyone to get what they want out of the house, then we leave here to find Krysty and the others."

"What about that poor devil in my room, Ryan?" Doc asked.

"I'll go see him."

"Burn the house," Trader suggested. "Best with a plague hot spot like this."

"Yeah," Abe agreed eagerly. "Want me to start setting the fires?"

Ryan shook his head. "No. Leave a notice on both doors. And nail one to the barn. Put them where the weather won't touch them. Big red warnings. You set a fire, and it'll spread the radiation for a hundred miles or more."

"Could bury the missile," J.B. said doubtfully. "Cut the rad emissions."

Doc snorted. "Stuff and nonsense, John Barrymore Dix! You know so much about weapons and yet you can suggest something as crassly foolish as that."

"Wouldn't take more than a half hour if we all got to it," Trader argued.

Doc pointed an angry finger at the other man. "I saw secret files on a big rad leak before skydark. They brought in eight hundred and ninety-two soldiers. Most of them were youngsters, in their teens and early twenties. There was a pile of radioactive material piled on the edge of a river. The lads were each given a pair of goggles, gloves and a shovel, then ordered to go out and run to this mound of rubble. Each man to take a single shovelful of the dirt and throw it into the river, then run back. That was all. One shovelful."

Trader sniffed. "So, what're you sayin' about it? I don't get you."

"Eight hundred and ninety-two young men."

"I heard you."

"Within less than two years seven hundred and sixty-eight were dead of various radiation-linked diseases. Virtually all of the rest were sick. Does that answer your question, Trader?"

"Sure. Yeah, sure it does," he replied, holding up both hands as though warding off a physical attack.

Ryan moved to the kitchen door, hesitating with his fingers touching the cold metal of the handle. "Doc, you and Sukie get some paper and do the notices. The rest of you check the wag and bring a couple of lamps. I'll go see to the man."

After the evening chill outside, the house retained the stuffiness and warmth of the day. The smell of decay and death seemed even stronger.

Ryan held the oil lamp in his left hand, entering what had been Doc's room. Ronny Warren lay in precisely the same position that he'd been in before, on his back, eyes shut. For a moment Ryan thought he spotted a glimmer of reflection from beneath the closed lids, but when he leaned nearer he decided that he'd been mistaken. After standing the light on the bedside table, he reached and tested the dying man's pulse.

He waited for several seconds, counting to himself. Even in the past half hour or so, it had slowed appreciably.

"Wasn't much of a treasure, was it?" he asked quietly.

The rise and fall of the chest was so slight as to be almost imperceptible.

Ryan weighed the options. There were only two, and they were both very simple. One was that he turn down the wick and walked out to join the others, the second choice to speed the man's passing.

Ryan's hand dropped to the butt of the SIG-Sauer, but bullets cost. It would take only a moment to draw the panga and slide it across Ronnie Warren's emaciated throat. But the one-eyed man felt an almost superstitious fear of having rad-poisoned blood on the clean steel of the cleaver.

He pulled up a handful of the blanket, careful not to touch any of the stains, then pressed it down hard over the man's face, pinching the nose between finger and thumb, the ball of his hand smothering the mouth.

The struggle was very small and very short.

Once it was over, Ryan turned down the wick of the lamp until the room was in total darkness. Then he turned on his heel and walked out to rejoin the others.

Chapter Three

The ruins of the bauxite diggings were just visible in the ghostly gleam of the rising moon, as were the stark ribs of ancient wagons, sunk deep in the drifted sand, with the rusted rims of the old wheels.

Only one of the front lights on the land wag was working, and Abe, in the cab, kept the speed down to a little over a brisk walking pace.

"Better arrive a little late, but all in one piece, than run early and end up in little pieces," Trader said, amending one of his war wag sayings to suit the moment.

He was sitting in the back of the rebuilt Volvo, next to Sukie, but they hadn't exchanged a word since the sudden burst of violence over the purloined letter.

"Here comes the fork," Ryan warned. The blacktop had turned into a dirt trail a mile or so behind them.

"Which way did Krysty say?" the little gunner asked.

"Left. Watch out for the remains of an old dam someplace around here."

"Then what?"

Ryan thought about it. "Didn't really say. The others are going to be up there anyway and it's full early. They'll hear us coming miles off."

THE MOON WAS GROWING and brightening, casting sharp-edged shadows from the towering saguaro that dotted the sides of the track.

"There's the dam," J.B. said, pointing with the muzzle of the scattergun. "Or what's left of it. Looks like it split clear down the middle with a quake."

It had once filled the broad valley, three hundred yards across and close to two hundred feet high. Now it barely hindered the progress of a fast-running river that coursed ahead of them, crossed by a sturdy wooden bridge.

"Keep going," Ryan said. "Once we get over there, pull off and shut down for a minute. See if anyone's around."

The planks and struts rattled and shook, but held firm as they inched over the foaming water. Abe steered in toward a wider place and heaved on the brake. He switched off the engine, and they all sat in the sudden, deafening stillness.

"Why not call out to them, Ryan?" Trader asked. "Night like this, it'll carry miles."

"Could carry to the wrong people," he replied. "They'll have heard us, if they're near."

"Long as that bastard rad sickness don't have them in its bloody claws," Sukie whispered to Doc, loud enough for them all to hear.

The sound of the desert night gradually crept back around them. A hunting owl swept low overhead, making Doc start, and they all heard the nerve-shivering cry of a hunting pack of wolves, somewhere much higher up in the surrounding bowl of the mountains.

"Ten minutes," J.B. said, checking his wrist chron, angling it toward the moonlight to see the figures more clearly. "If they're around here, they should be about ready to show themselves to us by now."

"I would venture to suggest that they aren't able to make out who it is driving this truck," Doc stated. "Our dear friends might suspect that we are malefactors, pursuing them with a villainous intent."

Ryan considered the possibility. "Jak Lauren's got great night vision, with those ruby eyes of his. But, you could be right, Doc. I'll step down and walk a few yards clear, so they can see me if they're watching from hiding. Everyone up on full red alert."

He dropped cautiously from the rear of the wag, boots crunching among the small pebbles. The blaster was cocked in his hand, and he knew that the other men were covering him with their own array of weapons.

Ryan walked a little way up the trail toward a sharp bend to the left. He was straining to see or hear the first sight or sound of any danger, but the roar of the river behind him was drowning out most sounds. And nothing was moving.

Someone was there.

Ryan felt it before he saw anything. The short hairs prickled at his nape as his index finger took up the tension on the trigger of the P-226.

A cluster of fallen boulders, rust red in sunlight, black as marble in the moonlight, stood off to the right of the trail, and Ryan moved quickly to their shelter.

Behind him he heard a flicker of sound as the others reacted in turn to his own instinctive reaction.

Hidden behind the great pile of rocks, Ryan waited, his eye raking the dark pool of shadow that lay spilled everywhere around him.

But the voice was behind.

"Getting old when watch wrong way."

Ryan didn't move at all. "Hi, Jak."

"Would have had knife between third and fourth spine bones, Ryan."

"I believe you, kid."

The youth laughed quietly at the old insult. "See J.B. in the rig. Catch moon off glasses. Doc blundering like buffalo in wallow. Loudest quiet mover I know. Who else?"

"Trader and Abe are in the back. And Doc found himself a woman up in the hills."

Jak stepped silently from hiding, appearing less than twenty feet away from where Ryan was crouching. "Good for Doc." His mane of white hair was tied back under a dark-colored bandanna for night movement.

"Where are the others? They all safe?"

"Sure. No sign of rad sickness. Mildred figures all right."

Ryan hoped privately that the woman was correct. Perhaps the worst bane of Deathlands was the varied forms of radiation sickness and the infinite range of genetic disorders that they propagated.

"We just got back to the house. Hour or so ago."

"What's going on, Ryan?" The loud bellowed query came from Trader.

"Everything's king-ace," he replied. "Coming back down with Jak."

"Saw note?" the teenager asked.

"Yeah."

"Warren dead?"

There was a momentary hesitation that Ryan couldn't avoid and knew that Jak would have picked up on, and interpreted correctly. "Yeah. Both dead."

"Best that way. Fire house?" He answered his own question before Ryan could reply. "Would have seen flames. Thought of it. You think of it, Ryan?"

"Sure. Not best idea. Left warning anyone came by." He realized how infectious Jak's clipped way of speech was.

"Bad rad leak," the albino said.

"How far to where you're camped?"

"Less than mile. Good wag?"

"Good enough."

They reached the Volvo, and Jak greeted old and new friends alike with a formal clasp of the hand.

"Come meet others," he said.

"Be good," Ryan agreed. "Been a long time."

THE TALK AROUND THE FIRE was like the most complex Navaho rug, intricately woven and interwoven, with everyone wanting to add their own strands to the pattern. Dean told his father about a bobcat he'd nearly shot, Mildred and J.B. whispered to one side of the fire, Jak was in earnest conversation with Trader and Abe about how best to balance a throwing knife, Doc and Sukie were the quietest.

Ryan and Krysty decided, unspokenly, to save their private talk for bed.

THEIR BLANKETS LAY between the land wag and the fire, giving them the best of seclusion and warmth. By twelve, the night had turned bitingly cold. Away beyond the truck, by a nest of young sycamores, the horses moved quietly.

Krysty lay on her elbow, her breathing returning slowly to normal. "That was good, lover," she said.

"Always is," he replied.

"That's glib. You know what I mean. After all those weeks away, that was *very* good."

He lay flat on his back, her thigh resting over his, just brushing against his cock, making it give the first faint stirrings of revived life.

"Good to be all back together," he said.

"I suppose so."

"Suppose?"

"Doc's new woman. Sukie. There's unease between them, isn't there?"

"Partly over that letter she took. But I think she's learned her lesson."

"She riding with us?"

Ryan smiled, his teeth white in the ruddy glow from the dying fire. "Who knows, lover? Still a lot of talking to be done in the next day or so."

"Doc was upset at leaving Judas at the ranch," Krysty said. "Funny. Best example of a love-hate relationship that I ever did see."

"Couldn't have gotten it on the wag. Judas would've kicked out the walls."

"You left it tied or free?"

"Free. Doc suggested, at the last moment, that he'd ride the mule up here. Too slow, we figured. But it can leave the spread if it wants to do that. Got enough sense. More sense than a lot of people."

She lay down again, staring up at the velvet sky. "Missed you, lover. No, don't just tell me that you missed me, too. Not what I'm saying. I'm saying that I *knew* I'd miss you. Knew that. But it was much harder than I'd figured."

"Hard for Mildred?"

"Sure. But she and J.B. don't go far back like you and me." She paused. "Or like you and Trader."

He read the message. "Saying that it worries you?"

"Some."

"Come between us?"

"Of course. Be triple stupe to think it might not raise a problem."

He sighed, moving his hand to touch her stomach, moving up, across her sweat-damp muscles to her breasts. "I swear on your life, lover, that Trader steps nowhere between you and me. Between me and any of us."

"Talk's cheap, Ryan."

"I know it. Just don't look for trouble when there isn't any. Fact is, being with the old man again hasn't been easy. Still thinks he runs J.B. and me, like when we rode the war wags together. Had some straight-edge moments."

"Better? Has it been getting—" Krysty gasped as he took one of her nipples between finger and thumb and gently squeezed and rolled it. "That's ... Yeah, lover ... Oh, yeah."

The conversation rested on the back burner for the next fifteen minutes or so.

THEY MADE LOVE for a third time, just as the faint glimmer of the false dawn was seeping into the canyon, over the jagged tops of the hills around.

Ryan had awakened, blinking his good eye open, feeling the remnants of a dream in which he lay in a bed with a dead man, whose bony fingers, gloved in dangling shreds of stale flesh and papyrus skin, were gripping his own mouth and nose, making breath impossible and death certain.

His heart was pounding, and he was aware on waking of the wonder of having the woman he loved at his side.

Krysty, deeply sensitive, felt Ryan's distress and came from sleep with him. She folded her arms around him and clutched him to her until the darkness of the nightmare had eased away and he was quiet.

"Bad?" she whispered, glancing around to see if anyone else had been disturbed, checking them all off in her mind: J.B. and Mildred, bundled together; four separate hammocks that were Dean, Jak, Trader and Abe; and a last blurred heap of bedding that concealed Doc and Sukie.

"Not good. Rad-sick man at the ranch."

"Ronny Warren?"

"Yeah, that was the name."

"Poor bastard. He and the woman thought they'd found their hearts' desire. Turned out they'd just taken their bane to their souls."

Pressed close together, Ryan felt his body reacting again to Krysty. He slipped his hand between them, finding her warm and ready for him, her thighs parting to grant him access.

"From behind this time," she breathed.

She rolled over onto her belly, sighing as Ryan slid above her, his erection thrusting. Reaching down she guided him in, breathing out as he filled her. She brought up her knees into more of a crouching position, feeling the hard walls of his stomach against the curve of her buttocks.

They began to move slowly together, with perfect rhythm. Ryan had one arm around Krysty's waist, under her belly, stroking her, his other arm gripping across her shoulders, keeping himself firmly in place.

"Not yet," she panted. "Soon, but not yet."

Faster, together. Once Ryan slipped out with the force of his lovemaking, but slid straight back on the next stroke, harder and deeper.

Krysty's long sentient hair was flowing down across her smooth back, seeming to move with her, caressing Ryan's chest, sparkling like fiery diamonds in the swelling light of the true dawning.

Ryan felt her begin the tidal wave of her orgasm, the powerful internal muscles contracting and squeezing him with a sensation so exquisite that it bordered on pain, sucking him in and on.

"Yeah, lover..." she whispered softly, warning him of her readiness, her head thrown back, pushing her hips into him. "Now..."

THEY LAY HOLDING HANDS, side by side, staring at the milky sky, aware of the dawn beginning to filter into the canyon around them. But it was still close to full dark, and they could only just make out the shifting shapes of the horses, all of whom had begun to stamp and whicker uneasily.

"What's up with them?" Ryan asked quietly. "Think it's that bobcat Dean mentioned?"

They both heard the sharp sound, from somewhere farther back down the trail, of one stone shifting against another. "Someone's coming up from the valley," Krysty whispered. "About a hundred paces off. Around the last bend, by the old dam."

Ryan swung out from under the blankets, pulling up his pants, the SIG-Sauer cocked and ready. He crouched flat against the condensation-slick flank of the land wag and stared into the misty morning.

A little way off, J.B.'s head appeared from his bedroll, as he quickly adjusted his glasses. "What?" he said, just loud enough for Ryan to hear him.

"Someone or something down the trail." He jerked with the muzzle of the automatic to point where he meant.

Jak was awake, like a ghost in the gloom, holding his satin-finish Colt Python.

Beyond him was the grizzled demon of the Trader, his Armalite flourished like a magician's wand, waiting patiently to see what was going down.

Though Doc was normally a solid sleeper, the flutter of movement around the camp jerked him half awake. He kicked off the blankets, revealing the half-naked figure of Sukie Smith.

"By the— What passes here?" Doc said in a loud booming voice that echoed around the hills.

"Fuck," Trader cursed, in an angry, flat voice.

"Get down and keep quiet, Doc," Ryan whispered urgently. "Something's out there."

Whatever it was had been provoked into action by the appearance of Doc. There was a strange, unearthly cry from the half-light, and the noise of stones rattling under charging feet.

Doc had stooped and drawn his Le Mat and stood his ground, squinting down the trail, trying to make out what creature was threatening him.

He began to laugh.

Chapter Four

From where he was standing, Doc could see farther around the bend in the trail than any of the others, and he saw the nature of their attacker before anyone else.

"Judas!" he called, doubled over with laughter, almost dropping his heavy revolver. "Upon my soul, but it is only proud, faithful Judas."

The mule came into sight, silhouetted against the brightening sunrise, galloping toward the camp at an uneasy trot, its long ears pricked.

By now everyone was awake, Sukie snatching at the blanket to cover her nakedness, Dean rubbing sleep from his eyes, Abe emerging from his cocoon of bedding. Everyone started to join Doc's amusement.

"Come here, you Deathlands Caliban," Doc called, the Le Mat down at his side.

Judas took him at his word.

Not altering his gait, he headed straight for the old man, who stood his ground until the very last moment, when it became obvious to him, as it had to everyone else there, that the mule really wasn't going to stop.

"Jump!" Trader yelled, starting to lift the Armalite to his shoulder.

Krysty saw the threatening movement and shouted for him not to shoot.

Doc dived sideways, landing clumsily on his shoulder, dropping the blaster, avoiding a vicious nip from Judas's curved yellow teeth as he fell.

The animal skidded to a halt, turning its head from side to side as if it had momentarily lost sight of its prey. Doc was sprawled on his back, dazed by the attack. Sukie moved quickly to stand between the helpless man and the animal, holding out her left hand toward the mule.

"Here," she said, her voice calm yet firm. "Come here to me, Judas. Now!"

The mule hesitated, its flanks shuddering with the effort of its charge up the hillside. Its eyes were bloodshot, rolling in the deep caverns of the angular skull. Slowly, very slowly, it lowered its head and began to walk toward the woman.

Doc scrambled to his feet, fumbling around for the gold-engraved Le Mat. He found the weapon and held it in his right hand, waiting to see if he was going to need it.

Sukie ignored him. "Come on, Judas. You clever animal, coming all this long way to find us. You must need some good grass and some fresh water." She patted it on the neck as it reached her, then turned to Doc.

"Shall I tie it with the horses?"

"Keep bit away," Jak replied, grinning at the tableau. "Judas spooks 'em."

So, the day began.

ONCE THE REMINISCENCES and the storytelling had begun to wind down, the talk turned from the past to the future. It was Ryan himself who brought the subject up.

Trader had just finished a long anecdote about a run-in with some bounty hunters over the old Canada line, which had ended in a collapsing mine shaft.

"Enough of then," Ryan said. "Time to start thinking about what we do now."

There was a long silence, while everyone switched their minds around. J.B. spoke first. "I don't see much hope of getting back to the house. Not for a long while."

Jak, who was most concerned, agreed. "Half-life rad poison could be forever."

"We got the wag and some fuel." Abe coughed. "I reckon enough to take us four or five hundred miles."

"I fancy trying out these jumps you told me about." Trader grinned at Ryan and J.B. "Would've made traveling easier in the good old days."

"Jumps aren't that easy," Ryan said. "We still don't have any idea of how to control them. Can't tell where we might finish up. Once it was in Russia. Another time we reckon it was on one of those circling space stations I heard about from old books and vids. Not the best fun in the world."

"Makes you feel sick," Dean offered. "Like when you roll all the way down a steep hillside."

Trader smiled at the boy. "My hill-rolling days are well past me, son."

"With the land wag and the horses, we could go most anywhere we wanted." Sukie flushed as everyone looked at her. "I got a sister, last I heard was living in Hope Springs. Could we all go visit her?" She spoke to the group in general, but addressed her question specifically to Trader.

"We'll do what most of us agree," he replied. "That has always been our way. If we are to enter the devil's caldron of the mat-trans chamber, then we shall go the Lord knows where. I doubt that it will be Hope Springs."

"Frontier pesthole," Trader muttered. "Was there years ago. Had a breakout of black-shit fever. Wouldn't want to go back there again. Not for a bag of jack."

"Well, I only got one relative that I know of, and if that's where she lives, then that's where I think I should go." She was stubborn, as though Trader's dismissive comment had sparked resistance.

Doc patted Sukie's hand. "My dear, madam, you shall go where you wish."

"You'd come with me?"

Doc stroked his chin, as if he were considering whether he needed a shave. "I think it is best to postpone such a decision until it becomes necessary."

"You said you went into the hills because you were tired of your friends, Doc."

"Not quite true," he argued. "I was far more tired of myself and tired of the life that the whitecoats had condemned me to. These people here—my friends and companions—are all that I now hold dear and who have sustained me through the long days and nights of darkness."

"I thought you cared for me, Doc?"

This public display of emotion was embarrassing the old man. "If the rest of you will excuse us," he said, "Sukie and I will take a short walk together. Perhaps to the top of the ruined dam. Look at the river and the hills and discuss our lives and what we might yet make of them."

They went close enough to the tethered Judas for the mule to try a halfhearted kick at Doc.

"She'll come with us," Trader said the moment they were out of earshot. "Woman can't do without a man."

"Woman needs a man like a turtle needs a helicopter," Mildred commented.

"Yeah, sure. Fancy little saying. One I like is the truth about what a woman needs from a man. The answer is just what the man happens to be out of at that moment." Trader laughed. "She'll come with Doc."

Krysty shook her head. "If I was into betting, Trader, I'd lay good odds that you're wrong."

Ryan clapped his hands. "Come on. Too many words and not enough talking."

IN THE END, after a good deal of talking, with everyone offering opinions, it became clear that there wasn't much of an argument.

Trader was keen to jump, having heard so much about the experience, and Abe, these days, tended to go along with everything that Trader suggested. Jak also made it obvious that the part of his life that had brought him to the Colorado Plateau, with his wife and baby, was ended forever and he wished to move far and fast.

Ryan inclined to side with them. He had told Krysty in the quiet moments between their lovemaking that he'd had enough of spine-jarring wags across unmade, quake-rippled highways. Even the brain-scrambling uncertainty of a jump was preferable to that for him.

Krysty was happy to agree to that, as was Dean. The boy quickly became bored with hanging around in the same spot for too long and was eager for fresh fields.

J.B. was less certain. "Could be interesting to drive up north and take a look around the Rockies."

Mildred sided with him. "I agree with John. Get in the jump chamber in the guts of some sepulcher of a redoubt, and you never know how things'll turn out."

Doc and Sukie had been away for a long time, out of sight of the others. When they eventually returned it was close to the middle of the day. Krysty noticed that the buttons on Doc's shirt had been unfastened and rebuttoned in the wrong order. There were also marks of red sand on the back of the woman's dark blue jacket that had resisted attempts to brush them clean.

"Well, Doc?" Trader asked. "What've you and the little lady decided?"

"We have discussed the matter at some length, thank you, Trader. Our decision is that we will go with the majority, while both reserving the right to alter our minds at some undecided future date."

"Still like to see my sister," Sukie mumbled. "Gotta do that someday."

"And so you will, my priceless pearl of the undiscovered Indies."

Trader laughed. "Told you, Krysty. Said she'd stand by her man."

Krysty didn't rise to the taunt.

Ryan looked around the group. "Breaks down that five are kind of definite about wanting to go and make another jump out of here. Two are less certain. And Doc and Sukie'll go along with the majority. That means we go."

THE NEAREST REDOUBT WAS the one that had auto-destructed, nearly killing them all, when first they'd met again with Jak and his bride. It wasn't that far from where they were camped, and there was enough room in the Volvo land wag for all of them.

"Means taking our leave of Judas. This time for good, Doc," said Ryan.

"I greet that news with the oddest mix of emotions that ever plagued a man."

"Could always put a bullet through its skull. That way you know it won't suffer in any way."

Doc shook his head. "I think not, but I appreciate the generosity of spirit that lies behind the offer, my friend. It is the rest of the wildlife of New Mexico that should walk from here on in fear and trembling."

"We'll let the horses go, as well. And Jak reckons that there are a number of wild mules in the hills. Figure Judas could find himself cock of the heap. Get a harem of pretty little ladies at his beck and call." Ryan grinned. "Come back here in ten years or so, and you won't be able to move without stepping on one of Judas's brood."

Doc smiled. "I believe that you speak with a straight tongue, Ryan. Allow me a few moments to bid the creature farewell."

The horses were gone, running free as soon as their bridles were removed. Everyone had walked to the wag, except Doc, who was standing near the mule, keeping himself carefully out of reach of hooves and teeth. He was talking to the animal, and once they saw him pluck out his swallow's-eye kerchief and dab at his face with it.

"Old fool's sun-stupe," Trader said. "Piping his eyes over a mule."

"Why don't you keep your opinion to yourself, Trader?" Sukie snapped.

"Well, forgive me for living, slut."

Krysty and Mildred both opened their mouths, catching each other's eye, but kept quiet, suspecting that anything said would make the tension worse.

"He's letting him go, Dad," Dean said, perched on the back of the land wag.

"Teach the old fool a lesson if that mule bites his skinny ass on the way out," Mildred commented.

The rope was loose, and for a moment the big mule just stood there, its head half turned to peer at Doc as if it suspected some sort of a trick. Even when the man patted it on the flank, encouraging it to go, the animal still didn't try to move away from him.

"Five gets you one it bites him," Trader offered.

"Wrong," Krysty said. "Look."

"I'll be damned." Mildred laughed. "Move over Saint Francis of Assisi, here comes Saint Theophilus Tanner."

The mule belied its normally vicious and malevolent nature, rubbing its head against Doc's legs, allowing him to throw his arms around its neck and hug it. Once again the swallow's-eye kerchief came into use.

Finally, reluctantly, the animal took a few hesitant steps away from Doc. Judas stopped, then kicked up its legs and gave out a great exultant bray that sent birds soaring into the air.

Doc waved a clenched fist as the mule trotted off into the hills, waiting until it had vanished, then turning and walking slowly back to the waiting land wag and his friends. His cheeks were still wet with tears.

"I had not thought that I would regret that parting," he said. "Still, it was well done. Now, let us move on and speed ourselves elsewhere."

Chapter Five

"There's that big comm dish," Krysty said, standing up in the back of the lurching wag, "the one that saved our lives when the mountain blew out."

The afternoon was nearly done, the sun hanging low on the western horizon, the shadows of the Volvo truck stretching far ahead of it down the dusty trail.

Ryan was taking a turn at the wheel, and he had already spotted the battered, rusting orange hulk of the communications receiver that lay on its side at the bottom of the steep, rugged hillside.

"Be inside by dark," he said.

"Jump straightaway?" J.B. asked, sitting at his side in the cab.

"Why not?"

"No reason."

"The redoubt got wrecked, didn't it?"

The Armorer took off his spectacles and began to polish the lenses. "Yeah. No cooking or sleeping facilities up there. Not now. Yeah, let's just do the climb, then do the jump. The sooner the better."

DEAN LED THE WAY up the sandstone slope, talking animatedly with Jak. Abe and Trader were next, the older man sometimes using the trusty Armalite as a stick to help him over the rougher places. J.B. and

Mildred were the third pair, climbing mainly in silence, as were Ryan and Krysty, following immediately behind them.

Doc and Sukie were trailing at the back.

Ryan overheard some parts of their conversation, realizing that Doc was attempting to explain the inexplicable concept of matter transfer and what making a "jump" would mean. He seemed to be doing his best to try to reassure her, but was generally making things worse.

"It is true that there is sometimes a small element of nausea involved."

"Bein' sick?"

"Just a little. I believe that I have made dozens of such jumps by now, and I have avoided being sick on several of them. So it isn't too unpleasant."

"You pass out though?"

"Briefly."

"I'm getting to think I should go look for my sister in Hope Springs, Doc."

"There is the rest of your life to try to do that, my dear lady."

"But if something goes wrong on this jump, then I won't have any rest of my life."

Ryan climbed a little faster and the conversation faded away behind him.

THE ORIGINAL ENTRANCE to the military complex had been wiped away by the explosion, and the way in now lay through a great scar in the raw rock. It was concealed from below by the angle and gradient of the mountainside and opened into the rubble-strewn remnants of a wide corridor.

Ryan wasn't surprised to find, when he reached the top, that there were no signs of anyone having entered the redoubt since their last departure from it. The dust that lay thickly over everything around the inner passage was undisturbed.

The rows of concealed lights in the curved ceiling had all been destroyed, and the carved-out interior of the mountain was almost dark.

Ryan stepped back to the brink and called out to Doc and Sukie to hurry up. "Time's running out if we're to jump tonight! Getting black."

"We are making our best efforts, my friend."

"Well, try making some even better ones," Trader shouted, "or you get up here and find we've all gone."

Doc said something to Sukie, but they couldn't hear what it was.

"SO THIS IS YOUR BOX of tricks, is it, Ryan?" Trader stood in the small anteroom, the main control consoles whirring and flickering behind him, staring at the door into the mat-trans chamber.

"Yeah. Inside, close the door. The metal disks in the floor and ceiling glow. There's a kind of a mist filters down from the top. You become briefly unconscious—"

J.B. interrupted him. "We figure that's the actual moment of leaving here and being transmitted or transferred, all the way to there."

"Wherever that is." Dean grinned.

Trader ruffled his hair. "Yeah, that's the most interesting part of all this, son."

"What's that panel of numbers and letters by the side of the door?" Sukie asked. Ryan noticed that her voice sounded high and strained.

"Control codes," Doc replied. "Sadly, at the time of what is called skydark, all of the relevant documentation and comp disks have been wiped clean or destroyed or have quite simply vanished. So we have no way at all of understanding what any combination might do."

"Why not just hit two or three at random?" Trader suggested. "See what happens?"

"No." Ryan tried to explain. "Some of the redoubts built at the very end of the twentieth century, before the big fires and the long winters came, were destroyed. Probably a whole lot of them were. We'll never know. And the rest have been mainly hidden since then. We kind of luck into them from inside when we jump. But some have been damaged."

"So?"

"So, the fact that we've never jumped into a vacuum, or into the middle of a million tons of powdered concrete and crushed steel shows there's a safeguard built in. Hit the buttons at random and not know what you're doing could, for instance, override that safety device."

"Oh, yeah. See what you mean, Ryan."

"So, is everyone ready?"

"You sure that little box of silvery glass will hold us?" Trader asked.

"Sure."

Sukie raised a hand. "Is there time for me to go back and find some place to take a leak?"

Abe cackled with laughter. "Make one of these jumps and you'll probably piss yourself anyway. So why bother?"

Doc hefted his sword stick toward the sniggering little gunner. "There's no call for that, Abraham."

"Just a small joke, Doc," he protested.

"Very small and not much of a joke, either. Rather like yourself." He glowered at Abe. "I would have thought that an apology to the lady might be in order."

"Let it be, Doc," Sukie said.

Abe shook his head. "No. I'm sorry, Sukie. Stupe of me. Guess I'm strung up and wound over for the jump."

One by one they filed into the six-sided chamber, all sitting in a circle, backs against the cool walls of silver armaglass. Here, in the heart of the mat-trans unit, there was ample lighting to see what was happening, powered by the original nuke gen that still worked diligently away somewhere in the bowels of the ancient redoubt.

Ryan waited outside, until everyone was comfortable, guns stashed safely. J.B. had taken off his glasses and folded them into one of his pockets, placing his fedora on the floor at his side. Then he locked his fingers with those of Mildred, sitting next to him. He winked up at Ryan.

Dean and Krysty had left a gap between them for when he'd closed the door and triggered the mechanism. Ryan noticed that Krysty's sentient hair was now curled defensively and tightly at her nape, its bright flaming color dimmed by anticipation of the jump to come.

Nobody liked jumping.

Trader had entered as though he half expected to see a panther lying curled in one corner of the chamber. He sat, stretching his legs, settling the Armalite on his lap, his finger ready inside the trigger guard. He looked around him in what Ryan knew, from long memory, as being something as close to nerves as the old man would ever show.

Abe perched happily beside him, next in the circle to Mildred, with Doc on his other side.

He waited until Sukie had sat, tucking her booted feet beneath her, nervously brushing her fingers over the divided skirt. Doc reached for one of her hands and pressed his lips to it in a gentle honorable gesture.

"I promise and vow that no harm shall come to you, my dear lady, as long as I live to be your champion," he said gallantly, receiving a watery smile in return. He sat, his knee joints cracking like firecrackers, and leaned back, closing his eyes.

Jak had entered the chamber like a cat, sitting in one corner, between Sukie and Krysty. He ran his long, pale fingers once through the mane of stark white hair and also closed his eyes and relaxed.

Ryan glanced behind him, from long habit, seeing that he was now quite alone, except for the banks of desks and tiny multicolored lights.

"Everyone ready?" he asked. No one answered. "Well, nobody not ready." He stepped inside the glittering chamber, pausing for a last second, hand on the edge of the heavy door, ready to pull it tightly shut.

At the frozen fraction of a second when the lock clicked firmly shut, and he moved to sit down, Ryan's eye caught the look on Sukie Smith's face.

He couldn't remember seeing such deep, superstitious terror on a human visage before. It was as though she had been dragged to the brink of the fieriest pit in hell and forced to stare into it.

At that moment Ryan knew that something was going to happen, and that he was the only one who could do anything to try to prevent it.

But Dean grabbed his one hand, Krysty clasping the other, and the moment had gone.

The metal disks above and below him started to glow brightly, and the lights outside seemed to have become much dimmer. There was a distant humming sound that somehow came from both inside and outside the chamber.

"No," Sukie said very clearly and distinctly, as if she were rejecting an obscene suggestion from a drunk in a back alley of a frontier pesthole.

"What?" Doc blinked his eyes open, struggling to focus, his brain fighting for understanding.

The gray-white mist appeared at the top of the silver-walled chamber, writhing lower.

Ryan battled hard to keep his one eye open. He wrenched his hand free from his son, who mumbled something in protest. But Krysty had a grip like steel, and he could do nothing to free himself from her. He saw J.B. reacting, but it was all much to little and an eternity too late.

Sukie was already up into a crouch, starting to move clumsily toward the chamber door, her mouth working. Odd words broke through the mind-scrambled barrier. "Have . . . sorry . . . Hope . . . sister . . . Doc . . . sorr . . ."

Ryan noticed that there was a small pool of liquid where the woman had been sitting, but that made no sense at all to him. "Don't . . ." he said.

Or thought he said.

Now the familiar black waters of the jump were sucking him down into their whirling center. The last thing Ryan saw was a dark figure, oddly opaque, cross his line of sight. There was the impression of the armaglass door opening and a hideous screaming, roaring noise that filled the universe.

Then the blackness became absolute.

Chapter Six

A darkness beyond any darkness, a cold beyond any cold.

The being that was known as Ryan Cawdor was reduced to a whirling speck of nothing, sucked into an infinite blackness and left there. He was deserted and alone, trapped either as a single neutron, in the sighing chasms that lie beyond the farthest limits of space and time, or as a molecule of matter, caught forever in the depths of his own body.

But part of his mind was still functioning, wrestling with the hideous dilemma of what had happened.

There was the obvious possibility that he had died during the malfunctioned jump, and that what he felt now was simply the endless doom of eternity.

But he was still sentient.

Unusually for the madness within madness that lay at the heart of a jump, he could remember what had happened in those last glassy moments.

Doc's friend, Sukie Smith, had lost her nerve and changed her mind, deciding that she wouldn't remain within the silvered armaglass walls of the chamber, but leaving it so late that the jump was already well under way.

Ryan could visualize the door swinging open, just as the shutters clamped shut on his brain.

But had it closed again?

Like a crazed stop-action vid, Ryan seemed to see and feel an infinity of images: a bleak moorland and cold steel in his hand and galloping hooves and the bristling of coarse hemp drawn tight around his throat; the pitching yards of an old predark ship and the bucking of yards, ratlines snapping in the teeth of a gale, the long fall to the heaving ocean, dark green, wind-tossed; a vast construction of stone and iron, like a giant's web, echoing and soundless, the liquid cement closing over him, silent and final.

Back again to space.

Ryan wanted to scream, but he had no mouth and could not.

For Jak Lauren, the jump meant listening forever and a day to a heartbreaking sound of a woman weeping and a small baby endlessly crying.

Mildred saw only fire and smoke, and was sick to her stomach at the overwhelming odor of roasted human flesh.

Dean was floating along vast passages, where the roots of unthinkable trees penetrated and twisted and turned in the stygian blackness. He was holding his breath, knowing that to suck in the darkness would be to lose his soul.

Abe was deeply unconscious, the electrical activity within his brain slowed so much that it was almost flat-lining.

J.B. stood completely motionless in the center of a whirling machine of polished steel and oiled brass.

Cogs and wheels rotated and meshed within fractions of an inch of his helpless, naked body.

To move was to die.

Krysty saw colors that had no name and came from beyond her world, colors that had weight, sound and texture, colors that surrounded her.

Doc wept tears that washed about him, salt and warm, slowly but inexorably filling the oblate spheroid of armored crystal that he realized was to be his tomb through all the ceaseless millennia of forever.

Trader found that someone had scraped all of the gray-pink sludge of his brain from the inside of his skull, leaving it squeaky-clean, like polished ivory.

But, particularly, that hadn't stopped him from thinking.

And it hadn't stopped him from being very frightened.

Chapter Seven

Ryan opened his eye and closed it again, immediately.

The sensation of vision, no matter how blurred and out of focus, was enough to bring on a gripping bout of boiling sickness. He swallowed hard, tasting the acid bitterness of bile at the back of his throat. He kept very still and took ten counted, spaced, slow breaths. His right hand reached down for the butt of the SIG-Sauer.

He decided to take the chance and carefully eased open his right eye again.

This time, the sickness was less insistent.

The first impression was the certainty that the jump had, at least, carried them away from the partly ruined redoubt in New Mexico.

The silver armaglass had gone, replaced by walls of vivid, flamelike orange, a color so hot and bright that it almost hurt to look at it.

The door was shut firmly, but there was something on the floor by the entrance that looked like the broken heel off a woman's boot.

Ryan glanced around the six-sided room, checked that everyone had made the jump.

Sukie Smith was missing, which was no surprise.

Doc had fallen sideways, into the space where the woman had been sitting. His hair was ruffled, a tiny worm of dark crimson blood creeping from the corner of his open mouth.

J.B. and Mildred seemed to have supported each other through the jump. Both still sat upright, though both were unconscious.

Abe had been sick all over his shirt and pants, his face the color of flour-and-water paste. His lips moved, but no sound came out.

Jak had pulled his bony knees up under his chin. His ruby eyes were slit open, staring toward Ryan, but there was no indication there that he had actually come around and was seeing anything.

Dean was showing signs of recovery, his tongue licking his dry lips. His right hand was trembling, the fingernails making a faint scraping sound on one of the metal disks in the floor.

Ryan glanced up and saw that the last swirling fragments of the mist were evaporating.

"Colors of all..." Krysty mumbled, her hand still locked in Ryan's.

He looked last across to his old leader. Trader had slipped sideways into a kind of hunched, prenatal position. It took Ryan several seconds to work out quite what had happened. As soon as he realized, he pulled himself from Krysty's grip and tried to move across the smooth floor, though it involved an enormous effort of will.

The Armalite was now cradled by the prone figure, the butt between the knees. Trader's index finger was snugly around the trigger of the blaster.

And the muzzle was between his lips.

"Fireblast!" The struggle to crawl to Trader, so soon after recovering consciousness from the jump, was immensely difficult.

"Hi, Dad." Dean had come around, with the natural resilience of the young. "What're..."

Jak was moving as well, with an exaggerated slowness, squinting across at Trader.

But it was down to Ryan.

If anyone disturbed Trader, or forced him into a sudden movement, then the finger would squeeze the trigger, the blaster would fire and the orange armaglass walls would be splattered with matted hair, ragged skin, splinters of jagged bone and a gruel of blood and brains.

"Don't touch hand," Jak whispered, stopping and doubling over, retching with a noisy violence.

Ryan had thought it through that far. Trying to move Trader's finger would also lead to the Armalite being fired. But his fogged mind hadn't yet come up with the answer.

He reached his old war chief, seeing the first flickering movements that meant he was coming around. Time was running out like gasoline from a ruptured tank.

"Safety," J.B. breathed from Ryan's right side. "Put on the safety."

He gripped the scarred barrel of the blaster in his left hand and carefully eased the safety from the fire position with his right.

Trader's eyes snapped open, staring blankly into Ryan's face, totally without any recognition. His lips mimed the word "Fucker," and he pulled the trigger, oblivious to the end of the muzzle jammed into his mouth.

Ryan knew better than to try to remove the Armalite from Trader by force.

Over the years he'd sometimes wondered what would happen if the two of them had ever gotten into a no-holds-barred fight. In the early war wag days, the idea that he might ever be able to beat his leader was nonsense. Trader would've simply broken him into small pieces.

Later, it had preoccupied Ryan to the extent that he had seriously considered trying to provoke Trader into a knockdown, kicking and gouging brawl to try to test himself. But he had enough sense to know that it would be a fight that he could not truly win. If he lost to Trader, then it would diminish the respect of the rest of the war wags' crews. If he beat Trader, then the old man would almost certainly have chilled him.

So it goes.

Now, he would have backed himself, younger, faster and stronger than Trader. But even now he knew the result wouldn't be a certainty.

"Who are you and why was my blaster in ... I'll be hung, dried and quartered for the crows! But I feel sicker than a gut-shot swampie."

"It's me—Ryan. We made the jump, Trader. Lie still awhile and get over it."

"I'm fine." But his eyes were rolling like pinwheels. He reconsidered. "Not fine at all."

Jak had just thrown up again, cursing under his breath. "Forgot how bad," he said, his voice barely audible. "Black hole in middle head."

Now everyone was lurching back toward consciousness, with the exception of Doc. Mildred had crawled to check him out, turning his head to one side, pushing her fingers into his mouth to make sure that he wouldn't swallow his tongue.

"I worry about him making jumps," she said, taking the old man's pulse. "It screws up his metabolism and his head is always badly muddled afterward."

"Only way to travel," Ryan said. He stood, steadying himself with a hand against the cold walls of the gateway chamber. "Air smells reasonable here."

J.B. and Dean were also vertical. Jak had lain down again. If possible, his face was even more pale than usual, with a light greenish tint to it.

Trader had carefully checked his Armalite, slipping the safety off again. "Puke color to the walls," he said. "They all different?"

Ryan nodded. "Most are. Seen red, purple, green, blue and yellow."

"Last one was silver."

"Right. How's Doc coming along, Mildred?"

"Pulse and respiration are picking up some. Should be back with us in a few minutes."

Trader was on his feet, drawing in gulps of the air. "You reckon this is good to breathe, Ryan? Tastes like the inside of a gaudy shithouse."

"Known worse. You have to remember that we're likely inside a redoubt that hasn't been entered in close to a hundred years. Only the reliable nuke gens keep power and air-con going. Always tastes a little stale and flat."

"Let's go recce."

Ryan shook his head. "No way, Trader. Place like this, we all stick together. You never know what kind of triple-red danger you might find."

"Enough of us with enough blasters to take anything and anybody out. If I'd had half a dozen well-armed troops with me when I started out trading, I could sure as shit be the baron of all Deathlands by now."

J.B. had quietly checked his blasters, then polished his glasses and replaced them. "Like we said before, Trader, that was then and this is now."

"Sure, sure. I'm just an old fart.... Like a fruit been sucked dry. Old rag been rung out and then thrown away. That's how you two see it."

Krysty laughed. "Love it when you try to turn on the self-pity, Trader. I never saw a man who looked less like an old rag been thrown away."

Grudgingly he grinned. "Mebbe, mebbe, Lady Red." Trader wiped his hand across his sweating forehead. "All these redoubts as hot as this one?"

Mildred interrupted him. "Doc's coming around," she said. "Why not open the door of the chamber, Ryan? Give us all a little more space and air."

"Sure. Everyone on triple red?" He looked around to make sure that all of them, except for Mildred and Doc, had their blasters drawn and readied.

He moved to the door, trying to make out any sign of anything beyond it. But the orange color was so vivid that it was impossible. The handle moved easily and he swung the door open, the others covering him from behind.

Trader started to push forward, past him, but Ryan held out his hand. "Hold it."

"What?"

"You heard, Trader. Times like this there has to be one voice, and it's mine. That clear to you?" Ryan turned and stared him full in the face, holding his gaze until Trader shuffled his feet and glanced away.

"Yeah, fine with me. Just that I always hated hangin' around a place."

"We wait for Doc."

"They always have these little bitty rooms stuck on the outside of them?"

"Gateway chambers? Yeah. Pretty well all of them. Most are just like this. No bigger than ten feet or so across. Majority are stripped bare."

"Beyond is the control room?"

"Like the one back in New Mexico, you mean?" Ryan nodded. "Yeah."

"Can we at least step into this room here?"

"Sure, Trader. But don't touch that other door."

Dean was looking around. "Doc's eyes are moving, Dad."

"Thanks, son."

Trader, Abe and Dean had stepped from the chamber, followed a moment later by Jak. Ryan, J.B. and Krysty waited, watching Mildred kneeling with Doc's grizzled head cradled in her lap.

His eyes opened, staring around like a newborn baby's, not focusing on anything in the glass-walled room. The tip of Doc's tongue moistened his lips.

"I am feeling better," he said. His eyes closed, and his head lolled back into Mildred's arms.

"Shit," she said.

"We still wait." Ryan made sure everyone heard him, made sure Trader understood him.

SEVERAL MINUTES LATER Doc made a second attempt to reenter the land of the living.

"I confess that I scarcely felt even the most nugatory pain from the extraction, my dear fellow. Best piece of fang carvery I ever knew." He smiled broadly. "I will commend you to any of my friends who seek the aid of a dentist."

Mildred patted him gently on the wrinkled cheek. "Come on, Doc. Nearly back with us. One more step." She built up the force of the blows a little at a time, until the chamber rang with the slapping sound.

His eyes finally clicked open again.

"Forgive me, Mama, but I truly believed that the bird was a ring ouzel."

The black woman shook him. "Snap out of it, Doc. We got places to go and things to do."

He closed his eyes for a moment, then opened them for a third time, nodding up into Mildred's face. "I had wondered whether I had passed into that dark bourn from which no traveler returns. But I would have woken to angel voices and sweet singing. Not to your ill-tempered visage, Dr. Wyeth."

She moved so quickly away from him that his head rattled on the floor of the gateway chamber. "Glad you appreciate my efforts to help you, Doc," she snapped.

He sat up, very gingerly, rubbing the back of his skull. "The typical action of a member of the esteemed medical profession whose bill has not been paid."

She showed him the extended middle finger of her right hand. "And fuck you, too, Doc."

Ryan grinned at Krysty. It looked like things were already back to normal.

THE ANTEROOM HAD two bare shelves of reinforced plastic, holding only a thin film of fine dust. Apart from that it was completely empty.

"We move into the control area," Ryan said, "still all on triple red. Ready?"

He opened the door.

Chapter Eight

"Good condition," J.B. stated.

"Go check the outer door, will you? Make sure the green lever's pointing—"

"Down," the Armorer completed. "I can remember that much, Ryan."

There was no trace of any fault or flaw in the main control area to the gateway chamber. Nor was there any sign of any human activity. It was as though it had been built and manned by robotic androids who had completed their set tasks and then quietly and tidily made their exits.

"Not even some fossilized chewing gum under any of the desks," Mildred said, stooping beneath the nearest row of consoles to check it out.

Binomial eyes clicked. A light film of the thinnest oil eased tumblers. On the control panels, dazzling arrays of changing colors—a rainbow of reaction. Wheels danced and numbers flashed.

The small black loudspeakers set in the corners of the control room suddenly hissed, one of them crackling. The voice that came from them had an oddly dead, automated quality to it as though everything human had been drained away.

"Midnight on fifth tone after message." A pause. "No message from central. All quiet." Another pause, then came five spaced tones, thin and metallic. "Midnight. Ends."

Abe laughed. "That thing been talking to nobody for a hundred years?"

Doc had sat at one of the comp keyboards, looking at the endless flow of data that was scrolling up the screen, like a reversed river of gibberish. "Once programmed, those 'things' as you call them, will loyally carry out their preset duties until time ends."

"I've never heard one in any of the other redoubts." Ryan looked at it. "Wonder why they left it on?"

"Better question is why they bothered to turn it off in the other places." Krysty looked around. "Nothing here for us. Let's go out and recce a little, lover. Might even find some beds for the night."

Trader had thrown his Armalite onto one of the desks. "Sounds good. You said that some of these places had plenty of blasters, and some had food and shit like that."

Jak had been leaning against the wall. "Some do, some don't," he said.

"Might as well go and take a look. J.B., you know the drill for opening the big sec steel doors. Rest of you get on watch. Still triple red."

Trader grinned across at Abe. "Triple-red warning must be in case one of these 'luminated screens gets off its ass and attacks us."

Ryan ignored him.

J.B. put his hand on the large green lever at the side of the massive door. It was down in the locked position. The Smith & Wesson M-4000 scattergun was propped against the wall next to him, the Uzi slung over his shoulders.

Everyone else had their weapons out and ready as they crouched in a semicircle around the entrance to the control room.

"Ready, Ryan?"

"Do it."

"Few inches for starters?"

"Yeah."

The Armorer started to tug the lever upward. Some of them, in other locations, had been stiff and resistant, but this one moved like a hot knife through ice cream. They could all just hear the distant, muffled sound of the gears engaging, slowly powering open the incalculable weight of the door.

A tiny slit of light appeared beneath the bottom of the sec steel, widening to eight or nine inches.

"Stop," Ryan ordered.

He dropped flat on his belly, the SIG-Sauer probing ahead of him, sliding to peer under the door. He could see the wall of the passage opposite, brightly lighted. By squinting he could make out the curve of the corridor, both ways. There was no sign of any sort of life.

For a moment Ryan thought that he might have caught a very faint scratching sound, but when he strained for it, the noise was gone.

"Watch out for the attack of the killer lemmings," Trader whispered.

Ryan found it interesting, and increasingly irritating, the way that his old war chief was reacting. If Trader had been in charge of the group in an alien environment where a danger could threaten them from anywhere, he would have been the first to insist on triple care being taken by everyone.

Now, conscious that Ryan was the man, he couldn't resist getting in the little sarcastic digs.

Ryan ignored the comment and stood. "Right, J.B., take her all the way up."

They all waited, taut and silent, until the vanadium-steel door had opened to the top. There was no movement from outside in the corridor.

Edging slowly around the corner, Ryan glanced quickly both ways. "Nothing," he said. "Let's go. Drop the lever once everyone's out, J.B., and we'll take a look."

One of the most common factors in all the redoubts that they'd visited through the mat-trans systems was that the passage beyond the control room almost always ran a short way to the left and then ended in a blank wall of bare stone, as though the gateways were always at one of the burrow ends of the complexes.

This one was no exception.

Less than thirty yards from the open door of the control area, the curved walls came to an abrupt stop.

"Other way," Ryan said.

"What's the sign say over the sec door?" Trader asked, pointing with the barrel of the Armalite.

Dean read it out. "It says 'Entry Forbidden To All But B12 Cleared Personnel And Above. Mat-Trans Unit. Project Cerberus. Overproject Whisper.' Did I get that last bit right? Real stupe long words."

"You did well," Krysty said.

Almost immediately they reached a side tunnel. But it was less than fifteen yards in length, with a lower ceiling, ending in yet another blank wall of concrete.

"Bullet holes," Abe said. "Look, took great scars out of the stone. Around four feet from the floor."

J.B. took a few steps into the side turning, stooping to pick something up that was laid against the bottom of the wall. He held it out to the others.

"A 9mm bullet," Jak said. "Got different look. Not like most."

"Equaloy," Trader observed, bringing it closer to his eyes to examine, angling it for the best illumination from the overhead strip lights.

The Armorer nodded. "Right. Hardly ever come across them. Think they must still have been sort of experimental when the big fires started burning."

Mildred took the unfired round from Trader. "What's so special about it, John? The coating's like plastic or..."

"Nylon. Self-lubricating."

"Feels too light." Mildred handed it on to Dean. "Why's that?"

"Aluminum. From what I know about them, the idea was that the bullet was high velocity, but when it strikes a target it checks momentum very quickly, so all of the kinetic energy goes flowing onward."

"Devastating," Ryan said. "Could do with a few hundred rounds of that. Must have had a massive effect on anyone who got in the way of it."

Mildred moved to the wall and ran her finger over the chipped holes. "You're right, Abe. They're bullet holes, all right."

Doc wasn't at all interested in the rare example of predark ammo. He had joined the doctor, staring down at their feet. "I suspect that if you were to analyze that black substance that stains the floor, my dear Doctor, you might well find that it is almost certainly human blood."

She stopped and rubbed her finger over it. "Old, old, blood, Doc. But you won't find me arguing with you over it." She straightened and looked again at the wall. "Firing squad."

"I fear that it was."

Everyone gathered around. Ryan was surprised. The evidence of some quasiofficial executions wasn't something that they'd come across before. It spoke of a violently traumatic episode in the last days, or hours, as the sky grew dark with the foreign missiles, of a mutiny or a rebellion.

"We'll never know," Krysty said.

They moved on.

THEY PASSED AN ENTRANCE or stairwell on the right, seventy paces farther along. But it had been sealed with shutters of sec steel. Without any plas-ex or some grens, they had no way of opening them.

"Getting bored," Trader said. "Thought these redoubts were treasure houses."

"Nobody told you that," J.B. protested. "This one looks like they did a good number on evacuating it. Odds are we won't find anything."

"Then we might as well make another jump and get out to someplace more interesting."

"Patience, Trader," Ryan said. "You used to say that a man who walks sees a whole lot more than a man who runs."

"I did?"

"You did."

"Anyway," Mildred said, "I'd like to check outside. Find out where the jump's taken us."

"I'd like some sleep," Dean said, yawning to prove his point. "Triple whacked."

"Yeah, me, too," Abe agreed. "Looks like there's another passage just ahead."

"Vid cameras following us." Jak pointed at the tiny boxes with the gleaming lenses that were suspended from the angle between wall and arched ceiling. They roamed ceaselessly, back and forth, sending their pictures to some distant, unmanned sec center at the heart of the redoubt.

Ryan held up his hand as they reached the junction with the side corridor on their left. It was more constricted and appeared to climb upward.

"Hold it here. I'll go check with J.B., just a little farther along. Rest of you wait here on orange alert. Be back within fifteen minutes."

"I'll take charge here," Trader said.

"No. Nobody takes charge here. Jak and Krysty been around with J.B. and me for long enough to know how things go down. Let it lie, Trader."

The older man nodded, stifling a yawn. "Make it quick. I could do with some sleep as well as the boy here." He patted Dean on his shoulder.

"Fifteen minutes at the outside."

IT DIDN'T TAKE ANYWHERE near that long.

They passed another sealed exit in the first hundred yards, then the passage narrowed and climbed much more steeply, with several flights of short, broad steps, a ramp at the side for wheeled vehicles.

The place was still spotlessly maintained, though the air quality seemed less good.

Neither man spoke. When you were on a recce patrol like that, you never spoke unless you had something to say.

Their search ended at the top of another, longer flight of stairs.

"That's it," J.B. said, moving forward to investigate the blank wall of pale cream sec steel that blocked off the corridor from floor to ceiling.

Ryan looked at the control panel at the side. "Been sealed off."

The coded letters and number buttons had been hidden behind a sheet of clear sec plas that would resist anything except some serious explosives.

"Not taking any chances of anyone getting into there, were they?"

"Right." Ryan tapped a finger on the cold steel of the huge door. "No point in wasting any time here. Let's get back to the others and try that side passage."

A SIGN OVER THE NEXT DOOR read Leaving Section 4— Entering Section 5.

It was a manual lock, a small silver button, arrowed for up and down.

"Can I, Dad?"

"Sure."

The boy pressed it. A red light glowed under the "up" panel, then went out. For a few moments nothing happened at all. Dean tried it again.

The red light stayed off, but the heavy door began to move upward, faltering three times before finally reaching the top and halting.

"First sign of malfunction," J.B. said.

"So it is human after all." Doc grinned.

It was almost the first sign of a normal response that he'd shown since coming out of the gateway chamber. He'd asked nothing about Sukie's absence, seeming to accept her last-second change of mind and disappearance.

Ryan had picked up the heel of a woman's boot that had been lying inside the chamber, slipping it in his pocket. His belief was that it had come off one of Sukie's boots, and he decided it would be better if Doc didn't see it—particularly as it seemed to have been sliced cleanly off, halfway up, by some unimaginable force.

Dean was going to run ahead into the section in front of them, but his father called him back.

"Wait. Keep together."

Krysty touched Ryan on the arm. "There's some sort of feeling in here, lover."

"What?"

She shook her head, her bright green eyes showing doubt. "Not sure. Just a sort of background.... I don't know...like a background *hum* of menace. It's both close and far away at the same time. Best be careful."

"Should we go back?"

"No. Just take care."

IT WAS WHAT THEY'D HOPED for—a self-contained area of the sprawling military complex, with a forty-bed dormitory, kitchen and ablution facilities.

The sleeping arrangements were single bunk beds, with plastic spring supports and shrink-wrapped mattresses.

The kitchen area was totally, hygienically clean, with nothing on any of the shelves or in any of the capacious range of polished steel cupboards.

Water ran from the taps there, as well as in the shower and toilet sections. It was flat, recirculated water that Mildred pronounced probably safe to drink, though she commented on how poor the air quality was.

J.B. and Jak quickly toured section five, reporting back to Ryan and the others that this part of the redoubt was also totally sealed off.

"Sec doors are locked at every exit. The only door open in the place seems to be the one between here and the gateway section," J.B. stated. "There's the vent grilles in the bathhouse, but nothing larger than a rat could get through there. And it's too clean for rats."

Trader didn't try to hide his disappointment. "No blasters or ammo?"

"Some you lose..." Abe said.

"I know that, you stupe, Lol!"

"I'm Abe, Trader."

The flash of temper evaporated as quickly as it had flared up. "Yeah, 'course you are. 'Course you are."

"Can we go to bed, Dad?"

"Sure. Place is locked up tight, so there's no need to post a watch."

He turned to Krysty. "How about your feeling?"

"Still there. Insistent. Not human. But I never felt anything quite like it. Definitely a sort of threat."

Ryan nodded. "Since we can't get anywhere else we'll use the beds. Then jump out of here in the morning. That way nothing much can go wrong."

Chapter Nine

Abe slept well.

It was an odd experience to have a real bed for a night, with a real mattress. Most times it was either rocks and dirt or a bare wooden floor. At first, the softness felt strange, but it eased the range of old knife and gunshot wounds that often gave him trouble.

As he dropped off he was wondering about Trader, remembering the burst of red-eyed rage that had been directed at him just before they all retired for the night, and the fact that Trader seemed to have so much trouble with his memory.

In the old days, Trader *never* had any trouble at all with his memory.

"Never," Abe whispered, dropping into the warm dark. "No, never."

ABE WOKE UP, aware of the pressure on his bladder from the amount of water he'd drunk before going to bed. He yawned and slowly rolled over onto his back, sniffing and wiping his mustache.

The overhead lights were still bright. It hadn't been possible to turn them off last evening. The Armorer had figured that there was probably a central control for them.

The others were all sleeping soundly. Doc had chosen to take the bed farthest from the entrance, and was snoring gently. J.B. and Mildred were in adjacent beds—they were all bolted to the floor, making movement impossible. On the far side of the prone figure of young Jak, Trader clutched his Armalite, though most of the others had kept their blasters on the floor, close at hand.

Abe got up, barefoot, and padded toward the closed door to the toilet and bath facilities. As he passed Dean's bed, he smiled fondly at the boy. He was sleeping on his back, sucking his thumb, looking even younger than his eleven years. Abe was struck by the strong resemblance between the lad and his father.

Ryan slept in the bed closest to the entrance door, with Krysty beside him. She had tied a strip of patterned material across her eyes to close out the dazzling lights, her hair burning like fire across the whiteness of the mattress.

It crossed Abe's mind to think how lucky he was to have fallen in with such a good bunch of friends—though finding Trader hadn't quite turned out like he'd somehow visualized it.

The old days seemed so long ago.

He was nearly at the door to the ablution facility to section five of the redoubt, already unbuttoning his pants, reaching inside, ready to take the leak he so badly needed.

The door had a built-in sensor, and it began to open as he approached it.

Abe took three steps inside, heading for the spotless porcelain stalls. The light in the bathroom, bouncing off the rows of mirrors, was even brighter and he closed his eyes for a moment, hearing the door hiss shut behind him.

He also heard a weird, scrabbling, scratching sound, like lots of children all gently scraping their nails along a strip of soft leather.

Despite the dazzle of the overhead lamps, Abe blinked open his eyes, squinting to see properly, and, blinking again, his jaw dropped.

Mouth open wide, Abe began to scream.

Ryan was off the bed, the blaster in his hand, and moved toward the noise before his conscious mind had recognized what had yanked him from sleep.

He was just aware of some of the others around him in the dormitory reacting to the sound.

The scream.

"Abe," he muttered.

J.B. was at his heels, fingers locked around the pistol grip of the folding butt 12-gauge, Trader a heartbeat behind him, Armalite at the high port. Jak ran at his shoulder, then Krysty, Dean and Mildred.

Doc lay flat on his bed, rubbing his eyes, mumbling to himself, unable to break his spirit free from the chains of the night.

The automatic door hissed open, liberating Abe's scream of shock and fear.

Ryan's first reaction was surprise that he hadn't noticed the night before that the floor of most of the bathroom facility was covered in dark brown fur.

Moving brown fur.

Trader was fastest to recognize the threat.

"Bastard spiders," he yelled.

Abe had staggered back against the white-tiled wall, kicking out, beating away with both hands at the hordes of spiders that were trying to swarm all over him.

Some of them were no bigger than sparrows, others close to the size of a rat. Ryan remembered what J.B. had said about the sealing-off of the section of the redoubt, seeing more of the spiders pouring through the wide-mesh grilles of the vent system.

Nobody had opened fire, recognizing the pointlessness of trying to shoot thousands of the scuttling arachnids.

"Get Abe out," Ryan snapped, holstering the blaster, drawing the panga from the sheath on his belt.

"They'll get out into the rest of the redoubt," Krysty shouted. "Me and Mildred'll try to chill any that make the door."

Trader, J.B. and Jak started to move across the rippling layer of hairy spiders, crushing them beneath their boots. Abe's bare feet had disappeared beneath waves of the mutie creatures. There was blood dappling his hands and arms, showing that the spiders had a vicious bite.

It passed through Ryan's mind, as he started to hack at the seething mass, that if the spiders were venomous, then Abe's life was already measured in minutes.

Now that he was in the middle of them, he could see that most were the size of a baseball, with dark brown furred legs that almost tripled their size. They had tiny black stalked eyes and large barbed pincers.

The three friends were only just in time to save Abe. His eyes had rolled back white in their sockets, and he'd almost stopped fighting for life.

Jak, as agile as an acrobat, was first to his side, grabbing his arm and sweeping off the most insistent of the spiders, holding the fainting little gunner upright until J.B. and Trader arrived to help him.

Ryan used the panga like a brush, slicing back and forth through the mass of scuttling insects. Liquid sprayed over his fingers, making them burn, but he carried on with the remorseless slaughter.

Out of the corner of his eye Ryan noticed that Dean was standing near the automatic door, just inside the toilets, using his turquoise-hilted knife to stab any of the spiders that threatened him.

"Get outside, son! Help Krysty and Mildred keep the shitters out of the rest of the complex."

The doors hissed and Dean vanished.

Fresh waves of the mutie creatures poured in through the grilles, dropping softly to the floor, joining the throng that was still surging forward to attack the invading humans.

Trader and J.B. had lifted the semiconscious figure of Abe clear off the floor, while Jak methodically swept away the spiders from his body.

The bath area was almost silent, the only sounds the grunting of the men, and the hiss of Ryan's scything blade as it decimated the mutated insects.

"Get him outside," Ryan panted. "I'll hold 'em off long as I can."

One of the largest of the horrors had climbed all the way up his back into his hair, dropping over his face with a sticky web projecting from its abdomen, blinding and choking him.

As Ryan plucked at it with his left hand, it bit him near the bridge of the nose, the needled pincers narrowly missing his good right eye.

The pain was agonizing, and he very nearly dropped the panga. But he grabbed the spider and squeezed, feeling the soft, brittle body turn to mushy pulp between his fingers. Ryan cast the squashed corpse away from him, where its fellows scrabbled around it, starting to devour the twitching legs.

Ryan rubbed at his eyes with the back of his hand, trying to avoid spreading any of the virulent ichor and blinding himself. The thought of being blind and helpless among the rippling carpet of spiders was so abhorrent that he came close for a few moments to losing control and sliding into panic.

But Ryan's combat experience surged forth and saved him. He turned, seeing that the others had managed to drag Abe to safety, leaving him alone for a moment.

But it was all right.

Control was back again.

Using the panga with devastating skill, he butchered dozens of the furry creatures.

Ryan slowly moved toward the exit from the bath and toilet area. He jumped at a sudden noise, but it was only the automatic water flush of the urinals, operating as it had hundreds of thousands of times since skydark.

The doors hissed behind him, and Ryan turned and dived through, rolling around and kicking out his feet, shaking off and crushing the last of his attackers.

A few dozen spiders made it through the gap, others being pulped as the doors closed. But there were enough people out there to stamp and stab every last one of them.

By the time Ryan stood, Trader and J.B. had carried Abe to one of the beds, laying him down while Mildred quickly started peeling off his clothing. Krysty, Jak and Dean were finishing off the mutie arachnids, hunting down the last dozen or so that had scuttled into the dormitory.

"You all right, Dad?" asked his son, breaking off to help him to his feet. "You got a double-flash bite on your face. Like someone stuck a pigeon's egg under the skin. Bet that sucker's really going to hurt you!"

"You don't have to gloat." Ryan cuffed the boy playfully. "You get bitten?"

"No. Too quick for them. But poor old Abe looks triple sick, Dad."

Krysty wiped sweat from her forehead, then cleansed her knife on one of the mattresses and sheathed it. "That must have been one of the world's bad sights," she said.

"What?"

"Opening those doors and walking in on those..." She shuddered. "On those things. Without any warning. Gaia!"

Mildred called to Dean. "There's two drinking fountains down the far end of the dorm. Go and soak a rag in one and bring it back. Jak, help him. Need lots of water to wash these bites. Your hat, John?"

J.B. looked puzzled for a moment, then quickly picked up his fedora and went to fill it with water.

Ryan looked down at Abe, seeing the numerous speckled lumps all over him where he'd been bitten. They were particularly thick around his lower legs and arms, but his face was also badly swollen, streaked with blood.

"He all right, Mildred?"

"Does he look it?"

"No."

The little man was pale, eyes closed, breathing nineteen to the dozen, his scrawny chest rising and falling. His fingers kept moving, as if he were playing an invisible piano.

"He's gone into shock." Mildred was taking his pulse. "Enough to send anyone into shock."

Water arrived and she used it to sponge off the blood, peering closely at the area of the bites. Everyone stood around in silence, watching.

"I think that we'd be already seeing a traumatic reaction if those furry little sons of bitches had been seriously poisonous. There's some localized swelling." She looked up at Ryan's face. "Like that bump on your nose. But I reckon they should go down. Everyone better wash any bites they've received. Be on the safe side."

Abe's body jerked and he suddenly opened his eyes, seeing Mildred's face looming over him. "Time to rise and shine?" he asked brightly.

"How do you feel?" Trader asked.

"Like I been through a mesquite hedge backward. Where's my clothes? Why's..." His face revealed revulsion. "Them spiders. Look, there's billions of fucking spiders in the bathroom! Don't go in, whatever you do."

Everyone laughed, easing the tension, puzzling the little gunner.

Krysty answered him. "Spiders, Abe? Yeah, funnily enough, we had noticed them."

Chapter Ten

Ryan glanced at his wrist chron, seeing that barely two hours had elapsed since they'd all been tugged out of sleep by Abe's screams.

Once he'd calmed down and Mildred had bathed the spider bites again, the gunner had recovered fast, keen to get his clothes back on as the ambient temperature in the redoubt was only just above comfortable.

The rest of those who had been bitten found that the initial swellings had quickly gone down, leaving only patches of red on the skin that itched rather than hurt at all.

J.B. went and sat on the bed by Ryan. "Noticed how bad the air's become?" he asked.

"Yeah."

"I wonder if those mutie insects have blocked off part of the vent system?"

"Could be. I guess they must have felt the vibrations of us moving around the complex. Probably the biggest even in Spidertown in the last century. So they all came looking for us."

The Armorer nodded. "Have you thought about what might've happened if those automatic doors to the ablutions had malfunctioned and let them in during the middle of the night, while we were all asleep?"

Ryan grinned and shook his head. "Not something I want to think about at all, thanks, brother."

Krysty had been dozing on the adjacent bed. Now she sat up and ran her fingers through her hair. "If we're all well enough, could we move and make a jump out?"

"Sure." Ryan stood and stretched. "No real hurry, though, is there?"

"Just have the feeling that our little furry friends might've found some way through the heart of the redoubt and they'll suddenly pop up in the gateway chamber."

"I reckon not, Krysty," J.B. said. "I didn't see any of those big grilles anyplace else."

She stood, sniffed and made a face. "Why's the air gotten so bad?"

Ryan started to answer. "We reckon that—" But he was interrupted.

The same disinterested, bland computerized voice as before came through the speakers in the ceiling.

"All personnel in sections four and five. All personnel in sections four and five."

"That's us," Trader said, standing and grabbing at his blaster.

They waited, listening, but there was no immediate follow-up to the message.

Abe cleared his throat. "Don't know if you're all hangin' here for me, but as far as I'm concerned, we could get moving out of this place real soon."

There was a hissing over the speakers. "This is a Code J for Juliet emergency in sections four and five. Repeat, a Code J for Juliet in sections four and five.

Immediate action is required by all personnel. Immediate action."

Ryan looked at J.B. "Fireblast! What's going on here?"

"Who knows? Sounds urgent."

The group of companions clustered together in the center of the room. Abe kept glancing toward the closed door of the bathroom.

"What do we do, Dad?" Dean touched his father's hand for reassurance.

"Wait a little."

"Man runs the moment he thinks he hears danger finds he's stuck his head right into it," said Trader.

"Code J for Juliet imperative action soonest."

"Mebbe we should head for the mat-trans right away," Ryan said uncertainly, thrown by the disembodied voice that implied urgency yet gave no clues to what was happening.

"Purging begins in five minutes from now. Ninety percent vacuum in ten minutes from now. Personnel evacuation soonest, repeat soonest, repeat soonest."

"What's a vacuum, Dad?"

Mildred snapped her fingers. "These places have overall computer control, don't they?"

Ryan nodded.

"And they monitor everything to do with the redoubt?"

"Sure. Old predark days they'd have had human controllers to override any problems."

"Yes, yes. But they're programmed to act independently if necessary?"

"Yeah. Some of them certainly have been. But I don't understand what's happening right here. What's all this 'purging,' and this 'vacuum'?"

"I suspect it's linked to the diminished quality of the air in here."

Doc nodded. "I believe that your deduction could be correct, Dr. Wyeth. We have all commented on the singularly unpleasant odor in here, particularly since that disgusting incident with Miss Muffet's companions."

"Four minutes. Four minutes to purging in sections four and five. Nine minutes to terminal vacuum. Any personnel remaining must exit now."

"How long did it take us to get here from the gateway?" Ryan looked at J.B.

"Fifteen to twenty minutes. But we went slow and stopped now and again."

"Looks like we're goin' to have to do a lot better than that. Grab everything and let's go."

RYAN SENT DEAN TO RUN ahead of them to press the button that would send the sec door crawling upward, while the rest of them snatched up their scant possessions.

"Door wouldn't work right on the way in," Trader panted.

The eleven-year-old's voice floated back to them. "Won't open, Dad!"

"Big fire!" Abe had just dropped his blaster, stooping to collect it from where it had rattled under one of the narrow beds. "Got it. What'd the kid say?"

He found that he was alone in the dormitory. With a hasty glance toward the ablution facility, Abe raced after the others, to find them by the locked door.

"Put a couple of rounds through the controls," Trader suggested.

"And jam the whole thing!" J.B. pressed the button twice more.

"Allow me," Doc said, stepping forward, blowing on the tips of his fingers like a master safe breaker.

He was interrupted by the amplified voice. "Three minutes to purging in sections four and five. Eight minutes to terminal vacuum. All personnel to leave instantly or use breathing facilities as instructed under J for Juliet."

Doc pressed the small button once, let it go, then pressed it halfway in, finally pushing it all the way in and holding it for a few seconds. The light came on and, after a trio of heartbeats, the door began to rise.

"Well done, Doc!" Mildred exclaimed. "Probably just pure luck, though."

"No. When I was a student at Harvard, I had a single-room apartment with a shared water closet. The flushing mechanism was, to put it mildly, very erratic. So, I simply administered a similar technique to the door and..."

It was nearly eighteen inches off the floor. Ryan ducked, peered quickly into the passage beyond, rolled underneath and called to the others to follow him.

Krysty caught Mildred by the sleeve as they waited their turn. "What's going to happen here?"

"If it's what I think it is, honey, then you don't want to know. Believe me, the faster we get and jump, the better."

She bent and crawled under the door, which seemed to be moving more and more slowly.

A few seconds later they were all safely through the gap, facing the stairs and the long expanse of curved passageway.

Ryan looked around. "Jak, you're fastest. Go straight to the outer door and throw the green lever up. Rest of us'll follow at our best speeds. Go!"

The albino vanished, running almost silently, quickly out of their sight.

"Time's snarling at our back," Ryan said calmly. "Everyone go for it."

They'd hardly started to run, Doc still at the top of the first flight of steps, when that calm, unflurried comp voice broke in on them again.

"Two minutes to purging throughout sections four and five. Seven minutes to terminal vacuum. Unless personnel are in proximity to exits, they must, repeat must, use emergency air facilities as instructed by code J for Juliet. These sections are now on full alert."

It seemed to be much longer returning to the gateway than coming from it had been.

Everyone did their best. Dean was lightning, only yards slower than Jak. Krysty was probably the next fastest, even in her Western boots, with Ryan and J.B. all capable of great speed. Then the problems began. Trader wasn't bad at keeping up, but his breathing quickly became hoarse and he had to stop twice—once by the scene of the firing-squad executions—to double over and cough. Abe had so many old injuries to legs and feet that running was always difficult.

And Doc would never have claimed to be God's gift to the eight-hundred-meter dash.

A siren had started up, seeming to come from everywhere and nowhere. Above it, they all heard the warning from the now familiar voice.

"Final warning of purging of air supply to sections four and five in sixty seconds from the tone." The high, thin sound was barely audible over the siren. "Sixty seconds and counting. Six minutes to terminal vacuum. Personnel to take emergency precautions now, repeat now."

"Not going to make it, lover," Krysty panted, feeling a tightness across her chest.

"Will. It'll take five minutes before all of the air's sucked out."

"Doc won't make it." She glanced over her shoulder to see the ominous way that the group was stretching out behind her. Doc and Abe were now out of sight.

JAK STOOD by the raised sec door, looking for the others. Dean had joined him, but the rest of the group still hadn't arrived.

The siren suddenly cut out, and the tomblike passage was flooded with almost total silence. The only sound for several long moments was the distant clattering of running feet, gradually getting closer to them.

"Dad's in the lead," Dean announced, fighting for breath. "Then Krysty next."

The albino didn't seem at all distressed by the headlong desperate charge through the corridors of the redoubt. "Time's done," he said.

The voice chimed in from the speakers, confirming his judgment. "Purging has now commenced in sections four and five, and will be completed in four minutes and forty-five seconds from now. All personnel must follow the prescribed emergency procedures immediately.''

''Here's Dad.''

There was a faint hissing all around them, as the comp generators began to remove the tainted air from the two sections of the complex. Once that was done, then fresh air would be drawn in from exterior vents and flooded through the passages and rooms.

But that would be too late for anyone trapped inside during the purging procedures.

Ryan arrived, sweat beading his forehead, the rifle clattering on his shoulders, with Krysty at his side. ''Get inside,'' he ordered, barely able to speak from the efforts of the run. ''I'll wait for the others.''

Krysty, Jak and Dean obeyed him without a moment's hesitation, going through the open doorway into the brightly lighted control room.

Mildred and J.B. were next to arrive. The Armorer had handed her the Uzi, carrying the Smith & Wesson scattergun in his right hand as he put on a last burst of speed. ''Go straight into the chamber,'' Ryan said, feeling his breathing ease a little, though he was now becoming conscious that the air quality was diminishing all too quickly.

Trader was in sight, stumbling toward the entrance to the mat-trans section. Ryan didn't say anything, simply waving him on through after the others.

''Want me to stay and help, Ryan?''

''No. It's under control.''

The hissing seemed louder.

"Purging of sections four and five is forty percent completed and will terminate three minutes from now."

Trader vanished behind Ryan, clattering into one of the consoles as he nearly fell.

There was only Abe and Doc still to come. Ryan could hear the sound of feet coming his way, but they sounded like walking feet, not running feet.

The air was definitely much thinner. Ryan could already feel that his heart was working harder, his lungs beginning to struggle for a share of the deteriorating oxygen.

"Come on!" he shouted, aware that there was also something wrong with the acoustics. There was a bizarre kind of flat echo wrapped around his words. "Quick!"

"Coming." Abe lurched from side to side like someone in an advanced stage of jolt intoxication.

"Two minutes to total vacuum in sections four and five. Two minutes and counting."

"How far is Doc behind you?"

"Don't know. Don't know, Ryan. What do...where do I go now?"

"Into the gateway. Listen, Abe. Triple important. If I don't make it, tell them not to wait until it's too late. Tell them to shut the door and jump. Got it?"

"Sure. Don't wait until too late. Jump. Yeah. Want me to come and—"

"No. Just go."

Ryan raced into the corridor. It seemed to be shrinking in front of him, and the lights overhead were moving and dancing, like figures at the end of time.

The air was very thin now, and every step was labored and painful.

He'd started to try to run his mental clock, but the effort of concentrating was too great.

All Ryan knew was Doc would irrevocably die if he wasn't helped, and that he might die with him, trying to help.

The floor was surprisingly hard, and he yelped with pain as he banged his knee. But that was before he even realized that he'd fallen.

Ryan pulled himself upright with the aid of the right-hand concrete wall of the corridor, slipping as he started to walk back again.

He had a moment of horrific doubt that he might have lost his bearings, that he was now walking away from Doc, toward the gateway entrance.

A booming voice told him that there was one minute left before terminal purging of the air supply.

Ryan could hear his own blood pulsing through his ears, deafening him.

"Dear friend . . ."

"Doc?"

"Here."

As Ryan fumbled across the floor, his fingers brushed against clothing. A hand gripped his. Heaving at it, he dimly made out the figure of the old man. He tossed an arm around his shoulders, then the two of them stumbled forward together.

"Like three-legged racers," Doc wheezed, but the words made absolutely no sense at all to Ryan.

The air was almost gone.

Time and distance had blurred into a tortuous metaphor for existence.

For living and dying.

Ryan retained enough of his atavistic combat skill to keep to the left side of the endless wavering passage, knowing that he and Doc would eventually fall in through the open door to the mat-trans section.

Miss it and they were doomed.

It seemed as though they fell down, and he lost contact with Doc. For a paralyzed moment he reached out and found nothing, nobody.

Then the fingers were in his again.

Brighter light.

"Nearly there," someone said.

But the air was gone.

As Ryan fought to breathe, his lungs resisted, finding nothing to draw on, no sustenance.

The brighter light grew dimmer.

He saw the rows of desks, meaning they were so very close now to safety.

"Come on, Doc. Last fucking mile." The croaking voice was dragged from gods knew where.

A small part of Ryan's memory knew that it was already over and done.

The others would have closed the door to the gateway chamber and would have jumped away to safety. Knowing that made it easier to bear dying—and made him angry at the thought of being abandoned by his lover, son and friends.

At least they would...

Then the lines went down, and Ryan Cawdor became involved with the enigma of his own passing.

Chapter Eleven

It was a pleasant sensation, floating in a lake of dark water so saline that his body lay effortlessly on the surface, unmoving.

The temperature was so close to Ryan's blood heat that it was almost like floating inside his own body.

Everything was calmness. A gentle, placid glow suffused him, filling him with well-being.

Whatever else he might have done in some previous, bleak existence, this was all that Ryan now wanted to do for the next hours, days, weeks, months, years. For the whole remainder of infinity.

"Stop fucking smiling."

He had a vague, satisfied smile on his face as he floated on and on.

There was a tunnel around him, just visible if he opened both his eyes, walls and ceiling of slick, black marble, moving quietly by him.

"He's slipping away, Krysty. I don't... It's like he's stopped fighting."

The walls were coming closer. The ceiling was lowering, drawing nearer to him.

But none of that mattered to Ryan, not compared to the wonderful lethargy that wrapped itself around him like a grinning serpent.

"Dean. You try. Speak to him. Loud. He's not hearing us. If we don't bring him back right now, then I'm afraid he's gone from us forever."

Ryan drifted faster down the shrinking tunnel. Some old predark song filtered into the parts of his brain that hadn't closed down, about having no regrets and, mostly, about having done everything his own way.

Drifting faster.

"Quick, Dean. Pulse is still going down. He's drifting faster away."

Faces. Faces from old photographs. What had happened to them all?

Mother and father. Brother. The smile eased away from Ryan's face. Tumbling hair, burnished and brighter than the most heavenly sunrise.

A young boy. Dark, curly hair, serious eyes. Himself when he was about eleven years old?

"Dad?"

For a brief moment the water that bore Ryan along seemed to ripple, and the walls of the passageway retreated.

"Dad, you gotta fight. Gotta come back to us, Dad. Don't just give up."

Ryan swallowed, closing and opening his eye. The temperature of the water around him seemed to have dropped a little, making him less snug and comfortable.

"Pulse steadied."

"Come on, lover. For me."

"Dad..."

Ryan swallowed and opened his eye.

He was lying flat on his back, feeling cold, with a circle of faces staring down at him.

"Yeah," he whispered.

"I GATHER from our preeminent medical authority, as Dr. Wyeth likes to see herself, that I had passed out from oxygen deprivation rather more quickly than you did. As my body had, effectively, closed itself down on all fronts, the damage from the air being sucked away was, consequently, rather less for me than for you."

Ryan nodded. "They dragged us in and started the jump and we got away just in time?"

Doc lay on the bed next to him, still looking pale and shaken. "Indeed, yes. It rather seems that you had somehow pulled me that last hundred yards or so, despite having zero oxygen in your lungs." He coughed. "Yet again, my dear friend, I find that I must thank you for saving—"

Ryan held up a hand. "Forget it, Doc. You'd have done the same for me. The others did the same for us. You go out on the edge when you have to."

He had a ferocious headache and kept fighting back swimming waves of gut-deep nausea. But it was only an hour since he'd been heaved back from the wrong side of the grave.

"I confess," Doc continued, "to having felt a great deal less than well when I eventually recovered from the jump. Now, having a bed to lie on, I am a man new-made. Fresh made. Dairy maid. Sorry. Tongue running away without first contacting the brain. Awfully sorry."

Krysty walked across the room, joining them. "How are the two invalids?"

Doc grinned. "The agony, madam, has somewhat abated. That is a quote from someone like the philosopher, John Stuart Mill, who fell as a two-year-old and bumped his knee. A lady said 'Has little chappy hurty-wurty oozleself then?' To which the infant prodigy is alleged to have replied 'Thank you, madam, the agony has somewhat abated.' Jolly, good, eh?"

Krysty and Ryan both laughed.

She sat on the bed and took his hand in hers. "Getting better, lover?"

"Sure."

"Close call."

He nodded. "I know it. I had an ace on the line for the last train to the coast."

"Seat booked and paid for and almost occupied. It was Dean who brought you back from the brink. You responded to his voice. Saved you, lover."

"I heard you, as well."

She looked at him gravely, head to one side. "That the truth, lover?"

"Yeah. Yeah, it is."

She smiled at him. "Glad."

"Where are we?"

"Somewhere else. Gateway chamber walls were a kind of dark gray color. That's all we know."

"Big redoubt?"

"Looks it. We found this dorm with all facilities. A lot like the last stop we made."

His eye turned to the closed door with the word *Bathroom* above it.

Krysty laughed. "You can go and piss in complete safety. J.B. checked it out and reported back that it's a completely spider-free zone."

"Explored any farther?"

"No. J.B.'s taken charge. He and Trader..." She hesitated. "Well, they had a kind of frank and free discussion. J.B. won it. They finally agreed not to go recce any farther until everyone felt up to it. Bad jump for all of us."

"Second one always is."

Doc sniffed and wiped his nose with his sleeve. "Oddly, I can recommend making a jump while already deeply unconscious. I feel better than I normally do after a matter transfer."

"What sort of condition is the redoubt in?" Ryan tried to sit up, moaning at the stab of pain across his temples.

"Lie down, lover."

"Felt like someone pushing my eye out of its socket from inside," he commented.

"Just rest. Mildred reckons it's a good idea for us all to take a break after the two jumps so close together, before we explore and then think about leaving the complex."

"Makes sense. Can't say I feel like naked mud wrestling with a stickie just yet."

Doc sat up. "Mud wrestling! I wonder whether I ever mentioned the occasion that I was in Montana, not a hundred miles from the Little Big Horn, and there were two ladies of the night—soiled doves—in a huge bath of mud and neither of them—"

Ryan held up a hand. "Some other time, Doc. Right now, I'd like an hour's sleep."

"Of course, of course, dear friend. May choirs of angels sing thee to thy rest."

But Ryan's good left eye was already closed and he was snoring gently.

WHEN HE AWAKENED everyone was sitting or lying on adjacent beds in the dormitory. The room was smaller than the one in the previous redoubt, and the air smelled notably fresher and cleaner.

Mildred saw him wake and came to check his pulse. "Back to around normal. You got the healthiest constitution of anyone I ever knew, Ryan."

"It's eating lots of greens and going to bed with the sun," he replied.

"Sure."

Trader had stood, shuffling his feet restlessly. "Can we get moving?"

J.B. also stood. "We've checked out the wall plans here, Ryan. One of the biggest redoubts we've come across. All the signs are that it was well evacuated. There's writing on the map shows nuke damage to the southern flank, but that's a good long way away from us. Seems the Russkies' rockets took out the motor pool and missile stores. Also the armory. But the way it looks, it was a double-clean stripping. So there probably wouldn't have been much left to interest us."

It was one of the longest speeches that Ryan had ever heard J.B. make.

"How about the main entrance?"

"Seems clear from what the map shows. The passages, as far as we carried out a recce, haven't been sealed at all, so, when everyone's ready, we can go take a look."

Ryan swung his legs over the side of the bed. There was another jagged flare of pain behind his eye, but it subsided quickly. "Far as I'm concerned, let's get to it."

THEY STARTED MOVING in a skirmish line through the silent, long-abandoned corridors.

Progress was uneventful.

The Armorer's description had been as concise and precise as Ryan expected. The whole place had been swept clean before being evacuated.

The plan of the redoubt showed where someone had scrawled in faded crimson paint across an entire section, writing the simple message: Nuked.

The way to the main entrance led them up several levels, through intersections and past dining and medical areas. Mildred had been interested in the latter, but they all accepted that this wasn't going to be one of the complexes where they'd come across some long-buried treasure.

Finally they passed through a number of raised sec barriers, and along the sides of some armored and fortified MG emplacements into the vaulted hall that lay just within the main doors.

"Fucking ginormous!" Trader exclaimed. "I have never seen sec doors of that size."

They were sixty feet high and painted dark green. To Ryan's relief, he saw that there was the usual basic entry and exit code control at the side.

"Three, five and two to open them up," he said.

"How do you know that?" Trader asked suspiciously. "You been here before?"

"No. For some stupe sec reason, every one of the redoubts we've ever landed in has the same three-figure code. Look, it's painted at the side of the control panel."

"Oh, yeah."

"Can I enter it in, Dad?" Dean ran eagerly toward the controls, heels ringing in the stillness.

"When I say. First everyone spread out to both sides. Blasters ready. If I say close it, Dean, then you press two, five and three as the closing code for the doors. And you do it instantly. Understand?"

"Yeah, Dad."

"Instantly."

"Sure."

It took only a few seconds for the rest of the party to take up positions. Ryan, Krysty, Doc and Jak on the left of the massive double doors, J.B., Mildred, Trader and Abe on the other side.

"Now," Ryan said.

The boy carefully punched in the numbered code, stepping back out of the way.

"Moving," he called. "Can hear it."

There was the first tiny razor's-edge opening, letting in a sliver of bright sunshine.

"Least the weather looks like it's fine out there," Krysty whispered.

The doors moved back slowly on self-lube runners, vanishing into the slabs of bare rock on either side. The operation was almost soundless.

"Looks like we're high up," Trader said, at a better angle to see through the widening gap.

Now there was blue sky visible, with just a few fluffy white clouds.

"What wonderfully clean air," Doc commented, taking a deep breath. "So bracing."

Once the gap was wide enough, Ryan moved to it and glanced quickly around. He turned to wave his hand at the others. "Looks safe," he said.

Chapter Twelve

"New England." J.B. slowly lowered the miniature location finder, having squinted up at the bright sun through the delicate lens. "That must be the Lantic that we can see over there, so my best guess would probably put us in the south of what used to be called Maine."

The companions were standing together, grouped like tourists waiting to be captured for a commemorative strip of vid. The main entrance to the redoubt had been skillfully carved from the flank of a mountain, as they so often were, that it was probably all but invisible from the flatter land below. There was what would obviously have been a turning area for vehicles and a small parking lot. But the tarmac had been cracked and rippled as the result of some minor quakes, and the indelible yellow hatched lines wavered like the waves on a shore.

A two-lane blacktop wound down the side of the mountain, diminishing with distance and then vanishing among seemingly endless strands of dark conifers.

"No sign of anyone getting in," said Ryan, who'd checked the sec doors and their surround for indications of damage. There were the usual scratches and a number of tiny bullet marks pocking the expanse of almost indestructible sec steel. At the right-hand side, waist-high, opposite the recessed controls, there was the dark flare smear of a grenade, but it had made almost no impression on the place.

"No sign life." Jak shaded his red albino eyes, so vulnerable in the glare of bright sun. "No smoke."

The expanse of water that J.B. had guessed was the Lantic Ocean was off to their left, rolling away to the smudge of the horizon.

Mildred stood with eyes closed, head thrown back, breathing in the pine-scented freshness. "My Lord," she said. "After that stinking claustrophobia this is wonderful. Can we go and explore some? It looks like paradise."

"Sign, Dad!" Dean called. "Just over the edge of the highway."

Ryan pressed the reverse code and watched the doors begin to slide shut. Only when they'd met at the center did he join the rest of the friends.

"Come on," Trader snapped. "We don't all have the words! Can someone tell me what it says?"

Doc clasped the lapels of his tattered frock coat in a theatrical gesture, and began to declaim loudly from the tilted steel sign. "It warns all personnel from the Cadillac Mountain Redoubt that many parts of the Acadia National Park remain open to the general public and that care must be exercised in driving military vehicles at excessive speed." He laughed. "Pray all take heed that it does not say they shouldn't drive at speed. Just that they should take care to speed carefully. How typical of the logically illogical military mind."

"Acadia," Mildred said. "You're right on the mark, John. Ace on the line. Southern Maine. Not all that far from Stephen King country."

"Who's he?" Abe asked. "Local baron?"

"Sort of." Mildred grinned. "Maybe even more famous than that, back in predark times."

Doc's face had become angered. "By the three Kennedys! If all of the faceless politicians and bureaucrats of what was once this fair and decent land of ours had but a single throat, then I would be the first in line to volunteer to slit it open."

"Why, Doc?" Krysty asked. "Because of skydark and the long winters?"

"That and ten thousand crimes more. Here we stand in one of the most beautiful places in the world. I visited it long before it became a national park in 1919. When I was a mere sprat I was honored to meet the immortal Ralph Waldo Emerson. He once said that 'Nature is a mutable cloud, which is always and never the same.' He could have been thinking of Acadia."

"Still looks beautiful," Dean said. "Don't really understand you, Doc."

"When the politics of the old prenuking world began to deteriorate at the very end of the twentieth century, the United States was one of the countries to realize that Götterdämmerung could be just around the corner."

"What the fuck's that?" Trader asked.

Doc bowed toward him. "I am delighted at your fascination at my pronouncements, my dear fellow, but I confess to finding that your phrasing is becoming both tedious and repetitive."

"How's that?" Trader hefted the Armalite.

Doc ignored him. "Götterdämmerung. The twilight of the gods. The end of the world, perhaps, Trader, would be more easily understood by you. Shorter words, eh?"

"Be real careful how you go, Doc," Trader warned with serious anger and menace in his voice. "Nobody loves a smartass, and I love them less than most folks."

"Of course, of course."

He turned to Dean. "I shall finish swiftly. The government, in its dubious wisdom, decided on its policy, under the Totality Concept, to build a number of these ultrasecret hideouts. These redoubts. And they chose the most beautiful and isolated parts of the country to site them." His voice boomed with rage. "And the running mongrels picked some of our finest national parks!"

"Like this?" Dean asked.

"Indeed. Acadia. Jewel of the Northeast, set in the silver sea."

"Still looks good, though," Mildred said.

"That is not the point, madam, as well you know. Something perfect has been marred forever."

"Nature finds its own way of getting back, doesn't it, Doc?" Trader shook his head slowly as he stared across the scenic vista.

Doc was taken aback. "Well, I suppose you could say... Yes, my dear Trader, I believe it has those powers of healing and regeneration. Shrewdly observed, my dear fellow, very shrewdly observed."

"Thanks," Trader said dryly.

"We talked enough, Dad?" Dean asked impatiently. "Only it looks a real dude kind of morning and we should get moving down the mountain."

"So wise, so young..." Doc said, then he stopped, looking embarrassed. "I disremember the rest of the quote. But the lad is right, is he not, Master Cawdor?"

"Yeah, he is. Let's go see what New England's looking like today."

AS THEY WOUND THEIR WAY down the hillside, it seemed like New England was looking particularly good.

The upper granite slopes of what they believed was Mount Cadillac were fairly bare of vegetation, with patches of scrubby heather and lichen here and there. But the lower they descended, the richer the land became.

"Look at the forest," Mildred said as they paused at one of the snakeback turns in the blacktop. "This must be what the land looked like before the white man came storming in with his alcohol and his smallpox and loggers and strip miners. One of the rare moments I'm glad to be in Deathlands rather than back in my old life. Least I can taste fresh air and smell the woods. It's a good-to-be-alive sort of day."

"What's that?" Abe asked, pointing to a large, blue-tinted bird with an enormous wingspan that had risen from a glacial lake behind a bluff. It flapped its serene way toward a larger body of water to the north.

"Blue heron," Jak said. "Used to be rare. Christina had predark book on birds. Saw it there."

NOW THEY WERE CLOSING in to the timberline.

Doc had paused and was staring back at the top of the mountain, shading his eyes with his hand. "It is impossible to make out the entrance to the redoubt, even from here," he said. "Such cunning concealment."

J.B. pushed back his fedora. "I reckon I once read that this place, this Cadillac Mountain, was about the first place in the whole of the predark States to see the rising sun. Guess it could well be true."

"Everyone's so full of fucking useless facts," Trader exploded. "Blue heron! It's just a big bird, and if we'd been close enough, it would make good eating." His voice became more sarcastic. "And who gives a splash of flying bat shit what place sees the sun first. You see it when you see it."

Doc pointed a bony forefinger at him. "Listen to me, if you will."

"What is it now? More words, Doc?"

"During the time that I have ridden, unbidden, hidden in the midden... Damnation! That I have ridden with Ryan and the estimable John Dix, your name has come up in conversation on countless occasions. Nearly always in circumstances that reflect favorably on you."

"So I'd fucking hope." Trader grinned.

"Wait before you allow smugness to advance too far. I was more than happy to meet with someone who had played such a vital part in the lives of two of my best friends. We have now only spent a few hours in each other's company and..." Doc hesitated. "And I am disappointed in you, Trader."

"That so? My heart is weeping, Doc."

"I am sure it is. You are an arrogant and bitter man who appears to have lost sight of humanity and humor. I do not know whether that condition is irredeemable. I hope not. But I hold out little faith in your changing. And for that I am deeply sorry."

Doc turned on his heel and strode off down the highway, the ferrule of his sword stick rapping out a merry tattoo.

Nobody spoke.

Trader looked around, finding that most of the group wouldn't meet his eyes. He settled on Ryan. "You got anything to say about that?"

"Some. Doc may seem like he's sometimes missing a few cards from the deck, but he's one of the wisest, truest men I ever met. Proud to call him my friend. I'm not saying he's all the way right. But there's a lot of truth in it. All I say, Trader, is to give it some thought."

"Oh, yeah, I'll do that all right."

He stalked off after Doc, shoulders hunched, the Armalite trailing in his right hand. Ryan glanced at J.B., who simply shrugged.

"HEMLOCK, SPRUCE, half a dozen different types of pine and three or four kinds of fir." Mildred had been ticking them off on her fingers as the blacktop entered the massive stands of timber on both sides.

"Never seen so many squirrels." Dean drew his huge Browning Hi-Power and aimed it at a group of the tree rats that were gamboling around the base of a lightning-scarred spruce. "Bang," he said. "Get us some dinner."

"Squeeze the trigger on that and you'd be picking up bits of fluff and gristle and a few splinters of bone," Trader said, his good humor seemingly restored. "Apart from bringing everyone running for miles around."

"Yeah." Dean looked rueful. "Wish I hadn't left that .22 back at the ranch."

"The Remington 580?" said the Armorer. "Nice little rifle. Would've been fine for those squirrels, Dean. Not an awful lot of use against bears or stickies. Just get them riled up. The Browning's a real stopper."

"Should think about getting us some meat," Ryan said. "Find a camp for the night."

"Along the side of that big lake could be good." Abe pointed below them, where the water glittered, blue-gray in the sunlight.

"Be plenty dry wood. Broken branches. Get smokeless fire going." Jak blinked in the bright sun. "Saw deer tracks side road back ways. Must be plenty game."

THE SMOKE FROM THE FIRE was almost colorless, rising in a narrow pillar between the trees, dissipated by the light westerly breeze that was blowing off the land, toward the nearby ocean.

The haunch of venison was cooking nicely, browning and bubbling on the outside, the greasy juices dribbling into the flames, crackling and spitting. The rest of the slaughtered animal was piled at the water's edge, where Dean and Abe were busily finishing the bloody process of butchery, singing a song together, taking alternate verses. The boy looked over his shoulder to see whether Ryan was listening.

Krysty watched him from by the fire. "You know your dear little boy is singing with Abe?"

"Sure."

"Know what he's singing?"

"Sounds like 'Black On The Outside And Red On The Inside' to me."

She smiled. "Disgusting song. The boy's only eleven. Some responsible father you are, Ryan Cawdor."

"Least I brought home the meat for the larder," he protested. "Fine shooting."

"With that SSG-70 Steyr? Starlite night scope and the laser image enhancer? All to shoot a baby deer from twenty yards from deep cover. You could have thrown the blaster at it and chilled it that way. Saved the bullet."

"I didn't..." He laid his hand on her shoulder, leaned forward and kissed her on her fire-reddened cheek. "Well, yeah, I guess I did. Not too hard a shot."

"You think anyone would've heard it?"

"Big round, but the trees would've muffled it. Shot it over an hour ago. If we were getting guests, I figure they'd have arrived by now."

"This is really one of the loveliest campsites we ever found." She kissed him, then leaned back, fanning at her face. "Good fire, that."

"I don't recall ever being this close to the sea in old Maine before," he said. "One of Trader's stomping grounds, New England. Met Marsh Folsom and the Magus around these parts."

Trader had gone for a walk along the side of the lake, with J.B. and Mildred. They had just emerged out of the dense forest onto a narrow promontory, a couple of hundred yards away to the left.

"Where's Doc?" Krysty asked.

"Dozing over there, at the bottom of the tall pine. Seems to have gotten over the disappearance of the woman real well. I was worried."

"Me, too. I think...no, I'm *sure* that they had a brief but active couple days of sex. But she wasn't right for Doc. Reckon he knew that."

"Do him good."

"How about what he was saying about Trader? Seems like Doc can't stand him."

Ryan knelt down by her. "What do you think, lover? You like him or not?"

She shook her head, solemn. "Too early to say. Ask me again in a few days."

Chapter Thirteen

They all ate ravenously from the dead deer, Trader in particular stuffing himself with roasted meat until he could hardly stand.

"Not good for your health," Mildred said reproachfully. "Starvation and then gluttony are a classic prescription for gut trouble."

"Trader had some real bad kind of rad cancer in his belly, didn't you?" Abe grinned at his old chief, until he saw from the expression on Trader's face that he wasn't particularly amused by the discussion.

"Yeah. But that was long times ago."

"You still get problems?" Mildred asked with a professional interest.

Trader controlled himself with a visible effort. "Know you're a doctor and all that, but what goes on inside my clothes is my own business and everyone else can mind their own. Is that clear?"

Mildred grinned and nodded. "'Course. But if you do get trouble, you know who to come to."

"Yeah, thanks."

THE AFTERNOON DRIFTED BY, with several of the group snatching at the rare chance of safety and stillness to catch up on lost sleep and relaxation, allowing their bodies to recuperate from the physical and mental horrors of making the double jump.

Dean wandered to the lakeside, picking out flat pebbles and flicking them underarm at the serene water, whooping occasionally at a specially long duck-and-drake skimmer.

Ryan and Krysty were lying together in the shade of a feathery blue spruce, watching the sylvan scene.

He broke the silence. "Know what you're thinking, lover."

"Probably."

"Shall I tell you?"

She smiled, her emerald eyes fixed to his face. "I love you so much, Ryan Cawdor," she said. "Now, go on and tell me what I was thinking."

"First you were thinking how much you loved me, which made me remember that I felt something kind of similar about you."

"Bastard." She gave him the finger. "Wish I hadn't told you my secret. Go on."

"You were thinking that this seemed like a nice place to settle and raise a family."

Krysty's smile vanished as quickly as a late frost off a summer pasture. "Yes," she said, the single word flat and dull, like a spade full of wet earth on a coffin lid.

"Well," he said defensively, "you were. I knew you would. Anytime we come across somewhere like this— woods, water, sun, mountains and all that shit—"

"All that *shit?*"

"You know what I mean, Krysty. And don't get pissed at me, because I feel the same."

"Do you, Ryan?"

"'Course."

"But?"

"But what?"

"There always has to be a 'but,' doesn't there, lover. What is it?"

Ryan sat up and looked around. "You used that word..." He thought about it. "Sounded like idle?"

"Idyll?"

"Yeah. Something that's triple ideal. Way this region seems. But it never has been. All of the other times and all the other places."

"There's always a worm at the heart of the apple, you mean, lover?"

"Something like that. Evil and death. A rotting skull underneath a pretty Mardi mask. I've had my hopes raised a few times in my life. Don't like the feeling."

"Fair enough." The smile was back again, tenderness in the fathomless green eyes. "Let's spend awhile in this particular paradise and see how it goes."

"Sure. It's such a good place, brimming with game, fish in the lake. Could stay here a week or so."

"That would be... What?"

Ryan had jumped to his feet, staring through the fringe of trees toward the lake. "Heard something."

Simultaneously they both heard the sound of Dean's voice, calling out in alarm, and a sinister, snarling noise.

"Wolf?" Ryan asked, drawing the SIG-Sauer and running to the side of the lake, looking to the left. Krysty was at his heels, Jak close behind. The others only just started to waken from sleep.

The boy was at the edge of the water, backing away toward the camp, crouching, his right hand held out defensively. He was around a hundred paces off, but Ryan could see the bright flash of silver off the blade of the knife and the sparkle of the turquoise from the hilt.

The animal facing Dean was nearly as big as a full-grown timber wolf, but it looked to Ryan more like a German shepherd. It was belly down, looking ready to spring, its red-rimmed eyes fixed on its prey. The brindled coat was marked by three distinctive white blazes on its chest, like stars. It was growling deep in its throat as it crept closer to the boy.

"Get the rifle," Ryan said to Krysty. "Best chance."

"No," Mildred breathed, arriving with Trader, J.B. and the others. "Mine."

Trader had his Armalite, and he shouldered the woman aside. "Boy's part in line of fire. Won't do anything with that fucking little gaudy toy. I'll take it out."

Ryan glanced sideways, seeing that Mildred had already drawn the six-shot revolver she always carried, the Czech ZKR 551, chambered to take the big Smith & Wesson round.

He'd watched J.B. fieldstrip the weapon, admiring the solid frame side rod ejector and the practical short-fall thumb-cocking hammer.

And he'd seen what Mildred could do with that special blaster.

"She shoots, Trader."

"Does she fuck?"

Dean had jabbed out quickly at the dog, holding off a charge, making it wait a little longer. But time was passing and time was lifeblood.

Ryan felt the old familiar crimson mist of blind anger seeping over his mind. He cocked the 9 mm P-226 and jammed it into Trader's side.

"She shoots," he said through gritted teeth, knuckle white on the trigger.

Trader said nothing, his whole body stiffening, eyes narrowing, lips peeling back in a feral snarl of anger. But he didn't try any movement.

"Do it, Mildred," Ryan whispered.

"Killing your son," Trader breathed.

Mildred stood very still, shuffling her boots in the shingle to gain a sure purchase. She lifted the revolver in her right hand, staring down the barrel, two-eyed, took a single breath and held it for several seconds.

Ryan also held his breath, seeing the way the big dog's haunches were quivering with barely repressed tension, ready to spring at the boy's throat.

The sound of the blaster was surprisingly flat, out in the open.

"Told you . . ." Trader growled, still braced against the muzzle of Ryan's SIG-Sauer.

The animal didn't move for several seconds.

"Again?" J.B. asked.

Jak answered the question. "No need. Chilled it."

The dog's head went back as though it had been distracted by a bird flying near by. It gave a strange, growling bark, then its muzzle dropped to the shingle, its flanks shivered, and it was motionless.

Mildred holstered the revolver.

She began to walk toward Dean, who was still carefully watching the dead animal. Jak and the others all followed her, boots crunching in the quiet.

Neither Trader nor Ryan moved.

"Well?" the older man said.

"Mildred won a silver medal in the free-shooting pistol event at the last ever Olympic Games, in Miami. She's the best shot with a handblaster that I ever saw."

"What 'bout three-eyed Charlie, lived near the Sippi back in—"

"The best," Ryan insisted firmly. "I knew she could pull that shot off and save Dean from, at best, a bad mauling. Better than any of us."

"Could've said. Didn't have to ram that blaster into my ribs like that."

"No time." He sniffed. "Reckon I can put it back in its holster now?"

"Sure."

Ryan put away the SIG-Sauer, every nerve on the alert for Trader swinging the butt of the Armalite at his head. But there was nothing.

The others had gathered around Dean, but Ryan noticed that Krysty was watching the dramatic scene behind her, and her hand was on the butt of her own five-shot Smith & Wesson double-action 640.

"That dog had a collar on," Trader said.

"Didn't notice."

His laugh turned into a cough. "Never did see everything, Ryan, with only one fucking eye."

"See more with one than you do with two."

Trader grinned. "That'll be the day, pilgrim. Yeah, that'll be the day."

They walked together across the sloping beach. Ryan thought that the moment of extreme tension had passed, until Trader grabbed him by the forearm, his fingers like steel traps.

"Just before we get to the others, partner."

"Sure."

"Known me a long time. Know that not many men stick me with a blaster and ever eat another meal."

"I'd do it again, Trader. If I had to, I'd do it again, just the same."

"I know you would. Just so's you know I might not react so slow next time."

"If there is a next time."

The fingers relaxed their grip. "Let's go see how pretty a shot the lady is."

The dog lay on the beach, surrounded by the rest of the group of friends. Ryan walked up and patted Dean on the back. "All right, son?"

"Sure," he replied, though the pallor of his cheeks told a slightly different story. "Came out of the woods at me. I reckon I could have taken it with my knife."

"You thanked Mildred?"

"Yeah, he did," she replied.

"Good-looking animal," Ryan said, noticing that Trader had been correct. There was a metal collar around its throat, above the three white stars.

"Real big." Abe bent down to stare at it. "I don't see the bullet hole, Mildred. No blood."

She leaned over to look, nodding, so that the beads in her hair clattered softly. "Yeah. Where I aimed. I couldn't see much, because of Dean being in the way. Just part of its head. So I shot it through the right ear."

Trader laughed. "You hit a dog in the ear at a hundred yards! With a fucking handblaster!"

"There," Krysty said, pointing with the chiseled toe of her boot. "See the tiny trickle of blood. Absolutely perfect shot."

"Told you." Ryan grinned.

BEFORE RETURNING to the campsite, Ryan unbuckled the collar from the dog's throat.

"What does it say?" Doc asked. "Mayhap that his name was Rover and he lived at Sunnydown Cottage?"

"No. I reckon it was called Three Stars," Abe suggested.

"Killer Bastard" was Dean's own offering for the dog's name.

"Well, lover? Tell us?"

"According to this collar tag, the dog was called '279792493A.' Funny sort of a name, isn't it?"

"Shows a sad lack of the romantic. Why not Stoutheart or Valiant?"

"There wasn't any other marking on it, was there, Dean?" Ryan said.

"The three white patches. One foot was white, as well. And the collar."

"Nothing else?"

"No, Dad. I can't go and look because I threw the body in the lake."

"That wasn't very ecologically correct," Mildred said. "Couldn't you have buried it?"

"No, 'course not, Mildred. That's a pretty triple-stupe sort of idea, isn't it, Dad?"

Ryan hesitated. "Well, different people have different ideas. Truth is, I'd probably either have left the body where it was or...or I'd have thrown it in the lake."

"Well..." The boy beamed at Mildred, who tutted in disapproval.

"Point of fact, son, I wish you hadn't heaved it in the water. There was something about it that made me wonder."

"Wonder what, Ryan?" J.B. asked. "About how healthy it looked? And that weird collar?"

"Yeah. I'll go and walk along a ways, see if it's still floating where I can get at it."

"I'll come," Jak offered.

"Sure thing." He looked at the sky. "This is such a good place, I think we'll camp here for the night."

They made their way toward the spot where the dog had come out of the undergrowth and menaced Dean. The afternoon was wearing on, and the shadows were lengthening. Out in the middle of the lake, a huge trout leapt and sparkled in the spray. And across the far side the two men saw a small herd of deer, browsing quietly.

"Could live forever here," said the albino teenager.

"Nobody lives forever, Jak." Ryan looked around. "Was it near here?"

"Think so. Before bit of land sticking out."

Ryan stood with his back to the forest, trying to make out the corpse of the dog, which should still have been floating, sodden, in the lake.

Then he heard a noise that raised his hackles, a deep, menacing growl.

He and Jak both spun to face what at first looked like a wolf, but which they realized was a German shepherd dog, snarling at them, with three white stars on its chest, a white foot and a silver collar around its powerful, bristling throat.

"Holy shit," Jak said. "Ghost dog."

Chapter Fourteen

The dog started toward them, tail out, moving one careful paw at a time. Its teeth were bared, and a yellow dribble of froth was sliding from its jaws. The sunlight danced on the silver collar.

"It's the same dog," Jak breathed, his right hand reaching behind him for the taped hilt of one of his leaf-bladed throwing knives.

"Can't be. Got a .38 bullet buried in its brain. It was chilled. You saw it. I saw it." Ryan drew the SIG-Sauer as the dog approached, stiff-legged, closing within thirty feet of them. "It was an ex-dog, Jak."

"So, what's this? Ghost? Manitou? Shape changer? Come on, Ryan. Tell me."

The dog hunkered, bloodshot eyes fixed on the two men, as though it were trying to decide which was going to have his genitals ripped from his body.

Ryan's finger tightened on the trigger. Despite his undoubted nerve and combat bravery, he couldn't shake off a feeling of near superstitious dread.

It wasn't just a similar sort of animal.

It was the *same* dog.

"Do it," Jak whispered.

Ryan shot the big dog through one of the trio of snow-white patches of fur in the middle of its chest. The 9 mm round went clean through the animal's body, blowing out a ragged, bloodied chunk of flesh the size of a grapefruit from under the ribs on the left side.

The animal went down kicking, trying to bite itself in the center of the exit wound, legs scrabbling in the small stones of the beach. Blood gushed from its body, pumping slower and slower. It toppled over, after trying to make it toward the safety of the forest, twitching and lying still.

"Now that's a dead dog," Ryan said, holstering the warm blaster.

He turned at the sound of running feet, everyone brought by the gunshot—everyone except Abe, who had chosen that moment to go into the woods to relieve himself. He had just appeared, pants at half-mast, trying to see what had happened.

"Not another dog," said Dean, first there.

Trader stopped in his tracks. "Not another dog. It's the same fucking animal!" He grinned in triumph at Ryan. "Told you the slut didn't... I mean Mildred couldn't be that good with a revolver. Nobody could be. Grazed it and it recovered. Got to be the fucking answer, don't it?"

J.B. reached in his pocket. "Very clever animal, if you're right, Trader. Didn't just recover from a brain shot with a .38, but it also made itself a brand-new collar." He produced the original strip of silvered metal and let it dangle from his fingers.

Jak sheathed his knife again. "Ryan said was ex-dog."

Doc glanced at Mildred, who grinned. They chorused, perfectly together "It has ceased to be," and broke into laughter.

"What's funny?" Abe asked, joining them. Seeing the dog, he added, "Why did you shoot a dead dog, Ryan?"

"It's identical," Krysty said quietly. "Same three white stars. Same white paw. Same collar."

Ryan stooped and removed the metal strip, angling it to the sun so he could read it.

"Says 279792493."

"Same number, exactly as this one," the Armorer said, checking each digit. "This one ends in the letter *A*. That one got the same letter?"

"No. This is a *B*, instead. Precisely the same coded sequence, but just a letter different."

They all stood in silence, looking at the corpse, already attracting the first of a swarm of blowflies.

"This passes belief," Doc said. "They must surely be from the same litter. Brothers, perhaps?"

Ryan looked at his son. "Did you notice anything else unusual about that first dog? Anything about it we could check with this one?"

Dean considered the question. "Gee, Dad, that's... I nearly pissed in my pants when I saw it coming for me, you know. The way it was snarling and baring its teeth at..." His eyes widened. "Oh, yeah, the teeth."

"What about the teeth?" J.B. probed.

"Well, I noticed that instead of the usual big curved tooth on each side, here—" he pointed to his own mouth, at the front "—it had like double teeth."

"The canines?" Mildred asked. "Really big and hooked over. Two? You mean two on each side at the top?"

"Yeah. Certain. I remember noticing it. When I was living with my mother, Rona, we were on the run a lot, skipping from villes at night, you know. Often had the baron's dogs set on us. I saw more hounds' teeth than I had hot soup."

Trader was already down on hands and knees, reaching for the blood-flecked muzzle, forcing open the jaws with an effort. "Strong bastard, it was," he said. "There." He finally managed to get them apart.

Everyone leaned forward, seeing that the dead animal had double canine teeth on both sides of its upper jaw.

RYAN HELD THE TWO COLLARS, laid flat across the palm of his hand, staring at them. "Doesn't make sense. Not to be that alike."

"Identical twins are not that unusual among human bipeds, are they, Dr. Wyeth?"

"I don't know the stats on that. Not my field. Twins must be odds of around a hundred to one. Identical siblings can only come along about one time in fifty sets of twins. That's all I know about babies. What I know about animal genetics can be written large on the head of a damned pin."

"But that engraved code." J.B. took the pair of metal tags from Ryan. "Absolutely identical apart from that last letter. Like some kind of experiment. Mebbe the woods are alive with twenty more, all with the same numbers and different letters. Or a hundred more."

Trader had been picking small pebbles from the deep tread on his combat boots, flicking them into the lake, where the corpse of the second animal was floating gently by them, about twenty yards out in the water.

"I reckon we should move from here," he said.

"Why?"

"Spooked, Ryan, that's why. When you meet something out of the ordinary, then it's time to hit the trail again. That was always my rule with the war wags."

"Like when?"

"Onyx woman in Houston. Giant rats in Allegheny. The purple creeper in Tuscaloosa. And the gold eagles up over the border snows in Canada. How about—"

Ryan held up a hand. "All right, Trader. You made your point. You say we should go back and make a jump again up on Cadillac Mountain?"

"No. Just move on. Away from the lake."

"I agree." J.B. looked around the circle. "Trader could be right. Something strange in those dogs. I can feel it. Guess we all can."

Ryan turned to Krysty. "You got a feeling on this one, lover? Good or bad?"

"Felt good for a while. Now..." She shrugged. "Now, I'm not so sure."

The doubt was there on everyone's face, and Ryan realized the decision had, for all practical purposes, been taken. "Let's move on," he said.

THEY WALKED AROUND the flank of the lake in a single, strung-out skirmish line. The region was full of wildlife, and they disturbed a mutie moose with antlers that had a spread of over ten feet. Trader went for the Armalite, but checked himself.

"Still got enough meat," he said, after a long pause, adding, "didn't want to chill something as grand as that giant booger. Wouldn't be right."

The trail forked at the neck of the lake, and Ryan stopped, considering the options.

They stood in a bowl of hills, those behind them taller than those ahead. In the one direction, Ryan could see that a fresh blacktop cut up higher through a fork in the rocks, looking as though it might lead into a valley.

"There," he said, pointing. "Try up there."

KRYSTY HAD MOVED FORWARD to join him at the head of the group. "Dark's not far off," she said.

"Yeah. You noticed that this has been kept clear, like it's used a lot?"

"I thought I saw some old wag wheel marks a way back, where the road split."

"We passed a number of side trails, and quite a few of those showed marks of wheels and feet."

"Yet it seems deserted. If there's lots of people, then the game would be more scared and a lot less." She touched him on the arm. "Good feeling's already gone, lover, on this place. Like we talked about—the worm in the apple."

"Go back and jump again?"

"Not yet. Mebbe find a good safe camp for the night and think about it in the sane light of morning."

IT WAS an excellent site for an overnight camp.

Halfway up the main blacktop, Ryan had picked a narrow trail to the left, which headed a little higher up,

ending at a small lake, really no more than a large
pool. But it was fed by a fast-running stream that fell
six or eight feet over a lip of granite, giving good, cold
water.

There was a view out to the west between two hills,
heavily wooded, with plenty of broken branches all
around them for a fire. Abe and Dean quickly got
flames dancing and started to cook some of the venison that they'd carried with them.

"Think we should post a guard," Trader asked,
"after those twin dogs?" He spit in the dirt. "And we
all saw them wag and boot tracks on the way here."

Ryan and J.B. had just been discussing that very
question when Trader joined them, both agreeing that,
with nine of them in the group, they could easily do a
one-on-and-eight-off watch.

"Yeah," Ryan said. "We'll fix the rota later, after
we've eaten."

THERE WERE DIFFERING times of danger during a
night in the open in unknown and potentially hostile
country.

Just as dusk subsiding into full dark was a particular threat, similarly the hour before the false dawn
brightened the eastern sky. Generally Ryan's long experience had shown that the small hours, between
about two and four, were also higher risk than earlier
in the night.

This meant using the less combat-skilled for the
safer times—Doc, Mildred and Dean. Abe and Krysty
for the midrisk times, then dividing the rest of the
hours of darkness between himself, Trader, J.B. and
Jak.

The white-haired teenager had the best night vision, so it was sensible to utilize him for the period of poorest light.

There was a sliver of moonlight, flirting with an endless range of frayed clouds that were being carried across Acadia from the Lantic Ocean.

SEVERAL TIMES while he was sleeping, Ryan came awake at the distant howling of what he was certain was a hunting pack of timber wolves. But they sounded far off, among the mountains, and didn't worry him.

Doc had awakened him once, whispering that he thought there was something drinking at the pool. "I fear that my vision is veiled at such times."

He was so close to Ryan that he could feel the old man's breath tickling the tiny hairs in his ears. "Stay still here, Doc. I'll take a look."

It hadn't entirely been a false alarm.

As Ryan inched toward the pool, blaster ready, he could hear a faint sound above the tumbling of the fall. He flattened out and crawled the last few yards on his stomach, parting a fringe of long sedge grass, peered out and smiled. He turned back and rejoined the waiting Doc Tanner.

"You were right to wake me," he said quietly. "Anything out of the ordinary has a capacity for turning into danger. But not this time."

"What was it?"

"Water shrews, about as big as your little finger. Couple hundred of them, like a regular army. Probably come up here together for a drink every night about this time."

JAK TOUCHED HIM on the shoulder. Despite the almost total blackness that met Ryan's eye, it was easy to see the great flare of white hair that tumbled about the young man's shoulders. "Time," he said.

"Anything?"

"No."

But there was a faint note of reservation. "What, Jak?"

"Thought heard dogs and man calling. Quarter hour back. Not repeated."

"Wolves?"

"Not wolves. Dogs. Then quieted."

Ryan stood, pulling on his coat. Despite the warmth and sunshine of the day, the temperature had dropped sharply and was now very close to freezing.

"Fine," he said, watching Jak pick his way to his own place around the dull embers of the fire.

As he moved from the camp, Krysty stirred and lifted a hand. Ryan stopped and took it, squeezing it between both his. He stooped and kissed the woman on the forehead, feeling the tendrils of sentient hair stirring and brushing at his own stubbled cheeks.

"Take care, lover," she breathed.

After a few minutes Ryan found that his night vision was slowly creeping back. It wasn't as good as Jak's, but a deal better than the average. The night was very dark, with the moon having finally given up the struggle and settled down for the rest of the night behind a wall of dense cloud.

As Ryan looked around him, he saw a chem storm in the distance, pink and purple streaks of lightning flickering across the sky like threads of fine silk in an antique shawl.

He'd read old crumbling books that showed men on guard in the night. They'd been marching around and around, like little clockwork sec men, making themselves an easy prey to any attacker. That wasn't the way to do it, as Trader had taught him.

"Slow and easy. Stop a lot, look and listen. Go back every now and again in the opposite direction. Avoid any pattern. Most important is to stop and listen. Best way of picking someone up who's trying to get in."

The other thing was to work a different perimeter. No point letting any enemy see that you were always walking the same pattern over the ground.

On his third walk around the camp, Ryan decided to strike off deeper into the woods, following a game trail down past the pool, into a steep-sided, narrow valley. It was filled with a tangle of brush and fallen trees, but the path wound its way around the obstacles.

Despite the covering of dry wood, Ryan moved silently, ghosting through the darkness.

He spotted the sinuous progress of a tiny, thick-furred, weasellike creature, crossing the trail less than ten feet in front of him, yet totally unaware of the human predator that had invaded its hunting territory.

The wind had eased in the shelter of the ravine, and Ryan stopped and held his breath, straining to hear any sound that didn't fit the mosaic of the night. He could just hear his own blood thudding in his ears, and he remembered that Mildred had told him that the great pistol shooters, back when she was on the Olympic team, timed their shots *between* heartbeats. Something that he found barely credible.

But he'd seen the astounding way that Mildred could shoot, so mebbe it was true.

Ryan waited, deciding that he'd gone far enough away from the camp, intending to climb back onto the ridge and walk around the pool, over the stream, when he heard a noise a little way farther down, where the path dipped sharply. The noise was like heavy breathing, or sighing, or moaning.

It took Ryan only half a minute to find the tortured, dying man.

Chapter Fifteen

Dean and Abe had built up the fire, blowing on the almost-dead ashes until they flickered into reluctant life, the flames catching at the dry twigs, spreading to the thicker branches until the camp was brightly lighted. It was risky, as the crackling flames could easily attract attention. A bright fire was visible for twenty miles at night.

Ryan had gone back immediately, after a cursory examination of the man, seeing that there was nothing he could do in the pitch-dark undergrowth. He figured that moving the victim to the camp was unlikely to do him much more damage.

Enough had already been done.

Jak, Trader and J.B. had accompanied him back into the steep ravine, working together to haul the moaning man up the slope, laying him by the growing fire, where Mildred could look him over.

Faced with a medical problem, she immediately slipped into doctor mode.

"Male, Caucasian, possibly with Native American blood a generation back. Five feet eight inches tall. Weighs...oh, around one-thirty. Naked. Been walking in the backcountry for several hours, mebbe days. Based on the condition of his feet. Very blistered. Multiple abrasions, cuts, bites, bruises and stings.

None of those look serious, though some of them have, I think, become infected.''

"Like saying that a bastard who's exploded a frag gren in his own mouth also had a fucking pimple on his ass. Not the bruises and stings that are chilling him.''

Mildred turned to Trader, her eyes cold. "My definition of a fool is someone who talks first and thinks afterward. I'm doing this so's all of us have an ace on the line about the poor devil's precise condition.''

"Go on, love,'' J.B. said quietly. "Don't take any notice of Trader.''

The older man turned away in anger and walked across the clearing to sit again by the side of the pool, presenting them with his hunched shoulders.

"Shaved head. Also shaved body. Complete depilation.'' Seeing the question rising to Dean's lips, she added, "I don't know why, son. Almost like he's been readied for a surgical operation, back in predark times.''

"That would correlate with the way he has been so sorely injured. Maimed, one might say. To my inexperienced eye, Dr. Wyeth, I would have said that the wounds had been inflicted with an almost-surgical skill.''

She nodded. "Can't argue with you on that, Doc. Scalpel or a straight razor's been used on some of those incisions around his chest and throat. Tracheotomy's been done by someone who knew exactly what they were doing. Tell the truth, I'm quite surprised to see this degree of clinical professionalism here in Deathlands. Thought that had all died out and all you had now were the butchers and the medicine-show quacks, the leeches and the tooth drawers. This was a surgeon.''

"What's a trackon?" Abe asked.

"The hole in his throat. This doesn't make sense, friends. There's needle tracks in his arms and small, partly healed sores where he's spent time in bed. Look at his elbows, heels and around his buttocks.''

"Those marks on his wrists and ankles look more like he'd been cuffed," J.B. observed.

"Agreed, love.''

The man had been placed gently on his back. He seemed to have sunk into a coma, though he kept making the tiny mewling sounds that had first attracted Ryan's attention. He had twice opened his eyes, but it looked as if they were fixed far off on someplace else. His breathing was ragged, bubbles of pale blood fluttering at the corner of his mouth.

"How long's he got?" Krysty asked.

"Hour. Might live to see the dawn.''

"You didn't tell us about all the other wounds, Mildred," Dean said.

"Holes in his guts and chest. Look to me like what we called a laparotomy. Kind of like keyhole surgery. You go in and take a look at what's in there, decide whether it's remedial or whether it might be inoperable or terminal. But, I don't see why the poor son of a bitch would possibly have needed three. Like they did them just for the sake of doing them. I can't understand the ethics of all this.''

"The stitches?" Ryan queried. "I've had some in my days, but he looks like a map of the Everglades.''

"Two or three hundred, easy." Mildred stopped and peered at them more closely. "Some are recent. Some look months old. But it's like the other factors. There's no illness known to man that would need so many stitches, all over the place."

"Not knife wounds?" Jak asked.

"No, definitely not. Look, they relate to different major organs." She touched him gently as she spoke. "Lungs. Liver. Kidney. Large intestine. Several around the urino-genital system. Joints have been opened. Knee, elbow and shoulder. Looks like a human guinea pig."

"What's killing him?" Ryan asked.

"Too much surgery. That's the simple, facile answer. But what he's doing way out in the wilds of Acadia National Park defeats me. Lost a mess of blood. I think he must have some serious disease, as well. Streaks around his thighs show he lost control of himself, way back. Maybe it's cholera or typhoid."

"Contagious?" Krysty asked, taking a few steps back from the dying man.

"Could be. Doubt we need to worry. He's so weak that a kitten fart could sweep him away."

Trader's curiosity had overcome his brief anger, and he had rejoined the group. "Looks to me like he escaped from some kind of baron's torture."

"If that's the case, then we should keep well clear of the baron who did this." Mildred turned away.

Dean knelt. "He's trying to speak."

"Doubt it," Mildred said. "So far gone I reckon... but his lips are moving all right. See if you can hear, Dean."

The boy laid his head close to the man's face. The blue eyes had started to open, gazing blankly at the lightening sky that was heralding the coming dawn.

Ryan was staring down into the eyes, and he actually saw the precise moment that life became extinct, the fraction of a second when life departed and eternity flooded in.

"Gone," he said quietly, touching his son on the shoulder. "It's over, Dean." The boy straightened, standing up, looking puzzled. "What did he say? Anything?"

"Not too sure, Dad."

Ryan held his son by the arm. "Doesn't matter if it sounds stupe, or if you aren't sure. Could be important. What did it sound like?"

"Thought he said 'twins.' Then another word that sounded like 'coning.' Didn't make sense."

"Coning?" Mildred probed. "Not 'coming'?"

"No. Might've been 'moaning,' I guess."

"Doesn't much matter, does it?" J.B. said. "We'll probably never know what happened to the poor man. What do we do with the corpse?"

"Leave it," Trader responded instantly. "We move on in another couple of hours. Let it lie."

Jak had stiffened, head to one side, eyes narrowed as though he were concentrating. "Hear dogs and men."

Everyone froze.

Krysty made a small gesture with her right hand. "Yeah, I can hear them."

Ryan shook his head. "Fireblast! Wish I had your hearing! How far? Coming this way?"

The albino turned to Krysty. "Could be little as mile? Water noise makes difficult be sure. This way?"

She nodded. "Agree on all that, Jak." Krysty glanced at the pale body by her feet, saying to Ryan, "After him?"

"Mebbe. They'll almost certainly have spotted our fire. Must stand out like a bunch of stickies at a baron's wedding. If they're looking for the chill, then it's probably better they don't find him here."

"I fail to see why having found the doomed wretch should bring us into difficulty," Doc said. "We are totally innocent, if they be his friends."

"What if they don't be...if they aren't his friends? What if the men coming are the ones that did this to him? Might not want witnesses."

"Might not even get around to asking any questions," Trader added.

"In the woods?" Dean looked behind them into the circle of blackness that surrounded the fire.

"They got dogs." Abe sniffed. "Be light soon."

"Put him in the pool." Ryan rubbed the side of his nose, considering his own suggestion. "Don't know how deep it is."

"Be a floater. Just chilled." Trader drew his own knife. "Unless we open him up and fill his guts with stones."

"Spill a lot of blood." J.B. was also looking around, as if he were trying to memorize the terrain about the camp. "Dogs'll scent it."

With the exception of Doc, they all turned simultaneously at the sound of barking hounds, seeming to come from only a little way down the trail.

"On a scent," Trader said. "Best get ready for a firefight. Get into the trees. Ring the camp. Take them all out as soon as they come in range of the firelight."

"The fire!" Ryan punched his right fist into his left palm. "Everyone get as much dry wood as they can. Big branches as well. We'll lay him on it and cover him."

"The smell!" Mildred exclaimed. "And you can't just burn a corpse like it—"

"Chuck on a couple of the pieces of deer we got left. Say it was spoiled. That'll explain the roasting scent."

"Sweet Lord, save us all," Doc said sorrowfully. "It has come to this. And such a long way down."

TRADER HAD SUGGESTED that he and Abe should go into the trees and wait under cover. "Ready in case the shit and the lead all start flying."

Ryan had disagreed. "We don't want to give them any reason for trouble. They might be hunters or trappers. Might not be after that dead man at all. Any suspicion and that's when the shit and the lead start to fly."

"We could still take them. Probably won't be more than three or four of them."

"Sorry, Trader, but I still say no. We all sit around on red alert. Blasters right by our hands. And we start shooting at the first sign of hostile action. Their dogs could easily smell you out in the forest, close by. Then there's ammo spent and some blood spilled."

"Yeah, I guess you could be right, old friend. Boy, that fire is blazing away."

The flames were fifteen feet high, obscuring any sign of the naked and mutilated corpse hidden within the bonfire. They could all hear fat crackling and spitting, and the air was filled with the rich, delicious scent of roasting meat.

"Throw that last hunk of venison on as soon as they come within sight, Dean," Ryan ordered. "Don't wait for a word from me. Don't want them seeing it's not spoiled."

"Sure, Dad."

"Yo, the camp!" a voice called out of the blackness. "Care to stand up and show your hands?"

"Care to take a flying fuck at a rolling doughnut?" Trader shouted.

They all heard laughter and a pair of dogs starting to bark furiously. The crack of a whip and a bellowed command shut the animals up.

"You want to come ahead, then do it," Ryan called. "We're out of food." Dean conspicuously threw some meat on the flames. "Burning some spoiled venison. Flies got into it. But you're welcome to warm yourselves."

Dawn was now very close, and the blackness around the camp was beginning to soften and lose its sable edge.

"We got blasters on you."

"Then you better use them." Ryan held up both hands. "We were out fishing along the coast. Squall blew up. Found ourselves on the rocks a few miles east of here. Other side of that big mountain. You see men?"

There was no answer at first, and Ryan had a gut feeling that a whispered conversation was taking place, somewhere out in the shadows.

"Couple of us are coming in. That all right with you in the camp?"

Ryan nodded. "Sure."

The first man to appear was tall and heavily built, mustached, wearing a white quilted plastic jacket over black trousers, tucked into ankle-high boots. He carried a silvered Mossberg 12-gauge pump-action shotgun under his arm.

His companion was of a different caliber.

He was less than five feet in height, with a long thin skull, showing a few strands of wispy hair pasted across. He wore a long cloak over padded pants and jacket. His spectacles were almost identical to the Armorer's—wire-rimmed—perched on the bridge of his bony nose.

He carried a spindly walking stick, the end coated with thick mud.

The two men stopped and both peered at the roaring blaze, sniffing the air.

"Big fire for dawn," the sec man said.

"You aren't roasting an ox in there, are you?" the smaller man asked. "Or some other animal, perhaps?"

Ryan's fingers itched for the butt of the SIG-Sauer, but he maintained a poker face. "We just rose early, ready to make a good start on the road. We still feel chilled from the ducking in the Lantic."

"What was the name of your ship?" the puny-looking man snapped, pointing at Ryan with his stick.

"It was…" To his horror, Ryan found that his mind had gone completely blank. He'd been so preoccupied with the problem of the burning corpse that he wasn't ready for that question.

"*Pequod,*" Doc Tanner said quickly.

The man nodded. "A good name. A good New England name, though ill-fated in history."

Ryan noticed that Krysty's eyes had been caught by something in the fire, though she had quickly looked away. He followed where she'd been staring.

The flames were so fierce that they'd already burned through most of the dry wood that had been piled on. One arm of the dead man had flopped out of the side, clearly visible. Each blistered finger carried a tiny flame, like corpse candles. The skin had peeled away, revealing the structure of the muscles and tendons beneath, blackened and charred.

Trader had quickly risen and brushed past Ryan, putting himself between the macabre spectacle and the two newcomers. He threw another handful of branches on the fire, covering the offending limb. "Best keep it going," he said with a knockdown, friendly smile.

"Where do you come from?" Krysty asked.

The smaller man turned and saw her for the first time, gaping at her dazzling hair. "Who— Where— I mean, I shouldn't have stared like that but— Where do we come from? Oh, not too far away." He recovered his self-possession. "Perhaps you would all like to come and be our guests for a while. Outlanders are very few and far between around Acadia."

"Keep it that way," his armed companion muttered.

"Yes, yes, I know. But there are good reasons why we— But that is none of your business." He pasted a smile in place. "My name is Buford. Professor Ladrow Buford."

"Professor!" Doc exclaimed. "You mean you're some kind of rad-blasted whitecoat scientist?"

"Of a sort, old man, yes. But we can talk so much more about this when you come to the institute."

"Institute!" It was Mildred's turn. "What kind of place in Deathlands gets to be called an institute?"

Buford tapped his stick in the dirt. "Too many impertinent questions! I will not—" He stopped abruptly and gathered some shreds of his former bonhomie. "I'm sorry. This has been a trying time...." The sec guard leaned and whispered in his ear. "Ah, of course. Thank you, Ellison, for the reminder."

To Ryan and the others he said, "First things firstly. We believe that you might well have knowledge of something that has gone missing. Something that belongs to us. Well?"

Chapter Sixteen

"Missing?" Ryan repeated. His senses were honed so fine that he was totally aware that every one of the nine friends around the blaze was waiting for one tiny clue from him, a signal to draw their guns and start a firefight.

"Indeed. Something has recently disappeared. Something that had been proving rather useful to us. I don't suppose that you would have any knowledge at all of this 'something' of ours, would you, sailor man?"

"I think I need a bit more of a description," Ryan replied, his mind flooded by a sudden vision of the raggled and tortured nameless chill that was currently being destroyed, only a couple of yards from where he was sitting.

"Yes," Buford drawled thoughtfully. "Perhaps you could tell me if anything unusual had crossed your path, so to speak, since your arrival here on our land."

"Couple hundred dwarf shrews, all drinking together." Ryan rested his chin in his left hand, pondering the question. "Little ferret. Real double-big moose."

"I don't yet know anything about you, not even your name. But I would not be pleased if I considered you were being willfully stupid and obtuse. I have only to say a single word, and there would be many deaths here."

"Including yours, you four-eyed little prick." Trader had the Armalite in his hands, trained at Buford.

There was one of those moments when time ceased to exist, the moment when the rocks crumbled away beneath your feet at the edge of the crevasse, the moment when the prairie rattler was poised to strike at your throat, the moment when the finger had tightened on the trigger.

"Insults are the last resort of the intellectually impotent," Buford said.

Trader laughed. "Well, you sure got some nerve for a four-eyed little prick. I'll hand you that. Just don't threaten us again, all right?"

"We shall see."

He returned his gaze to Ryan. "A sensible answer to my question?"

"Tell me what it is you're looking for," Ryan said, keeping calm.

Buford hesitated for a moment, glancing at his companion. "Very well. Have you seen a dog? Or, possibly a pair of dogs? Quite similar to a casual glance, with silver collars?"

Dean's mouth had opened and the little man spotted it. "Yes, lad? And don't now try to tell me that you don't know what I'm talking about."

Ryan answered him. "Sure we saw them. A long ways off. Yesterday, about five miles or more behind. Near the shores of a real big lake."

"You didn't catch them? Or see them close?"

"No. But they did look kind of similar, now that you mention it. Like German shepherds."

"Yesterday. By the lake. Both of them." He stood completely still as though he were receiving a secret communication from the Almighty.

Ellison nudged him, whispering, loud enough for the others to hear. "We can come out tomorrow, Professor. Could find them if they haven't gone far."

"No. Too labor intensive. The collars would have been useful to us."

Ryan was conscious of the weight of the two lengths of silver in the pocket of his coat.

Buford reached a decision. "We will all now go back to the institute and break our fasts together. I know that my colleagues will be most interested in such an unusual group of outlanders. Shall we go?"

"Why not?" Ryan said. "Let's move, people."

BEFORE LEAVING THE CAMP Ryan used the excuse of wanting to take a leak to throw the two collars far out into the middle of the pool, hoping that the sec men from the institute didn't come back later in the day to see the heat-broken skeleton of the dead stranger among the ashes.

THERE HAD BEEN six other sec men with the scientist and Ellison, all armed with identical Mossberg scatterguns. Ryan noticed that, oddly, none of them carried either a holstered handblaster or a rifle of any sort. Nor did any of them show any inclination toward conversation.

They all wore the same uniform of white quilted plastic jackets and black pants tucked into ankle-high boots. Unusual for sec guards, they didn't wear any kind of ville badge or identifying insignia.

As they walked through the swelling opalescence of the dawning, Ladrow Buford attached himself to Ryan, recognizing him as the leader of the group. He asked him for the names of all the other members, pausing to jot them down in a small notebook of maroon morocco leather.

He had also asked a little about their fishing trip. Ryan had explained that they had come from a tiny settlement way down the coast, called Miskatucket. That seemed to satisfy the little man, who changed the subject.

"We are a closed community at the institute, Ryan. Have been since before the long winters."

Ryan was taken completely by surprise at the bland statement. "How do you mean, from before the long winters? How can you have done?"

"A lucky chance. Freak of nature, winds and the ground-zero locations of the enemy missiles. We were preserved. Of course there were a number of fatalities in the months that followed, from the radiation-induced cancers. A sad number. We have never recovered from that in terms of our population. Which is, sadly, still shrinking slowly. Fertility has not been our strong point. But with the new . . ." He stopped, giggled and clapped his hand over his prim mouth in a girlish manner. "But I go before my horse to market, Ryan. We should be there in a couple of hours, and you will see what you will see, and hear what you will hear."

THE FOREST WAS THICK on both sides of the trail while the game was noticeably diminished.

Buford wasn't capable of making much speed, and the time dragged by for some of the party, particularly for Dean.

With his father's permission he kept scampering off ahead of them, investigating side trails, reappearing perched high in the branches of a lofty spruce, flicking cones at the sec men, who ignored him.

"The boy has great spirit," Buford observed. "When we are a little nearer the institute, he must remain with us or he could come to harm."

IT HAD RAINED on the part of the woods they now walked through, water still dripping off the long needles of the pines, making the path muddy and treacherous.

"Fallen tree ahead," Ellison called, coming forward to join Ryan and Buford.

"Ah, yes. It has come down very recently and blocks the path. We must detour."

Ellison tapped a finger to his forehead. "I'll warn the others, sir." Ryan had noticed that the man had an unusual curling scar that tugged down the corner of his mouth, partly hidden by the luxuriant mustache.

As the word was passed along, Krysty called out to Ryan. "Dean's somewhere up front of us, Ryan. Should you go and call him back?"

"Don't fuss about the kid," Trader said. "Boy needs adventure. Way of the flesh. Can't raise him as some little wimp who only wants to cook and sew."

Mildred laughed. "I see that political correctness is a concept that never reached you, Trader."

"What's that?"

"It's a sort of idea that being a misogynist redneck peckerwood isn't necessarily being wise and godlike."

Jak interrupted the argument, pointing ahead of them where the trail dipped into a shallow valley. "Dean," he said. "In dropped tree."

It was a tall spruce, the dry brown of its foliage showing that it had already been dead before its roots lost their grip on the soil beneath it. It was a tangle of jagged branches, some of which had already snapped off, some of which were now perched at dangerous angles.

Dean was sitting astride it, as though on a horse, waving to his father and the others. "Come on. Safe enough to crouch under," he called.

"Come down," Ryan said, seeing the way that the big tree was perched at a perilous angle, its broken tip swaying on top of a bank of loose earth.

"No, Dad, it's—"

There was a deafening crack, like a dozen large gren mortars being fired simultaneously. The spruce dipped and rolled, its branches exploding into flying shards of splintered wood, sending everyone ducking out of the way.

When Ryan opened his eye again, his son had vanished.

"Dean?" He started to run toward the tumbled giant, boots slipping in the mud, feeling his heart leap into his throat, almost choking him.

There was a cry from beneath the tree that was so piercing and shocked that it didn't seem to bear any resemblance to any human sound.

Ryan stopped, fighting against a blood rush of panic, knowing that he had to overcome his own fear for Dean's life before he was able to do anything to help him. He stood a few yards off and studied the horror of the situation.

Once the mud and dust had settled, it was easy enough to see Dean. Or part of the lad. His head, shoulder and arms were visible, pinned beneath a massive branch, that was itself poised and restrained by the main trunk of the fallen spruce. One wrong move and it would rock free and roll all the way down, crushing the boy.

The rest of the group, including the sec men, were moving behind Ryan. He held up his hand and shouted for them to stop. "Everyone keep the fuck back out of the way!" he yelled. "Krysty and J.B. here."

Buford insisted on joining them, stooping and peering owlishly over his glasses. "Most perilous," he lisped. "If the fulcrum is disturbed, then the pivotal motion will rotate about the long axis and it will—"

He stopped as Ryan turned on him. "That's my son, you piss-ant little bastard. Get out of the way or I'll snap your neck like a rabbit's." When the man still didn't move, Ryan called to Trader. "Shift him for me."

Buford squealed as Trader stepped up and dragged him away by the upper arm, the pincering fingers probing beneath the cloak and nearly pulling the biceps muscle away from the bone.

Ryan ignored them.

Dean was conscious, his head strained back, the sinews in his throat corded with the effort of trying to look at his father. "I'm triple sorry, Dad, about—"

"Shut up. Can you move?"

"No. Branch is across my stomach and the tops of my legs and feet."

Krysty spoke to the trapped boy, keeping her voice calm and reassuring. "Soon get you out, Dean. Can you move your arms and fingers, all right?"

"Yeah." The boy's voice was fragile and feathery, trembling like the beating of a bird's heart. "I can feel my toes wriggle, as well."

Ryan nodded. "Good. Means you got no bad injuries. We'll have you out, Dean. Don't go away."

Something like a laugh. "Try not to, Dad."

Ryan led Krysty and the Armorer a little farther away, dropping his voice to whisper urgently to them both. "What do you reckon?"

J.B. answered. "If we got time, we can send a sec man to fetch some good ropes from their ville. Not far. And pulleys. We can jury-rig a tackle and heave that branch off him." He paused. "If we got the time."

"Dad?"

"Hang on."

"No, Dad, listen. I think the branch is getting heavier on top of me. Like it's moving, real slow. I can feel it."

Ryan gestured for the others to keep well off. Going alone, he picked his way through the scattered detritus from the broken branches, taking the ultimate care not to slip and somehow disturb the delicate balance of the lethal trap that was crushing his helpless son.

"Can you see anything, Dad?" Anxiety nearly swamped his brave efforts at control.

"Yeah. Yeah, I can see what's happening. The sharp, broken end of the branch that's got you is sinking into the soft, muddy ground. That's gradually increasing the weight on you."

"Will it stop?"

Ryan hesitated. From where he stood, it was possible to see that the other end of the spruce branch was very slowly slipping from the trunk. Once it lost that residue of purchase, it would then fall and wipe Dean away.

"Sure it'll stop."

There was no way of getting anything else under it to check the inexorable progress downward. The other branches were brittle and dry and would snap. The trees all around had strong healthy branches, but to cut through one or two of the necessary breadth would take far too long without a power saw.

And, because of the configuration of the ground and the way the tree had fallen, there wasn't room for several people to get in and lift it. There was barely space at the point of balance of the shifting branch for even a single person.

"I'll take the weight, lover, and you have everyone else ready to try to hold some of the strain, if necessary. And get Dean out the moment I lift it up. Have to be quick."

"Use the Gaia power?"

"Yes." Krysty's face was calm, as though she were already starting to focus some of those hidden, mysterious strengths, the secret skills taught to her by her mother, Sonja, linked to the Earth Mother herself, Gaia.

"You know what it does to you. It comes close to chilling you when you use it, Krysty."

"I know."

"Dad, getting heavy!" Dean's face was turning red as his chest was compressed and his breathing became more and more difficult. "Be quick."

Ryan hugged Krysty, kissing her on the lips. "You can do it?"

"I can try."

Ryan had to draw his SIG-Sauer to force Buford away with his men, explaining in a few words to the others what was going to happen.

Trader had opened his mouth to protest at the absurdity of it, but then shut it again when he saw the cold death in Ryan's eye, contenting himself with the barely audible whisper of "Fucking triple impossible. Im-fucking-possible!"

Krysty had thrown off her dark blue jacket and stood by the tree in her white shirt and blue pants.

Dean gasped for air, sucking in rapid, shallow breaths, his eyes closed.

"Everyone dead quiet," Ryan ordered. "I'll kill the first person who makes a sound."

The midmorning forest was silent. Not a bird flew anywhere near them. Not a squirrel chattered in the high branches. The lightest breeze rippled the tops of the pines all around, and the air carried the faint flavor of salt from the nearby ocean. The sun sailed across a cloudless sky, peeking down and casting dappled shadows.

Krysty's lips moved, the words just audible to the watchers. "Gaia, help me here. Aid me, Gaia, and lend me your strength for this action, only to save another's life." Her green eyes were closed, and she was deliberately controlling her breathing.

"That hunk of wood must weigh three or four hundred pounds, easy," Ellison muttered, not loud enough to disturb Krysty's preparation. "Just can't be done."

Ryan glanced sideways at the sec man, who caught the look and shook his head slowly.

"Can't get no air, Dad!" The boy's voice was ragged with blind fear.

But it didn't disturb Krysty, who had locked herself into the trance that she needed, moving below the great branch, touching it gently with the tips of her fingers, tensing herself.

"Gaia, help me with your power... now!"

Chapter Seventeen

Ryan had seen Krysty use her mysterious, mutie powers just a few times before. On each occasion it had left her totally exhausted, drained of all energy, needing care and rest to restore her to normal.

He had watched as she performed acts that transcended all the normal laws of motion, energy and strength, and seen the toll it took.

But he had never known her take on a challenge that was so obviously impossible. The sec man was right. Trader was right. There was no way on God's earth that a hundred-and-fifty-pound, five-foot-eleven-inch woman could even begin to move the mass of dead wood that hung over Dean, waiting for the slightest nudge to tumble and smear him into the dirt.

Krysty stood below the behemoth of timber, slightly crouched, taking the strain on her shoulders, steadying the branch with both hands.

J.B. was in charge of Trader, Abe and the sec men, waiting to try to step in if there was anything that they could do to help. Ryan and Jak were less than six feet away from Krysty, all of their concentration focused on the trapped boy, ready to move in at the first sign of movement from the broken tree.

In the stillness there was the sudden, harsh, explosive sucking in of air, a fraction of a second of utter silence, followed by the faint creaking of the wood as it began—so slowly—to move.

Ryan's concentration was so total that he didn't even hear the startled exclamation of amazement from many of the watchers. His eyes were on Dean, and the rough bark of the dead branch that held him pinned.

His son had slipped into unconsciousness, his eyes closed, his face suddenly pale.

"Ready, Jak?" Ryan whispered.

"Yes."

It was moving.

He risked a glance up at Krysty, then looked quickly away, shocked at the naked agony that was etched deep in her face. Her bright green eyes were wide open, staring blindly, her mouth in a rictus of pain, teeth clenched so hard he expected to see them splinter and break. A vein throbbed prominently across her forehead, on the left side. She wasn't breathing at all, gradually straightened her back under the immense deadweight of the wood.

For a moment she supported the entire bulk, rock-solid, not even staggering.

"Now," Ryan said, diving in past her legs, Jak moving on the other side. Both of them grabbed Dean by an arm and started to pull him free.

For a single fraction of stretched time, nothing at all happened. The boy's lower half still seemed totally pinned down, immovable. Ryan braced himself, his boots slipping in the wet dirt, heaving until the muscles in his shoulders and back felt like cracking. Jak was fighting alongside him, whistling between his teeth with the enormous effort.

"Quick!" The single word was hissed in a voice that bore a vague resemblance to Krysty's, but it sounded as though it came through thick fog, from an infinite distance, a lonely and desperate voice.

Dean's eyes opened, gazing blankly at the tree that hung, suspended, over his head. "Free," he whispered.

One moment the boy was immovably trapped, the next moment the crushing pressure was removed and Ryan and Jak were able to pull him out.

"All the way," Ryan panted.

Scrabbling for purchase, they backed away, each holding a slender wrist, heaving the semiconscious lad out of the shadow of the branch. Trader and Abe jumped in to lend a hand and pull him completely clear.

"Let it go!" Mildred shouted. "Krysty! He's out. Let it go and get out yourself."

The tall woman, her fiery hair in a tight knot at her nape, stepped back, allowing the branch to slip from her shoulders. It rolled a little, then fell completely free of the main trunk of the fallen spruce. It landed with a terrifying crash on the very spot where Dean's head had been, narrowly missing Krysty's own legs.

Ryan had been kneeling by his son, but he stood and started to move to support Krysty.

But he was way too slow as she crumpled like a dead leaf, toppling to the ground on her back, her eyes wide open and staring blankly at the sky.

"She's fuckin' chilled herself," Trader whispered with an almost superstitious awe.

"No," Jak said. "Just strain."

Ryan crouched at her side, holding her hand, chafing her wrists. "Happens when she calls on the Gaia power," he said, speaking more quickly than he'd intended. "Always happens. She'll be fine in a minute or two."

Behind him, he was vaguely aware that Dean had started to recover, rolling over onto hands and knees and being noisily, copiously sick.

Mildred put a hand on Ryan's shoulder and eased him to one side. "Let the dog see the rabbit," she said. "Need to examine her properly."

"She's fine, Mildred."

Doc's voice called from the group of watching sec men. "I confess the poor soul looks less than well, though I am no judge of medical matters. As Dr. Wyeth is, of course."

Krysty hadn't moved, her face like ivory, her eyes still blank and lifeless. A thread of brilliantly crimson blood inched from her nose and mouth.

Mildred was checking for a pulse. She looked up at Ryan, her face bleak. "I'm sorry," she said quietly.

Chapter Eighteen

"No." Ryan looked down into the lifeless eyes of the woman that he loved above all else in the world. "No, Mildred."

"There's no pulse, Ryan. I can try artificial respiration and chest massage. I could even open up—"

"I've seen her before. The Gaia power takes all her life force. Sucks everything from her. I don't know how she does it, Mildred, nor does she. Krysty learned it from her mother, and she only uses it in the direst emergency."

"Like now," Trader said.

"Yeah. Like now."

"But the pulse. All the life functions are—"

"Take it again, please."

The woman reached and laid a hand below the angle of Krysty's jaw, feeling for the carotid artery. She shook her head, the beads rattling, loud in the stillness. "No, I told—" Her eyes widened.

"It's there," Ryan said flatly. It was a statement, not a question.

"Yes. Not as strong as I'd like, but it's surely there. But it was gone. I'd have certified Krysty as clinically dead. How does she *do* that?"

"She doesn't know. Nor do I."

Ladrow Buford was standing just behind the one-eyed man, nudging him with a bony elbow. "Was that some kind of magic trick?" he asked.

"What? Why don't you just fuck off out of the way and I'll come tell you when we're ready to move on again."

The scientist persisted. "It was a miracle, Cawdor. I don't want to cause you trouble, but the work we are doing at the institute would benefit unbelievably! Unbelievably if we could secure the cooperation of Miss Wroth and her powers. Do you think that might be possible?"

Trader took the little man by the scruff of the neck. "You don't take to telling, do you?" he snarled. "You come with me and we'll sit quiet together, and I'll tell you about the time I chilled eighteen swampies with a plastic spoon and six ounces of plas-ex I'd hid up my ass."

Ryan watched them go off, Buford's feet barely trailing the ground.

"Pulse is growing stronger," said Mildred, who'd totally ignored the brief altercation.

Krysty's eyes moved, life returning to them. With a struggle she concentrated on Ryan's worried face. "Did I do it?" she whispered.

"Sure. He's fine."

"That's good," she said, and slipped back into darkness.

DESPITE THE FUSSING of Buford, aided by the repeated concern of Ellison, his sec boss, it wasn't possible to move Krysty for three hours.

She lay in a semicoma, Mildred constantly checking pulse and respiration. Dean, fully recovered from his ordeal, kept scampering to a nearby stream for supplies of fresh water to bathe her forehead.

Every now and again she would briefly surface from the deep sleep. Twice she asked whether the boy was safe. Once she called out to her mother, Sonja.

Ryan sat on the grass beside her as the day wore on, holding her hand, occasionally talking to her in a quiet voice about small, personal things—about how he was missing her, how she'd saved his son's life, how he wanted her well again.

It was just over three hours by his wrist chron, when she finally opened her eyes, yawned and stretched, managing a weak smile for him.

"You look terrible," Krysty said. She coughed and cleared her throat. "I'm as dry as the bottom of the driest well in Drytown."

"Dean, bring us some more water," he called.

The boy was at Ryan's side almost before the words were out of his mouth. He knelt and held the beaker for the woman to sip at. "Thanks, Krysty," he said. "I owe you."

"Do the same for me one day, Dean. Thanks for the water. Feel better now."

She pulled herself up into a sitting position with Ryan's help. But her eyes clouded and her head lolled to one side. He patted her cheek.

"Take it easy awhile longer."

Buford had broken away from Trader's glittering eyes and his endless tales of heroism past, and paced up and down nervously. "We must get back to the institute. We should have returned by noon at the very latest. There will be concern at the highest levels, Mr. Cawdor."

"They can piss their pants at the highest level for all we care," Abe called, overhearing the scientist. "We move when Krysty's well and not before."

"Triple-well said, Abe," Trader added.

"Could carry her. Two men linking hands. Be like a chair." Ellison rubbed a hand over his mustache, just touching the deep scar beneath it.

Ryan glanced at J.B., who shrugged. "What do you think, Krysty?"

"Normally I'd like to stay right here and sleep for three or four days, lover. But if this place he talked about isn't too far off, then a clean bed might just be the next best thing to paradise."

"How far, Buford?"

"Be at the sec barrier at the neck of the pass in about an hour. Longer if we move slow for the mu . . . the woman. Steep uphill. After that it'll be all downhill. Another half an hour or so. No longer."

"Krysty, you feel up to this? Being carried the rest of the way?"

"Long as I don't get too shaken around, lover. Might just throw up if I did."

THE BARRIER WAS heavily guarded.

The installation obviously dated from before skydark, hacked at unthinkable cost in money and labor from living rock on either side of the highway. There were slits in the defenses for rifles and machine guns, and turrets on the top that would have raked the entire area, up and down the hill.

A number of oil drums had been rolled into the middle, with room for a man to walk by but no space for horses or any other sort of transport.

Ellison had gone on ahead of the rest of the group, giving a shout of warning. Immediately they were covered by at least a dozen uniformed men, all carrying either the ubiquitous Mossberg or M-16 A-1s.

"Boy, they look like they got a fuckin' army up there," Trader said grudgingly. "Them's some real smart and well-trained sec men, you got, Professor."

"We pride ourselves on the record that nobody has gotten into and out of the grounds of the inner institute unbidden, through the last hundred years or so that it has been functioning. Not a single soul."

"Into and out?" Ryan said. "You mean one or two got inside the place?"

"One or two. We counted them in and we never counted them out again, Cawdor."

"Only way to do it," Trader agreed in the first sign of friendliness that he'd shown to the little man.

"How many men you got, Buford?" Ryan asked. "Must be a regular predark army if you can put this many onto every entrance and exit."

The scientist covered his hand with his mouth and sniggered. "This is our only way in and out of the institute. Once we are over the ridge you will see that Nature herself has provided us with total security."

"IT PUTS ME WONDERFULLY in mind of the grandeur of Yosemite Park," Doc said.

"Looks like the biggest wag trap ever built." Abe cleared his throat and spit.

Past the barrier, the road continued as a two-lane blacktop, down an incline for about a half mile between walls of sheer rock. Walls carried on all the way around through three hundred and sixty degrees, forming a perfect bowl of unscalable cliffs. At the bottom was a thickly wooded valley roughly three-quarters of a mile across with a river flowing through it, the water cascading off a feathery fall to the east side.

And at the very heart of the valley was the group of buildings known as the institute.

There were two more levels of sec barriers down the road, both manned by half a dozen sec guards, all in the white quilted plastic jackets. There was a metal sign by the last of the barriers, its supports rusted through, leaning against the wall of quartz-silvered granite.

The words were still legible, despite a century of chem storm fallout and weathering: The Melissa Crichton Institute of Medical Research. Cryology and Gene Sculpturing.

"Cryology!" Mildred exclaimed. "Do I believe my eyes?"

"You know the word?" Buford asked.

"Sure I used to—" She caught the simultaneous warning cough from Ryan, Krysty and J.B. "I mean I read about it. Freezing and stuff, wasn't it?"

"It was, I believe. Sadly that is one of the main wings of the hospital complex that has been long closed down and abandoned to the ghosts of yesteryear."

"So, what do you do down there, then?" Ryan asked, turning the conversation from the potentially difficult one of the bizarre past of Dr. Mildred Winonia Wyeth.

Once again there was the irritatingly girlish giggle, partly hidden by the soft palm of his hand. "What don't we do? Much of our work has been undertaken over a long period of time, the research being handed on down the line from father to son and from mother to daughter."

"And from father to daughter and from mother to son," Mildred said.

"Yes, of... I see that's supposed to be some sort of a joke, isn't it?"

"Very nearly, Professor. Very nearly."

Krysty had fallen asleep, and Ryan went to where she sat in the arms of two of the bigger sec men. Only then did Ryan notice how alike the pair of guards looked.

"You two brothers?" he asked.

"No."

"Yes."

Neither offered any explanation of their answers. Ryan shook his head, checked that Krysty was as well as could be expected and turned to rejoin the others.

"Have your magical mystery princess safe snuggled in beddy-byes within the hour now," Buford said.

FROM THE BROW OF THE HILL that overlooked the secret valley of the Crichton Institute it appeared that the buildings were all in pristine condition.

But as they gradually made their way closer, the damage of the turning years became more apparent. The complex had originally been shaped like a star, with wings running off in five directions from a central area. This atrium seemed relatively untouched, though Abe pointed out that parts of the roof looked like they could do with some repair.

Three of the five main wings had clearly suffered serious structural damage. One had collapsed in its entirety, the one that Buford pointed out had once housed the finest cryology unit in the northeast.

Another had folded in like a pack of cards, with the end wall subsiding and knocking down all the interior sections, one after another.

The third one had a tilted, kinked roof, and all of the exterior glass was gone.

"Earth slip," the scientist commented, "about forty-five years ago."

"Earth's lip," Doc said. "Lip o'suction pump and never give up the ship boys and girls come out to play's the thing." He slapped himself on the wrist. "My deep apologies, ladies and gentlemen. I think my brain has become fevered at the thought of entering the de-mesne of those wonderful breed, the scientists. I can scarcely contain my excitement at the prospect."

Buford stared hard at Doc. "You seem a person of some education, outlander Tanner."

"Down in our friendly little ville of Miskatucket we were blessed with a marvelous library. Preserved in all of its predark wonder, where I misspent so much of my halcyon salad days. Housed in the spooky old Arkham house on Innsmouth Avenue. Including a rare copy of the *Necronomicon,* by the mad Arab, Alhazred." He smiled. "Though not of course that notorious edition bound in human skin with the er-ratum on page 116."

Ryan turned to him. "Doc?"

"You are about to suggest that I shut up, are you not, old friend."

"I am."

"Then I will."

Mildred touched Ladrow Buford on the arm. He jumped sideways as though a hot golden scarab had fallen onto his hand. "We are... My people are not used to sudden and unexpected physical contact like that."

"Sorry. Just wanted to know what the surviving sections were being used for?"

"They have been united for the core research that goes on in the institute."

"And what's that?"

He giggled. "Soon," he said. "All in good time."

Chapter Nineteen

"No attempt from the chickenshit bastards to take our blasters away from us," Trader said. "That's what's really making me suspicious."

Krysty lay recovering in one of the beds, a fresh white sheet pulled up to her chin, her hands outside, folded on her breast. Doc had already remarked that she looked like a statue on a medieval crusader's tomb.

Now she smiled at Trader. "I can see why you've lived as long as you have," she said quietly, "if you get suspicious just because there's nothing to be suspicious about."

"I don't see a threat here," J.B. said. "Trader's right. With the armament and manpower they have here in this ville, they could have taken us out more or less anytime." He stopped, looking puzzled. "But, why the dark night do they want us here in the first place?"

Dean nodded, sitting cross-legged on the bottom of Krysty's metal-framed bed. "Right. They tell us how nobody ever got in and out alive. Show us their barriers and their sec men." He hesitated. "Though I thought that Ellison guy was a flash dude. One with the mustache and the big scar by his mouth. Seemed friendly. What was I saying? Yeah, they got all this power and they smile and ask us in. Too friendly, I reckon, Dad."

"Will come into parlor said spider to fly." Jak was slouched on a folding chair in the corner. "Christina taught me that."

Ryan walked quietly to the door and tried the cream plastic handle. It turned easily, and he peeked out into the corridor, expecting to see a sec guard or two standing there watching him. But there was nothing.

He walked back to the others and sat on the bed by his son, reaching for Krysty's hand. Though it clearly took her something of an effort to move at all, she responded and gripped his fingers. But with only a fraction of her normal strength.

"I'll be fine by... by tomorrow, lover," she said. "You know using the power of the Earth Mother always leaves me feeling like the bottom of a cockatiel's cage."

"Seems a good place to rest. Buford said that the rest of us can meet up with the baron of the place. Or whatever he calls himself."

"I want to prowl around," Mildred said. "You know my specialty was cryonics, and the sign said this was a center for it. Well, I tell you that I never heard of any public research institute up in the middle of a national park."

"Military?" J.B. suggested.

"Could be."

Ryan considered the possibilities. "As there's already a redoubt in the park, I don't see why the government wouldn't have built a secret military hospital here, as well. But I don't see any real danger to us. No threats at all."

"How about the mutilated dead man?" Abe asked.

"And those weird dogs, Dad? Something sort of real creepy-chucky about that."

"True, Dean. We know the dogs came from here. But they never mentioned looking for the poor bastard with the scars. Might have nothing to do with them. I remember seeing in old predark mags that hospitals and research places used millions of animals in their experiments."

Mildred nodded. "That's right. Making beagles smoke hundreds of cigarettes and putting shampoo in the eyes of rabbits. Taking the tops off the skulls of monkeys to see what effect electric shocks had direct to the brain."

"Indeed all of that is true." Doc cleared his throat. "I confess that I am sometimes exercised by considering whether Deathlands is truly more barbaric than the great civilization of the twentieth century."

Trader had been leaning against the wall, cradling the Armalite. "Want to know what I think? Well, I don't mind if you want to know or not. Because I'll fuckin' tell you. What you just said, Doc, is the straightest ace on the line I heard. Living as long as I have in Deathlands means I've seen more chilling and violence and brute behavior than you can imagine. But it's mostly prompted by a wish to live longer or have a capful more jack or fuck another woman or get more land. Personal, know what I mean?"

"You're right there, Trader," Abe said. "I always thought that, too."

"Shut it, Abe. Personal, I said. But all I heard about the best of times before skydark and the long winters—it sounds like a few had it great. Cream so thick you could cut it with a razor. The rest had shit. And the violence was impersonal. Whitecoats pressing buttons and mixing germs. I figure we're better where we are."

Nobody spoke for a few moments, then Krysty slowly clapped her hands. "Good, Trader, good."

THEY HAD BEEN GIVEN some excellent coffee sub and some honey biscuits when they arrived, though Krysty was still too weak to take any interest in any sustenance. It had kept them going into the afternoon, and Buford had reappeared briefly to tell them that they would meet with the senior men and women of the institute over supper at six.

He had stared at the sleeping figure of Krysty. "When will she be well enough to get up?"

"Mebbe tomorrow," Ryan replied.

"And when could she give us another demonstration of her amazing powers?"

Ryan had turned at that, feeling a flicker of anger at the scientist's bland assumption that Krysty was some sort of performing windup doll.

"You saw how ill it made her, Buford. You think she's going to go through that hell again just to entertain you and some of your friends?"

The eyes behind the glasses widened with shock, and the little cupid's-bow mouth pursed in disapproval. "Not *entertain*, Cawdor. Most certainly not. Our needs, I should say, our interest in Krysty is purely scientific."

Doc snorted. "When I hear a whitecoat talk about 'scientific,' then I have this extraordinary tendency to want to reach for my revolver."

Buford had muttered an apology and quickly left the suite that they'd been given, saying that he'd see them all again at six o'clock.

Mildred had said that each of the rooms would probably have been a small ward on its own. Some had two beds and others three. Ryan and Krysty had the first along the corridor. J.B. and Mildred had poached the next one. Trader had taken the third of them, choosing to share with Abe, leaving the end three-bed room for Doc, Dean and Jak.

They were on the second floor of one of the two surviving wings of the institute, with a view out of the side windows across the river and up toward the impressive sheer face of the nearest mountain.

Each room had its own cupboards and shelves, along with a large sink with long-handled chrome taps for hot and cold water. Everything was spotlessly clean and hygienic.

A narrow closet held brooms, brushes, dustpans and cleaning cloths. Another closet contained hangers for clothes.

Around the top of every bed was a long steel rail that Mildred told them would have been for curtains, to give the occupants of the wards some privacy.

She had gone out during the middle of the afternoon, while the others rested, exploring with J.B. for company and protection, returning in about ninety minutes.

"Definitely a hospital," she reported. "I had a peek at the cryology section, but it was totally destroyed. Grass growing up through the floors. Same with the ruined wings we saw from back up the trail. But the other wing is closed off from us. Guards just said it

was for experimenting and research.'' She glanced at
J.B. for confirmation. He nodded, and she continued. ''This one has two operating rooms on the first
floor along with what used to be a path lab and an
X-ray department. Also a physio rehab unit at the far
end, with double doors opening onto the gardens.
They're real pretty, too.''

''Security?'' Trader asked.

The Armorer answered that one. ''Thorough.
Common weapon is the Mossberg. Silvered 12-gauge.
Original blasters, but beautifully kept. Worth a for-
tune to a handful of frontier barons we all know of.''

''How many men?'' Ryan queried.

''Difficult. Like Mildred says, we couldn't get access to the closed wing. Also, the atrium at the heart
of the complex had sections that we were steered away
from. Didn't like the idea of our going outside, either. If I had to make an informed guess from the one
short and partial recce, then I think I'd have to be
looking around the hundred mark. Saw about a dozen
or so of the scientists, as well.''

''Well-trained guards?''

J.B. nodded. ''You saw them working out in the
back country, Ryan. Can't add to what we all thought.
Efficient. Mebbe not combat-hard, though, is my
guess. Like they know in theory what to do when faced
with a firefight situation, but they've never actually
done it.''

''Makes it easy.'' Trader grinned.

''Sure,'' Ryan said. ''Just about as easy as taking
candy off a gorilla.''

RYAN LEFT KRYSTY sleeping soundly in their room. Some of the color was seeping back into her cheeks. The horrific effect that using the mutie Gaia power had on her was so devastating that he couldn't face the idea of her using it, ever again. There was the grim certainty at the back of his mind that the next time might be the last, that the force would ultimately be so overwhelming that it would rupture an artery in her brain or, more simply, burst her heart.

He went out into the corridor, passing a series of closed and locked doors, all with strange letter and number combination codes on them, in a variety of colors. A few bore their original predark signs—Nurses' Rest Room, Orthodontics—Do Not Enter When Red Light Shows; TV Room—Absolutely No Smoking; Dietician; Blood Bank, which had a small, homemade label fixed beneath it: Dracula's Castle.

He passed a pair of patrolling guards, each with a Mossberg slung over the shoulder. He nodded to them, and they both grinned cheerfully.

At the end of the wing he passed through two sets of double doors, finding himself in the main atrium area that Mildred had mentioned. Here the old signs had all gone, the walls painted fresh and clean. The closed wings were self-evident, the wreckage visible through some obviously sealed sec doors.

The other usable area, which had been barred to J.B. and Mildred, was the next one around the central core of the huge medical complex.

It had no sign to give a clue to what went on behind the guarded doors.

"Help you, outlander?"

Ryan spun, seeing a sec man holding his blaster, looking suspiciously at him. For a moment he thought the man was a stranger, then he realized that it was the sec boss, Ellison, the one with the vicious scar by his mouth. The reason he hadn't recognized him straightaway was that the man had shaved off his luxuriant mustache.

"No. Just stretching my legs, thanks."

"What's your name?"

"You know my name, Ellison."

The man's eyes widened, and his finger moved onto the trigger of the shotgun. "How the showering sheep shit do you know my name, outlander?"

Ryan could see that there was something wrong, but couldn't for the life of him figure what it was. "I know you because we spent hours together out in the park."

"Park?"

"Acadia."

The muzzle of the Mossberg was now aimed, very definitely, at the pit of Ryan's stomach. "You say you and me spent hours together, outlander?"

"Sure we did."

"I say that you're some kind of sneaking liar. I never seen you before."

"Why did you shave off the mustache, Ellison?" Ryan asked, trying to find some connection with the angry man. "Get bored with it?"

"I never had a fucking mustache in my life. I never seen you before in my life. And you're about to find out what it's like to buy the farm."

"Hold it, Ellison."

Ryan glanced over his shoulder. He'd been about to chop his hand at the barrel of the 12-gauge and take his chances, which he'd mentally put at around a hundred to one.

"Buford," he said. "Didn't think I'd be saying it, but I'm glad to see you."

The scientist pointed a trembling finger at the sec man. "Gun down, Ellison. Order! Do it or you'll be cleaning out the freak cages for the rest of your life."

"He said he knew me, the outlander."

With the threat of the blaster removed, Ryan was becoming angry. "'Course I know him. He was with you all of the time. Saw the tree fall and everything. I asked him why he'd shaved off his mustache."

"I never had—"

Buford reached across and actually laid his hand across the sec man's mouth, silencing him. "No more talking, Ellison."

"Let it lie," Ryan said. "I'll just go back and join the others. Doesn't matter."

"It was his brother who accompanied us into the forest in our pursuit of the animals that had escaped from our laboratory."

"Brother?"

"Yes. His twin brother." Buford took his hand away from the sec guard's face. "Now go and carry on the patrol, Ellison. I shall speak with you at a later time."

The man turned wordlessly and marched off, the Mossberg slung once more across his broad back. His whole posture was one of frustrated rage.

"There," Buford said, rubbing his hands together. "No problem too small and no solution too large. That's what we say here at Crichton."

"Sure. I'll go..."

"Of course. We'll meet at six. Everyone is so very excited about it. Krysty won't— No, of course. Too early. But, perhaps tomorrow?"

"Perhaps."

On his way back toward the rooms they all shared, Ryan wondered about the Ellison brothers. One with a mustache and one without.

And both of them with a precisely identical scar.

Chapter Twenty

"It was my dear departed grandmother, Melissa Crichton, who was responsible for the founding—and a deal of the funding." The scientist emitted a fragile, dry chuckle that sounded like the peeling off of a mummy's shroud. "Just my little joke. Many of my colleagues have heard it, I fear, many times in the past sixty years or more. So difficult to calculate the passing of time as one slips into the eighth decade of life."

"I would be the first to drink to that, Professor Crichton," Doc said gallantly, lifting his cut-crystal goblet of elderflower wine.

David Crichton was eighty-three years old, or eighty-three years young as he sometimes declared himself. He sat at the head of the table, with his senior staff ranged on either side, alternating with Ryan and his friends.

Only Krysty was absent from among the visitors, and Dean, who had volunteered he didn't want a formal supper and had offered to stay in the room to keep Krysty company. Ryan had been glad to accept the offer.

The food was terrible, a surprisingly large proportion of it recycled and artificial. Ryan had found himself sitting between Crichton and Ladrow Buford and had commented on the lack of fresh meat and vegetables.

"No need for it," the little scientist explained. "We can process much of what we need. It prevents any necessity for us to go outside the valley more than three or four times a year. Then we mount a large-scale expedition. Stock up. And dry and pulp and freeze and retexture the food to last us another three or four months. Tasty, is it not?"

"Tasty" wasn't the first word that would have occurred to Ryan.

There were printed menus spaced along the table, and the food, already in individual portions on rectangular green plastic dishes, was served by unarmed sec men.

"Soup of the Day" turned out to be a pale green liquid that matched the bowls and had a faint taste of dried peas and too much salt.

"Fish pâté and salad." The former was a pinkish gray color, with a watery constitution, and the latter was a single irradiated tomato and three shredded leaves of reconstituted lettuce that had neither flavor nor texture.

The main course was "Meat and three vegetables."

"What kind of meat is it?" Mildred asked.

The elderly woman whitecoat sitting next to her didn't know, but she thought it might once have been pork. The younger man opposite, with a hearing aid, decided after being asked six times that he believed that it was beef. A sec man, who was serving, suggested bone-stripped veal.

In the end, not one of the scientists could answer the question, though Crichton gallantly offered to send a message to the kitchens to try to find out.

"Don't bother," Mildred replied. "I guess it's still going to taste absolutely like nothing, even when I know that it's really something."

The vegetables were three dollops of mush, precisely the same size for everyone. Buford pointed out proudly that the machines in the kitchens were accurate to an eighth of a milligram in doling it out.

One dollop was pale yellow, one was off-white and one was dark green.

The desserts were a straight choice between cheese or fruit cobbler.

To Ryan's surprise, the cheese actually looked and tasted like cheese. The cobbler looked like crimson mush, reduced to the texture of watery porridge.

"The cheese keeps well, and we have not found a way, after all these years, to successfully deconstruct and then reconstitute it." Crichton smiled.

"Well," Trader said, "I guess that's one thing for us all to be grateful for."

The conversation was stilted. The men and women in their lab coats seemed to have little idea of the world beyond the rocky walls of the valley that held the institute at its center, like a powerful oyster gripping a pearl.

They asked a little about the fishing village that Ryan and the others had claimed to come from. But the inquiries were desultory and didn't show true interest.

The one subject that undoubtedly *did* interest them all was Krysty Wroth.

Every one of the outlanders was quizzed intensively by his, or her, neighbors.

"Where does she come from?"

"Who is she?"

"Are her parents muties?"

"Is it true that she has phenomenal powers, as Ladrow Buford claims?"

"When can we see her?"

The old man at the head of the table was persistent with Ryan. "We are true inquirers after all scientific truths, as was my father and his mother before him. There are so many tests that we could carry out on the woman in question."

Ryan didn't much like David Crichton. Sitting next to him made his flesh crawl. It wasn't the whitecoat's age. He'd seen, and liked, enough elderly people in his life.

Crichton was like an evil child. His skin was soft, like a newborn reptile's, his eyes milky and pale. He ate the food with a strange, infantile sucking action, dribbling a great deal. When he was speaking he sometimes forgot that he was also eating, and the food simply plopped back onto his dish.

"What do you actually do here?" Ryan asked. "What's the research you work on?"

Buford answered very quickly, as if he didn't trust his leader to be discreet. "Very secret, Cawdor. Known only to a few of us around this table. The second-stage workers and sec men, and the auxiliaries, of course, have no idea at all what we do. We are most careful about that."

Doc heard part of the conversation. "Little knowledge can be a dangerous thing, when in the hands of the wrong people, Buford? So we make sure that the right hands are our hands. Is that the basic idea?''

"Yes, it is," Crichton said so excitedly that his gleaming false teeth shifted and nearly followed the regurgitated food onto the table. "You are obviously a person of wisdom, Tanner. After we have finished what we have started, then there might be something for you to do here with us if you so wished."

Doc gave him his best and most sincere smile. "My thanks to you. But I believe I must claim a subsequent engagement, Professor Crichton."

"Are we going to learn what you do?" Trader called from lower down the table, on the same side as Ryan. "Or do we just stay here for a day or so, sucking up this pastel-colored snot, and then move on?"

"You are outspoken, Trader." Buford giggled.

"Doesn't answer my question, does it? You want something from us. What is it? Can we trade? Do we want to trade? You gotta tell us."

Crichton peered myopically down the room. "Your companion, Cawdor?"

"Yeah?"

"I see why he has been nicknamed Trader. It is most appropriate for him."

"Sure is." Ryan laid down his knife and wiped a few crumbs of cheese from his mouth. "And I don't hear an answer from you or any of your people to the question he just asked."

"Which was? Refresh my memory, if you would."

"This institute been running ever since before the birth of Deathlands, is that right?"

"My grandmother herself laid the foundation stone two years before what I believe has become known to outlanders as 'skydark.'"

"Helped by the military?" J.B. asked.

The rest of the men and women around the long table seemed content to become observers while their leader, and occasionally Buford, dealt with any of the questions from this strange crew of outlanders.

"Oh, yes. The Crichtons have always been patriots, Mr. Dix. We were there at Bunker Hill, looking deep into the whites of their eyes. A Crichton was at the Alamo, facing the red glare of the rockets, showing how a man of honor can die. A Crichton rode against the smoke-clustered guns at First Bull Run and a cousin stood alongside Lee at Appomattox. My great-great-grandfather was—"

Ryan held up a hand. "We get the picture. Yeah, we see."

The old man looked at him with the steadiness of a sun-warmed python. "Outlanders are rare as the mother lode here," he said. "We are not used to the direct way some of you have. Here we talk more carefully."

"Comes back to what Trader asked you," Ryan insisted. "Why do you want us here? Bearing in mind, like you say, that you don't allow outsiders into this valley."

"That can all wait until tomorrow." David Crichton stood, a little shakily. "Now, I shall go to bed."

Buford coughed, catching his master's attention.

"What is it, Ladrow?"

"If the lady is well, we were going to ask permission to spend some experimental time with her. The others could safely be shown some part of our lengthy labors here, couldn't they?''

"Indeed."

Ryan tapped on the table with the hilt of his crusted knife. "One thing to make clear. I understand that Krysty's special powers are of interest. But we come all together, or we don't come at all. No question of you seeing her while the rest of us tourist around the bits you want us to see. Understand?"

"A direct man, Cawdor." Crichton laughed, the sound like an owl raking its claws through dry shells. "Unusual in my experience. Very well. If you will all agree, and the lady herself gives consent when she is recovered, then your cooperation in this matter would be appreciated." He gave them a small ironic bow and began to walk slowly away.

"Hope you all enjoyed the meal," Buford said perkily, turning to trot at the heels of David Crichton, moving across the long room in a direction that would bring them into the wing that was closed to the visitors. The rest of the scientists filed silently after them, without a word or a glance either to the outlanders or to one another.

"'Enjoyed the meal,'" Mildred said, shaking her head in disbelief. "Tell their cook not to give up her day job. I've eaten better food at my Uncle Josh's house, and his wife could ruin breakfast cereal."

"What do you reckon, Ryan?" Trader asked.

Suddenly the door swung open again and David Crichton appeared. "You didn't see my pair of hounds, did you? Any of you? No? Pity. A lot of work went into—" A hand appeared on his shoulder and drew him out of the room again. The door closed with a hydraulic hissing.

Trader grinned. "Few cards short of a deck, ain't he?"

Ryan didn't smile. "I'm not sure. Way I see it, Crichton might be playing a totally different game to the rest of us."

Chapter Twenty-One

"They've been living here in this secluded valley for the better part of a hundred years?"

Krysty was making progress on the slow road toward total recovery.

After the meal, once they were back in their own wing, there had been a brief strategy meeting with everyone present. There had been no need for long talks and complex planning. They all agreed that the institute didn't seem to present any serious threat to them, either individually or collectively, and that they would follow Ryan's lead the next day.

"Must be inbred." Ryan had pushed the two beds together and slipped a small sec lock across the inside of the door, giving them a fragile privacy.

"They seem like crazies or stupes?"

"No, and they aren't really like those weird white-coats we ran into up at Crater Lake."

"So, what are they doing, lover? What's their big special secret?"

"Yeah, that's the rusty nail in the lumber pile. I keep thinking about those days."

Krysty lay back, sighing. "Sorry, lover. Wave of tiredness came over me. Yeah, the dogs. And don't forget that poor bastard who looked like he'd been gone over by a mad surgeon."

"Might not be any connection."

She nodded, looking steadily into his face. "But there was the last words he said. Dean heard them."

"Twins."

"And 'coning,' remember? Dean said that the last word of all sounded like 'coming,' didn't he?"

"Moaning? Someone's name? Going? Could've been that. He was trying to say that he was going."

"Still doesn't explain him talking about twins, does it? And Dean was certain on that." She paused. "The dogs were so similar they looked like identical twins, didn't they?"

"Yeah, that's true." Krysty smiled as she yawned. "Talk can wait. You need some more sleep."

"I reckon I'll be back up to about ninety percent by morning, though their mushy food didn't help. I'd kill for eggs over easy with back bacon and a pile of hash browns in the morning along with a glass of fresh-squeezed orange juice. And good coffee, hot and strong enough to float a horseshoe."

"Promise you it won't be that, lover." He stood and started to get undressed.

"You turning in this early?"

"I think my own batteries could do with a little re-charging, as well. Trader always said that you should take sleep when you want it and you can get it. Or you'll want it another time and you won't be able to get it."

Krysty watched him, seeing the lean, scarred body, with bands of muscle hard across the strong bones, waiting until he was peeling off his dark blue pants, laying them on a chair in the corner, where the Steyr rifle was resting.

"Lover," she said very quietly.

"Yeah."

"I'm tired."

"I know."

"But not that tired."

BREAKFAST WAS A GRUEL of watery yellow that the sec man claimed was made from real eggs but had some added goodies, and some white gunge, slightly browned, that he told them was radiated and constituted potatoes, better than they were when they came out of the earth.

The orange juice was nonexistent. Fresh fruit was difficult to keep in the institute for very long. To drink he offered some truly bizarre nut-roast coffee with vile soya milk that stayed in long, circular streaks around the mug.

"Professor Crichton said to tell you that someone would call for you in about a half hour and to ask how the lady was." He addressed the statement to Ryan.

"She's sitting right in front of you. Why not ask her yourself?"

"Because they all said she was...she had... You know what I mean?"

"You mean I'm a mutie?" Krysty sat up in bed, her long flame-colored hair tumbling free over her shoulders. Ryan had noticed how dulled and limp it had become immediately after she'd used the Gaia power and how it was now returned, almost, to its full brightness and glory.

"Yeah, I mean... They said you lifted a whole tree that weighed ten tons."

"Very nearly," the woman agreed. "And you can go and tell your baron or boss or professor or whatever he calls himself that the mutie lady is feeling herself...." She glanced at Ryan and grinned impishly. "Cut that. Just report back to him that she is feeling a great deal better and should be able to meet anyone at anytime, anyplace."

The man nodded and lifted an index finger to his forehead in a salute. Then he turned on his heel and marched out of the room, closing the door quietly behind him.

IT WAS THE EVER-PRESENT Ladrow Buford who appointed himself as the guide to the party, greeting them out in the atrium at three minutes after nine in the morning, the time checked with a large four-faced digital clock whose numbers had been clicking remorselessly over for the entire life of the Melissa Crichton institute.

"Greetings to all of you outlanders, ladies and gentlemen and children." He stooped forward to peer at Dean. "Sadly we have few children here in the institute these days. The records show a far higher birth rate back in the early days of the long winters, after skydark."

"Probably nothing else for them to do," Abe said in a stage whisper.

"Sample of outlander humor?" the scientist asked, wiping his hands down the sides of his long lab coat as though they'd suddenly become infected.

"Good sample, too. You want some more?"

Buford shook his head, wincing as though someone had wafted a foul-smelling rag under his nose. "No, thank you. I believe not."

"Can we see all around?"

He looked at Mildred and pasted a lopsided smile across his face. "Why, of course you can." He paused. "Eventually. But not today."

"Why? What the fuck do you have to hide from us?" Trader snapped.

Buford glanced around, checking that there were half a dozen sec men within easy call. "You must not be so violent. It will benefit you nothing. Today we'll have a look around the outline of our project, give you an idea of what we do. Then, perhaps tomorrow, Professor Crichton wishes to talk with you. Specially with you," he said, turning to face Krysty.

"Me?"

"It's obvious already that you are not the common, run-of-the-mill outsiders who have stumbled into our lands in the past. We believe you have not told us the truth about where you come from and who you are. Perhaps you have been utilizing some terminological inexactitudes. We think you might have skills we do not yet understand. But we will. Obviously Miss Wroth's supernatural skill has attracted our interest, and we would like the opportunity to carry out some tests. No harm will come, either to her or to any of you. I promise you that."

"That's fair," Ryan said. "You lay your cards on the gaming table. Something in what you say. You don't get to make old bones in Deathlands if you go around blabbing off to everyone about who you are and what you've done. Mebbe we don't come from a little fishing village. But that falls under the heading of being our business, the way we see it."

"You admit to being liars?"

Ryan considered the question. "Yeah. I'll put my hands up to that charge, whitecoat."

Buford pulled out his notebook and quickly wrote several lines in it. Ryan glanced sideways but couldn't read the crabbed, angular hand.

He put the book away in a pocket and smiled brightly. "Very well. The tour begins here."

It DIDN'T TAKE LONG to check out the atrium, which the short, balding man explained had once been filled with a variety of rare and exotic plants. But they had all died. Sleeping and eating quarters opened immediately off it, with the security section on the second floor. Buford also took them into the other story of their own wing.

The rooms were mainly filled with laboratories of differing sizes, manned by the men and women who'd shared their supper the previous night. But there was nothing to give an obvious clue as to what work they were doing there. One of the things that Ryan noticed immediately was the almost-total absence of anyone under the age of thirty in the whole of the institute.

Doc had been walking briskly alongside the diminutive scientist, his sword stick rapping away on the plastic tiles of the corridors.

"Elegant," Buford commented.

"Thank you kindly."

"It looks a true antique." He peered at it. "That beautiful animal's head in silver."

"Toledo steel blade within the ebony case, and it supports me in my frail old age."

"I sometimes use a stick myself," Buford said, "as you probably noticed when we were outside. Rough ground is hardship to me with my knee and hip joints."

Mildred overheard the end of the conversation. "Why can't you carry out replacement operations? Place like this must've once been geared up for prosthetic installations."

"Prosthetic? You use a word like that! A woman shouldn't have knowledge from predark times on such medical matters. May Hippocrates himself preserve us, but I think that you are all muties!"

Mildred smiled. "Like Ryan told your chief, we don't always tell everyone everything about ourselves. Not too wise. But I give you my word that I don't suffer from any kind of genetic mutation."

Buford stopped in his tracks, so quickly that Abe bumped into him and Dean bumped into Abe.

"Genetics! You read it!"

"Where?"

"Sign on the outside, coming in."

"Gene sculpturing was what that said. Didn't actually mention the word 'genetics' at all."

Buford's eyes protruded behind the magnifying lenses of his polished spectacles. "Mystery on mystery."

"Ossa piled upon mighty Pelion," Doc added, grinning slyly at Mildred. "As you might say."

"You speak gibberish. Total rubbish. It makes no sense at all to me. What is Ossa and who was Pelion?

I am considered one of the brightest and best of the workers, here, but I have never heard of such talk."

Doc put his hands behind his back, like someone delivering a lecture. "In the world of the famous myths of ancient Greece—in Europe—the Titans wished to attack the mighty gods in their heavenly home. In their stupidity they piled the mountain called Ossa upon the one called Pelion and then both upon Mouth Olympus. And still they failed. Because the gods will always remain untouchable, just beyond our reach."

"You made that story up, Doc," Trader mocked. "Good one, though."

Buford clapped his hands to his shining pate. "This is madness. Ragged outlanders filled with knowledge that not even the best minds here know about."

He turned to Ryan. "You!"

"What is it?"

"The one-eyed man from the country of the blind. You see, I, too, have wisdom. You are some sort of shaman. You are bewitching us all with magic."

"We have knowledge," Ryan said. "We all have different skills. Doesn't make us muties."

Buford pointed at Jak. "What about him? He is a pure albino. We know about that from our research. There is a team already working on pigmentation problems. We know what causes it, but none of us had ever seen such a person before. He, too, could help us with our work."

Jak took a single long step so that his face was close to the scientist's, almost at the same level, the red eyes reflected in the glasses like tiny fire rubies. He lifted a long white finger and touched it to Buford's lips.

"Shh," he whispered, and took a single long step away again.

Buford swallowed hard, licking his lips, sighing. "I guess we know where we stand on that one, don't we?" He nodded so hard that the wisps of hair pasted across his scalp trembled as if a tornado were passing by. "Yep, we sure all know where we stand on that one."

Trader nudged Abe. "Whitecoat'll likely have to go back to his room and change his pants after that."

Mildred touched Buford on the arm, making him jump again. "Sorry, I forgot you said you don't like being touched."

"We have what we call a PHZ."

She smiled. "A personal hostility zone. Common psychobabble back in the 1960s. I understand. You didn't answer my question."

"What was it? So many rivers have been crossed in the last minute or so that—"

"This was a huge hospital and research institute, massively financed. I realize that times have changed and the wheels have sure turned. But you still call yourselves professors and wear white coats and have labs and all that. So, how come you can't perform a simple operation like replacing a diseased knee or hip joint?"

"After the nukecaust, there was a dark period here, as in the rest of the world. Though we were miraculously sheltered and a significant proportion of us survived, many clinical skills were lost at this time."

"Many?"

He nodded, shuffling his feet. "We can look in a part of the main research wing, now, if you wish."

Trader led the group in following the little scientist, but Mildred wasn't done with him, yet.

"Hold on just a moment. When you said that many of the clinical skills were lost... What sort of range of operations can you carry out now? I've seen the operating theaters and they look ready to rhumba."

"Ready to..."

"Never mind, Buford. Can you carry out, say, a mastectomy here?"

"No, not quite."

"You mean you could cut off the nipple but not the rest? What does that mean, man?" She was becoming very angry. "Appendectomy? No? Tonsillectomy? You mean you can't even take out someone's tonsils anymore?"

"It would be difficult."

Ryan interrupted the argument. "You've lost all of the basic medical skills, Buford?"

"Not precisely lost, outlander Cawdor. More that they have been rather... mislaid."

Mildred closed her eyes for a moment, struggling for self-control in the face of this staggering confession. "Can you explain what 'mislaid' means?"

"There were records of all sorts. Vids and machines to play them on. Demos of every operation ever known, taken step by step. We still have most of the equipment. Books and micros and disks. It was one of the finest medical libraries in the whole world."

"And?"

He sniffed. "An electrical fault. Fire. All gone."

"When?"

Buford scratched his cheek thoughtfully. "Can't say precisely. About thirty years ago. Maybe nearer to fifty. Nobody who's alive here now remembers it, except for the great Professor Crichton himself."

Krysty spoke. "So, all you do here now is what you call your research? That right?"

"Yes," he replied miserably.

"No surgical or medical skills left at all? Not a single one?" Mildred probed.

Buford's face brightened for a moment. "Not quite. Last year, after some experiments, we rediscovered how to pull out a diseased tooth."

Chapter Twenty-Two

The standoff had been going on for nearly half an hour, while everyone stood around the atrium, waiting. Krysty, after a request from Ryan, was provided with a chair.

"Sure you're all right, lover?"

She squeezed his hand. "Sure. Nearly back to normal again. But this hanging around is getting on my nerves. How long's it been?"

Ryan checked his own chron against the big clock. "Twenty-eight minutes since Buford went tottering off like a gaudy slut in a tantrum."

"Here he comes, Dad," Dean called.

Buford had taken up his stick again. His face was even more pale than usual, and he was perspiring profusely.

"Well?" Ryan said. "Do we get to see the rest of this place or do we all simply pack our bags and blasters and leave?"

"The Professor didn't take it at all well, being threatened like that. His first reaction was to order the sec men to take remedial action against you."

Trader laughed raucously. "Bunch of soft stupes who mince around looking like oven-ready chickens! That's a serious delusion, mister."

Buford tried an ingratiating smile with the grizzled man, ignoring the fact that the muzzle of the Armalite happened to be pointing at his groin. "Professor Crichton, in his wisdom, made it clear he had no wish to have nine innocent lives laid on his conscience."

Trader shook his head sorrowfully. "You pathetic little triple stupe! Move a finger in here and you'd drown in the blood that we'd spill."

"Let him finish, Trader," Ryan said quietly. "You can see we've already won the argument. No need to carry on rubbing his nose in it."

Buford almost bobbed him a curtsy. "Thank you, Cawdor. I put to Professor Crichton your offer that Miss Wroth would assist us in our research. Subject to certain controls and conditions, of course. And in return we would conduct you through the remainder of the institute."

"And he agreed?" J.B. queried.

"Yes, yes he did. But he made the point that much of it would make no sense to you, despite your undoubted remarkable range of skills."

"Fair enough." Ryan helped Krysty to her feet. "Then let's go."

AFTER THREE QUARTERS of an hour, Krysty whispered to Ryan, "Buford was right. I haven't understood one word in every hundred. You?"

"Not much." He closed his eye and put his head to one side. "The research for the last many years here in the redoubt, I mean the institute, has been directed at recreating life but making it perfect. Removing all the rotten parts and replacing them with good bits from elsewhere. That it?"

"Like breeding horses or cultivating flowers, working to make them better and better."

Ryan nodded. "That's why they're interested in Jak. Want to study him and see what it is in his genes that makes him an albino. Then try and replicate... That the right word? Replicate? Yeah. Make a new Jak who's normal."

Krysty smiled. "I see that. But what do they want from me? Make another Krysty who hasn't got the Gaia powers? That wouldn't make any sense at all. Unless they could alter it in some way. Don't like the thought of that."

They had stopped for a break. Sec men had brought in trays of different colored drinks, pink, green and violet. The trouble was that all of them tasted the same.

"Mixed fruits," Buford stated. "Pulped and spun dried in a vacuum rotator, then reconned and liquefied with preservatives and color additives. Delicious, aren't they?"

Trader was the only one in the group to actively disagree with the whitecoat.

"Well, let me think about that. I recall being down in the Mojave having had a disagreement with a breed baron. Very much in my young and unwise days." Ryan knew the story, having heard it a dozen times, and he saw the point that Trader was about to make. "He taught me a lesson in manners. Chained me naked in a cell that was five-by-five with an old rippled-iron roof. Was one-ten outside. Must've been one-fifty inside. Nothing to eat or drink for a week. Had to do a kind of backroll and piss in my own mouth. Not a pretty thought, Buford. But I lived through all that and lived to see that baron choke on his own bloodied lungs. Now," he said, grinning at the others, "given the choice, I'd take my own piss rather than these sickly brews."

THEY'D COVERED MOST of the first floor of the long wing of the institute, visiting lab after lab, with benches and all kinds of arcane scientific equipment.

"We'll go up the stairs to the top floor," Buford told them.

"What's along there?" Ryan asked, pointing to the end double sec doors.

Buford looked up at the ceiling, as if he were trying to read the solution to an ageless riddle among the strips of neon lights.

"That's sort of secret," he finally said. "Professor Crichton said he was sorry, but he didn't feel able to include that in the guided tour."

"Why?" Mildred asked. "All you've shown us so far is standard advanced genetic engineering. Carried a bit farther than anything I'd heard of. Grant you all of that. But it's still not much more than tampering with elongated DNA chains, using your supercomputers to ease calculations."

"Here in the Melissa Crichton Institute, Mildred, we all believe in making yesterday's impossibilities tomorrow's possibilities."

Doc clapped his veined hands together, slowly and sarcastically. "Jolly, jolly good," he drawled in an exaggerated accent. "That's the sort of jolly phrase that my dear grandmother would have insisted on embroidering into a sampler. The sort of jolly phrase that echoes around the mouth like an overripe plum and means precisely nothing.''

"Mock not,'' Buford said with an effort at dignity. "The last tear of sorrow is the one that counts.''

He was adamant on not allowing them access, and there were sec guards there to back him up. Ryan had seen nothing in the place to make him feel particularly suspicious and could find no reason to push the matter.

As Buford led the rest of them up the stairs, Ryan remained a few moments, staring at the wall above the sec doors, where an old sign had been painted over.

AFTER THEY'D SEEN ALL that they were allowed to see, which Ryan calculated at about sixty percent of the closed wing of the institute, Ladrow Buford invited them to eat a little lunch with him.

A couple of the other scientists joined them and, without warning, the tottering figure of David Crichton appeared, taking a seat at one end of the long table.

The food laid before them was no better than before, a variety of mushed-up slops in several different colors and with several different names.

Dean put his spoon down halfway through the main course. "Don't you ever have any real food here,'' he asked Buford, "like meat or fruit or anything?''

Crichton gave them his croaking laugh. "I hear you've dug out our lack of real medical skills. It's a miracle I've lived this long. But we have this baby diet for several reasons. One of them is this.'' He put his palsied hand into his mouth and took out a full set of false teeth, laying them, trailing spittle, on the table alongside his plate.

At a nod from their leader, the other whitecoats also took out full sets of teeth and showed them to the outlanders, with Buford last to comply.

Crichton favored them with a gummy grin. "We have technical skills to replace the teeth we lose but not the medical ability to keep the teeth with which we are born. That answer your question, young man? Chewing is one of our more difficult accomplishments in the institute."

Mildred raised a hand to attract his attention. "We've seen some of what you do here. Not all, by a long way, but I think we get the overall picture."

"You do, do you? Then that's extremely clever of you, young lady."

Mildred smiled. "Been a long while since I've been called that, Professor Crichton. Thank you." He bowed as he readjusted his dentures. "Genetic engineering is the simple phrase that covers it all, but I have some questions."

"Fire ahead, and damn the torpedoes."

"What do you use as your raw material for the research? I saw nothing involving live tissue."

Buford cleared his throat. "We occasionally make use of animals that we trap locally. After use they are returned to the wilds unharmed."

"Like those dogs you were searching for?" Trader asked.

After a heartbeat's hesitation, he replied, "Yes. Only they had been bred specially here."

"Not humans?"

"No."

"Never?" Mildred asked, pressing him. "I would be amazed, considering the range of your explorative surgery if you didn't at least use cadavers."

"Corpses!" Buford looked shocked, like a maiden aunt on a country walk accidentally catching sight of a bull's genitals. "What do you think we are, Miss Wyeth?"

She stared steadily at him. "Now, that *is* the big question, Professor. And the other one is why you're doing all this. What's the aim? What lies at the bottom of the last page of the book?"

Crichton waved his hand at Buford. "I'll field that one, if I may, Ladrow. Originally there was military interest. That is long gone, of course."

"Of course."

"You are aware that there are all manner of mutations rampant in the United States, or, Deathlands as it has sadly become. Our aim, as you put it, is to genetically remove all the mutations and breed a normal race."

"All mutations?" Krysty asked.

He lowered his head at her question. "I would not be so ungallant. Obviously only those that harm and destroy. The poor wretches called stickies are prime targets. With our help, they can be removed forever in a single generation."

"I can remove stickies in thirty seconds flat." Trader grinned and patted the butt of the Armalite. "Quick and easy and definitely terminal."

Crichton beckoned one of the silently watching sec men and took the Mossberg from him, holding it with difficulty. "We have our own firearms, you see."

"Why me?" Krysty asked. "Because I have the mutie talent for drawing on a unique power?"

"Yes. We have used other muties, if you will pardon the expression. Most have had gross physical deformities or appalling social deviations. These are tolerable. I am most repulsed by the inner mutations."

"But mine is . . ." Krysty began.

Crichton shut her up. "No, no. It is physical, though it has an inner core that you can somehow tap. Once we examine your DNA we can . . . If it wouldn't be a stratosphere above your head, I would explain what those letters mean."

Buford jumped in his seat. "In fact, the black woman used—"

But Mildred was quicker. "Don't patronize me, Crichton," she exploded. "Deoxyribonucleic acid, as opposed to ribonucleic acid. They differ in the pyrimidines. RNA has uracil rather than thymine. Similar but different, Professor, as we both know."

The long silence stretched and stretched. Finally the old man broke into a smile. "Well, I'll fly to the moon on a three-legged duck, as my grandmother used to say. Perhaps you can stay here and help us with our work when the others have been . . . are . . . My tongue stumbles. After the others eventually move on."

"Maybe, but don't count on it."

Krysty wasn't satisfied. "I see what you mean about me. That my power is made manifest outwardly. How do you feel about inner mutie powers like 'feeling' and 'seeing'?"

"They are called doomies and seers," Crichton said. "Now you are talking about serious nucleus-deep evil.

Our experiments over the years have never found any physical reason for such powers. If we find them, then we destroy them.''

Dean was instantly on his feet, his mouth open. Ryan saw the movement and his heart sank. "You wouldn't destroy Krysty or—''

"You need your afternoon rest, son,'' Ryan said loudly. "Seems you've been dozing and not listening to the baron. The professor, I mean. He explained that the power Krysty has is fine, not like doomies and those others who are real dangerous and should be stamped on. *Real dangerous*. You understand me, son?''

Dean nodded slowly. "Sure. I'm real sorry, Dad, for not listening and nearly saying something triple stupe. Sorry everyone. Guess I'll go to my room.''

"Mebbe we all should,'' Ryan said. "Thanks for the tour and the meal. But Krysty's very tired....''

BACK IN THEIR OWN WING, Ryan called everyone together. "Interesting, huh?''

"Nasty moment about seeing,'' Krysty said, lying flat on her bed, eyes closed.

"I'm so sorry about...'' Dean began. "Just hearing him say that Krysty was evil and should be destroyed made me see red. Won't do it again, Dad.''

"That's all right. Didn't do no harm.''

"Any, lover.''

"Any what, Krysty?''

"It didn't do *any* harm. Not didn't do *no* harm.''

"Yeah. Anyways, who's got any comments? Mildred, you know more than the rest of us.''

She sighed. "Truly bizarre. There's equipment here to run the finest hospital in Deathlands. They could spare endless misery for thousands of people a year. And all the medical wisdom has vanished forever. So they spend day after day, this inbred collection of small-brained whitecoats, month after year after damned decade, researching and experimenting away, slowly vanishing up their own assholes."

Doc nodded. "That is precisely my own perception, too. My own feeling is that there is nothing to keep us here for any length of time. The food is execrable and the intellectual company is barely above the level of a brain-dead dung beetle."

"Agreed," J.B. said. "The sec men might be soft, but there's a lot of them. And you don't need to be a shootist to blow someone away with a 12-gauge. I think we should get ready to move."

"They threatened us." Trader stood in the center of the room, hands on hips. "We all heard it. The shit about those who get in don't get out. I say we walk careful, pick our moment and start blasting."

"Agreed with the first part. Not about the blasting away. Remember there's only one road in and out and it's guarded," Ryan said. "Mebbe it's better to let them talk to Krysty for a day or so while the rest of us recce and make sure that when we want to get out, then we all get out. No argument?"

"We split up for this?" The Armorer was sitting on Ryan's bed, checking the action on the Uzi.

"Yeah."

Krysty opened her deep green eyes. "I think I'd like to sleep for an hour or two. I don't feel any danger around. They don't have the balls for it."

Mildred laughed. "Truth is, they don't have any kind of equipment for anything, Krysty."

Dean nudged his father. "Can I have a look around, ready for the breakout?"

"Go with Doc. I don't want anyone isolated." Ryan raised his voice. "There's one other thing that you ought to know about this place. Ties in with what Mildred said about their equipment."

"What's that?" Trader asked. "You really do see more with your one fucking eye."

"When we were in the research wing. Just when Buford was leading us all up to the top floor, away from those closed sec doors."

"I didn't see anything." Abe looked around. "Did anyone?"

"It was a sign that had been painted over long time ago. But at a certain angle you could read the lettering underneath—Entry Absolutely Forbidden to all But B12 Cleared Personnel. And at the end was Mat-Trans Units."

"A gateway," Doc breathed.

Chapter Twenty-Three

"Snowing out."

Ryan pulled back the corner of the blind, looking across the dark green river to the towering walls of quartz-flecked granite. By bending he was able to make out the leaden sky riding low over the valley.

A few flakes of fluffy white drifted gently by the window, carried on a light easterly wind. Ryan stared at what had once been a massive parking lot for the Melissa Crichton Institute, now lying under a dusting of snow.

Krysty yawned. "Much? Is it white over?"

"Not quite. By the look of the sky, it won't be long before it starts coming down for real."

"I'll spend some time with the whitecoats today."

"Sure you feel well enough?"

"Only talk."

He started to get dressed, taking his clothes off the green ribbed radiator fixed to the wall beneath the window. "Might ask Buford or his baron whether we can go out. Getting cabin fever from being locked up in this artificial air."

"Professor, lover. You keep calling Crichton a baron. He's not that."

Ryan nodded, halfway through lacing his combat boots. "Yeah, you're right. I do. Just that I don't see

much difference between this place and any other fortified frontier ville. There's sec men and power, just
like a ville.''

"Not many frontier villes have a mat-trans unit of
their own, do they?"

He sat up, stretching the tight muscles across the
small of his back. Feeling the usual morning stiffness
that dated back years, when a performing camel had
rolled on him during a fight at a wild animal show up
near Peoria.

"It was only the sign. Painted over years ago.
Doesn't mean they still have an actual chamber.''

"It would make sense.'' Krysty peeled off the thin
cotton T-shirt that she slept in, revealing her breasts,
the nipples peaking from the morning chill in their
room. Ryan stopped and stared at her, but she shook
her head. "No, lover. I'm still a little tender after last
night.''

"All right. You were saying that it would make
sense if there was a gateway here.''

"Military sponsorship.''

He nodded. "You know what would be profoundly
triple exciting, don't you?''

"No. But I can tell from your face that you're just
about to tell me.''

"If they had a gateway and it worked, and they
knew *how* it worked. Still had instructions how to
control where you jump to. That would really be
something. Make such a fireblasted change to all of
our lives.''

Krysty's ability to get dressed in no time at all constantly dazzled Ryan. Most times in Deathlands he
wouldn't feel anywhere near secure enough to take off

any of his clothes when sleeping. But even when he did strip down, he always figured that he was a fast dresser.

One moment Krysty was standing by her bed, magnificently naked, her hair like a torrent of living fire, pouring over her shoulders. Next moment she had on her blue jacket and matching pants, tucked into the tops of her dark blue Western boots, with their chiseled silver points at the toes and the embroidered silver spread-winged falcons on the fronts, running her long, strong fingers through her hair, bringing it to some kind of stubborn order. She smiled at him.

"Like what you see, outlander Cawdor?"

"You could say that, outlander Wroth."

"You don't look too bad for an old man yourself, outlander Cawdor."

"Old! There's a whole lot less than ten years between us, as you know. And it's common fact that women grow older much faster than men."

"That so?"

"Yeah, that's so."

"Isn't."

"Is."

"I'll arm-wrestle you for it."

"No way. You'd cheat and use the Gaia power."

She shook her head. "Hope it'll be a good long while before I call on that again."

FOOD WAS SERVED TO THEM at eight-thirty in the larger, three-bed room by a couple of sec men, accompanied by the scar-faced man that Ryan had run up against the previous day.

His whole manner had changed, and he smiled at the group as he came in through the door. He noticed Ryan glance at his face, and he looked a little embarrassed. "Oh, the mustache," he said. "I figured it was time to get rid of it. Had it for three seasons through already. 'Ellison,' I said to myself. 'Can't hide behind that bushy growth for the rest of your days.' So, last night, before sleep time, off it came."

"Last night?" said Ryan. "Not earlier?"

The sec boss shook his head. "Allow a man to know when he shaves off his mustache, outlander Cawdor, if you don't mind. Last night."

"Fine." Ryan turned away to conceal his puzzlement, looking at the big plastic dishes of food that were being uncovered, steaming slightly in the cold. "Why isn't the heating turned up higher, with snow outside?"

Ellison sniffed. "Yeah. Way the sky's squatting on top of the valley, it's going to unload plenty of goose feathers. Professor Crichton's been sayin' for some months that the power source is starting to give up. Reckons that it's only important to keep it up in the labs. Rest of us poor folk can just shiver and pull on an extra layer of clothes."

Trader and Jak were both by the window, gazing out at the thickening blanket of white, ignoring the dishes of pallid gunk that were being ladled out.

It was Trader who turned away first, addressing the sec boss. "Ellison, just what do you do for sport in the dead-alive hole?"

"You mean gaudy sluts? We go out on a rota in one of the small wags, four days a month. There's a ville about fifteen miles away and the girls there—"

"No, no, fucking no!" Trader held his forehead in his hands, reassuming control of himself. "I didn't mean that sort of sporting. I meant hunting or fishing or something like that. That ever happen?"

Ellison smiled, the deep livid scar curling his lip like a purple worm. "Sure. Fact is there's to be a hunt starting off around noon today. Professor Buford said I was to ask if the rest of you wanted to come, figurin' that Miss Wroth would maybe stay and help out the whitecoats."

"What hunt?" Jak asked.

"Guards at the barrier have seen a big bear. Humpback grizzly sow with a cub. Seen her two or three times. Put her in the mutie class. Reckon she's up to fifteen feet on her hind legs. Take some stopping."

Ryan looked at Krysty. "Sounds good to me, lover. Sure you're well enough?"

"Sure."

"I'll stay with you," Mildred said. "Hunting down a mother bear with a cub sounds like my idea of murder, rather than sport. But, don't let me stop you, gentlemen."

"My orders was everyone except Miss Wroth. Professor didn't say anything about anyone else being around. Have to check."

"Go ahead," Ryan said. "Rest of us'll eat."

The sec boss hesitated, then went out of the room. Ryan followed him, closing the door of the old hospital ward behind him. Ellison waited for him to speak.

"What is it, outlander?"

"Anything going to happen to Krysty?"

The blunt face was immobile. "Why should it?"

"Things happen here. Dogs vanishing. Taste of blood in the air. Not obvious, but it's there, like a forgotten promise at the back of your mouth."

"I believe that no harm at all will come to her. I helped in one of their experiments, but I'm sworn to secrecy. Didn't do me no harm." He touched his mouth. "This was there before. Nothing to do with them."

Ryan stood close, almost brushing the whispering white plastic jacket. "Anything goes wrong with Krysty, the first person I look for is you."

"I'll be here, Cawdor."

"Good." He nodded. "Now I'll go take a leak."

The bathroom was clean, though he noticed that the water pressure in the faucets was intermittent.

Outside in the corridor he could just hear Ellison talking to one of the other sec guards, their voices fading away toward the staircase.

Ryan finished pissing, did up his pants again and washed his hands at the nearest basin. There was a slit window behind it and he leaned forward to find out whether the snow was persisting. It was still falling steadily, cutting visibility to less than a hundred yards. It was already layering on the branches of the nearby pines.

There was a movement below him and he could just make out a few figures, very dimly, moving toward the edge of the trees. From the shouting and laughter he could tell that they were playing in the freshly fallen silent shroud of snow.

Curious, Ryan clambered onto the narrow tiled sill of the window and pressed his face against the cold, frosted glass, peering through the slits.

Four or five sec men, wearing quilted white jackets, were sliding around, throwing snowballs at one another. It was a scene of unusual good fellowship, and Ryan felt a momentary pang of envy for the fun they were having.

His face had to have been visible, dark against the opaque window, as one of the men stopped and stared directly up at him, pointing to the others.

Though Ryan knew there was no way they could recognize him, he pulled away.

One of the men had a scarred lip and was either Ellison, who couldn't humanly have gotten out there so quickly, or a dead ringer for him.

Or his identical twin, as Buford had said.

Chapter Twenty-Four

Permission was granted for Mildred to remain in the Melissa Crichton Institute, along with Krysty, subject to the codicil from Ladrow Buford that there would be times that they would wish to interview Krysty on her own without anyone else being present.

Mildred thought that wasn't unreasonable. "Keeps your research untainted," she commented.

"Are you sure that you would not rather come hunting with us, to track down the great bear and mighty jackaroe?" Doc asked. "Chance of real meat for a change."

"I dare not go a-hunting, Doc, for fear of the little men in white coats. You know them better than anyone. Best to be careful."

Doc nodded. I cannot but agree with that, my dear Dr. Wyeth."

THE BIG CLOCK in the atrium clicked over from 11:59 to 12:00 while they stood and waited. Most of the group of friends were happy with their own clothes, but Doc had borrowed a heavy jacket as had Abe.

They were all armed.

J.B. had left his Uzi with Mildred, deciding that the big 12-gauge Smith & Wesson M-4000, with its murderous Remington fléchettes, was a better weapon for hunting bear.

Ryan carried the SSG-70 Steyr rifle across his shoulders, with the SIG-Sauer holstered, as ever, on his hip, balanced by the heavy cleaver.

Trader had his Armalite while the rest of them carried their usual handblasters.

A group of a dozen or so of the institute's sec men waited on the far side of the open hallway, glancing across at the outlanders, obviously discussing them in soft whispers. They were mostly armed with Mossberg scatterguns, five of them carrying the big M-16 A-1s that Ryan had seen them holding before.

Ellison strode through the double doors from the main accommodation wing, heels clicking on the plastic tiled floor. He nodded to his men, marching straight across to Ryan. "Your people all ready?"

"Sure. Did you enjoy your snowball fight, Ellison, outside there?"

"What?" The man's face showed bewilderment. "I ain't been outside since yesterday...no, the day before. When you and your friends were brought in here." He paused. "And there wasn't no snow then. Except on the high peaks."

Ryan smiled. "My mistake. Just that I looked out the window of the john and I could've sworn that I saw you and some other sec men fooling around outside."

Ellison sniffed and tugged at the lobe of his left ear. "I don't reckon... Well, it sure as shit wasn't me." He hesitated, as if he were thinking about saying something else.

"Yeah?" Ryan prompted.

"No. Nothing."

"Who's coming with us?" Trader asked, joining them. "Any of the whitecoats?"

"Probably Buford. Likes squeezing the trigger on something living, and maybe Professor Gibson."

J.B. joined the group. "Which one's Gibson? The woman with the squint?"

Ellison nodded. "Best you don't mention Thea Gibson's walleye to her, or you'll finish up under her knife."

"Knife?" Ryan queried. "I thought that the scientists were supposed to have forgotten all the medical ways of curing people with surgery?"

"You don't get cured with old Thea's knife." The sec boss grinned. "Absolutely the opposite, in fact." His face changed as he saw two figures come through the double swing doors toward them. "That's enough said, outlanders. Not a whispered word about this to any whitecoat."

Buford wore a full-length slicker over what seemed an amazing array of padded clothes. He carried a long gun over a shoulder and leaned on his walking cane. Ryan recognized the rifle as being a Winchester 94 centerfire carbine, a six-round lever-action weapon.

"What model's that, Buford?" J.B. asked. "Standard, angle-eject or the big-bore?"

"You surely know your firearms, outlander Dix," the diminutive man replied, shaking his long, narrow head from side to side approvingly. "It is the big-bore model. Chambered to take the .375 round."

The Armorer nodded. "Stupe of me. 'Course it is. Should've spotted the rubber recoil pad on the end of the stock. Put a good hole in a bear with that."

Buford beamed. "I most certainly hope so. Let me reintroduce my colleague, Professor Dorothea Gibson. Thea for short. You all met her at the meal."

Like many of the whitecoats, Thea Gibson was slender, standing close to six feet. Her iron gray hair was scraped back into a tight knot at the back of her head. Her bright blue eyes were as cold as Arctic pack ice, one looking at Ryan, the other seeming to have a life of its own, roaming off toward the overhead clock. On her shoulder she had a slender Anschutz Kadett bolt-action rifle with a scope sight.

"Kind of dainty blaster for going after bear, ain't it?" Trader said.

"A .22 bullet will kill the largest creature, if it is aimed correctly," she replied in a prim little voice. "And I have five of them in this rifle."

"Remind me to keep out of your way." Trader grinned.

"Like all men you have a preoccupation with size, outlander Trader," she stated. "As in other areas of life, you are totally under a misapprehension." She glanced toward her colleague. "Time is wasting, Ladrow. Shall we go?"

"Yes, of course, Thea. Is everyone ready? We have a day's provisions in packs carried by the security forces who are accompanying us."

"Then, let's do it," Ryan said.

"BASTARD BALL-FREEZING," Trader complained before the hunting party had even gone a hundred yards from the main entrance of the institute.

"Should've stayed home with the girls," Abe said. "Or you should've borrowed some warmer clothes."

"Day I need advice from you, Abe, is the day that hell freezes over." He shivered theatrically, clapping his hands together. "And that might just be today."

There had been an old predark thermometer fixed to the outside of the building by the doors, and Ryan had glanced at it as they walked past. It was showing an ambient temperature of minus eight degrees, but there was a biting near gale blowing in from the northeast that must have brought a windchill reading of nearer minus twenty-five.

The snow had eased, but there was still a scattering of fine, grainlike flakes whirling past. The wind was picking them up and spinning them around the parking lot like miniature tornadoes of white powder.

Everyone had covered as much exposed flesh as possible against the icy blast. Scarves and gloves were essential wear. Dean had on his dark blue peaked cap, pulled low over his eyes, and trudged behind his father, trying to use him as shelter from the worst of the wind.

Doc slapped the boy on the back. "Bear it bravely, young'un. Foot it featly. This is nothing compared to some of the cold times that I knew in old days."

"Don't care about old days. Care that it's so radblasted cold here and now, Doc."

"I can recall a time that the hairs up inside my nose froze into ice."

Dean grinned. "I known it that cold, Doc. I remember up near the Lakes one winter when I took a spit and it froze in the air and tinkled on the ground as solid ice."

Jak was walking with them, his long hair seeming to mingle with the snow, his face like carved ivory, ruby eyes glowing. "Once came north from swamps," he said. "Near Lantic. Birds dropped dead from sky with cold. Covered fields for miles."

Trader was exercising as he stepped along, holding the Armalite by the barrel and swinging it as if he were aiming for a homer into the heart of the bleachers. "You lot are just home babies," he said, scornfully. "Talking about how cold it once was. None of you can imagine the years that followed on the heels of the long nuke winters."

"Tell us, Trader," Ryan said, nudging J.B., both of them knowing that Trader had an infinite capacity for rattling off the tallest of tales.

"I remember falling asleep in a forest and waking with my eyes frozen shut. Got them clear and stood up in the snow to take a leak. I started to piss, and it began to freeze from the ground up, turning into a golden ladder of pure ice."

"Not very pure, Trader," Ryan commented.

"It's what they call a figure of speech, beyond your poor understanding."

"Go on," Dean urged.

Trader sniffed, wiping away a bead of moisture from the end of his nose. "Well, kid, the freezing ice was getting nearer and nearer to my...you know..."

"To your dick?"

"Yeah. I knew that it would freeze right the way inside me, until my bladder froze, then my heart and lungs would've turned to ice."

"What did you do?"

"Pulled out my knife and slashed down at the stream of piss, and I cut clear through it just in time.

Another inch or so and old Trader would have been chilled Trader. Now, what d'you think of that?''

The woman's voice from behind him was colder than the weather. "I think that's a pointless and triple-stupe outlander tale that contains not a word of truth from its pathetic beginning to its sorry end."

Trader spun, his lips peeled off his teeth in a feral grin that mixed disbelief and anger. "Well, now, whitecoat Gibson, I doubt you've ever had much experience of a man's dick anywhere near you, so how would you know?"

He turned his back on her and walked ahead, his head bowed against the blizzard.

Professor Gibson didn't reply to him. She looked around for Ellison, beckoned him to her and whispered something in his ear, looking angered when he shook his head and moved away.

THE WIDE, HIDDEN VALLEY seemed to exaggerate the force of the weather, trapping the wind and snow and whirling it around like a huge mixing bowl.

The group plodded back up the trail, passing the barrier, where the sec men were sheltering in their huts, over the ridge and into the more open country, where the wind wasn't as severe and the snow eased.

Ellison, who was running the hunting expedition, gathered everyone around him in the lee of a granite outcrop that was dusted with frozen snow.

"Grizzly and her cub were sighted around this area. In the past four or five years—in winter—they've sometimes come over the high land to the north of us, making their way across what's left of the causeway, particularly if there's been a very hard winter in old Canada."

Buford raised a hand. "I remember we killed two in the same month, not all that far from here. It was a long day's expedition, near Witch Hole Pond."

A frosty smile appeared on Thea Gibson's face. "We were able to try out a cub in the labs that time. Didn't work out too well. Adrenaline was an unexpected problem. But we've made such progress in the last couple of years."

Buford nodded. "But remember that we have been told by Crichton to take care about risking exposure of any element of our work to the outlanders." His glasses flashed toward Ryan. "However undeniably pleasant they might be."

"Of course, Ladrow. You were right to reprove me. My enthusiasm for my work sometimes carries me along just that few steps too far. Forgive me."

Ellison rubbed his gloved hands together. "You know that I'm more interested in your work, professors, than most anyone around the institute. But we should be moving. Want to get this over and back again before dark. Weather could turn real nasty."

Ryan agreed with that. The sky that had seemed the darkest gray at breakfast time had cleared and lightened a little, but over to the north it was now nearly black and the snow was already falling a little faster again.

"How're we doing this?" Trader asked. "There's twenty or so of us in this party."

Ellison looked at him, lifting a finger to rub the scar. The bitter cold had made it darker against the pallor of his face. "We'll split up is best. Three groups, I think. There's several trails to bring us to Witch Hole Pond. We can cover them all. I'll lead one group, Professor Buford can guide the second and Professor Gibson the third."

Ryan caught J.B.'s eye, getting a cautious nod in return. Dividing into three meant splitting their own party, and with a dozen sec men around that could prove risky.

But, there still hadn't been any kind of direct threat to any of them.

ELLISON TOOK four sec men, plus Jak and Abe.

Buford had four more sec men, along with Doc, J.B. and Dean, who had wanted to go with his father. But Ryan had persuaded him that it would be better to be separate. "If anything goes wrong, one of us has to be there for Krysty," he'd said to the boy.

Professor Gibson had five sec men, Ryan and Trader with her.

She took her party to one side before they all divided up. "Just one thing gentlemen," she said crisply. "I know that you two outlanders are not used to taking orders from a mere frail woman." One eye appeared to be glaring at Trader and the other directly at Ryan. Neither of them spoke, while the sec men remained silent and sullen in the background. "I know this land. I have hunted all game from bears to cougar. I am in charge of this group. Is that absolutely clear?"

None of the sec guards spoke, one of them hitching his pack higher on his shoulders. Trader simply nodded his agreement. Ryan shrugged.

"Guess so," he said.

They were to take the eastern trail, Buford the center and Ellison the west. They'd meet at the small lake by three. It would begin to get dark a couple of hours after that, so time was somewhat of the essence for them all.

"Anyone finds the grizzly or recent spoor, fire two spaced shots in the air. Rest of us'll come running." The sec boss looked around him. "Good luck."

Chapter Twenty-Five

"Wolves," Trader stated.

"Too far away to bother us," the woman scientist replied. "Off near the Narrows to the mainland."

"Sounded less than a couple of miles." Ryan put his head to one side, closing his eye, concentrating on listening.

One of the sec men, a short man with a pocked face, chose that moment to have a coughing fit.

"Shut the fuck up," Trader snapped.

Thea Gibson pointed a bony forefinger at him. "Watch your language, outlander. You aren't lying with your filthy stupe whores now."

Trader bowed to the scientist. "No. Plenty of times I wish I was."

"Shut up, both of you." Ryan held up his hand. "Yeah, there it is again. Definitely only a mile or so away. Sounds like a hunting pack to me."

Thea Gibson tightened her fingers in her gloves. "I have read research that there is no evidence whatsoever, throughout history, of wolves voluntarily hunting human beings."

"I *been* attacked by hunting wolves," Trader snorted. "So's Ryan here."

"That's right."

"Well, we have ample firepower, assuming that you are capable of using your firearms. Eight guns should be enough to hold off a few scrawny dogs."

It was a fair comment, unless it was a particularly savage mutie pack, in which case a war wag and a few cases of implodes and frag grens would come in useful.

DESPITE THE HANDICAP of his stick, Ladrow Buford led his group along the narrow trail that ran down the center of a steep valley, sparsely wooded on both flanks. It was far more rocky than any other section of Acadia Park, with a number of narrow streams flowing fast among the frost-riven boulders.

"We shall be at the rendezvous in good time," he said to J.B.

"This the easiest of the three routes?"

"I believe so. There are few places where we are likely to come unexpectedly upon our prey. To the east of us, where Ellison is leading, the trail is more hazardous."

"What about the other side, where my father is?" Dean asked. "That dangerous?"

Buford considered the question. "Possibly. Yes, in a couple of places, most certainly."

JAK WAS FEELING the cold, aware of the threatening weather that was looming from the far north. The wind was rising, blowing the lying snow into deeper and deeper drifts, some of them already deeper than a man's shoulder.

He moved forward, passing Abe who was struggling over an icy patch, catching up with the powerfully built sec boss. "Why not hunt tomorrow?"

Ellison glanced at him out of the corner of his eye. "Why?" He spoke again before Jak could answer him. "I wanna ask you a question. Been a lot of argument about this, you understand, back at the base. When you bleed, what color's your blood? I say it's white."

Jak's expression didn't alter. "I say better wait until you see it."

"Right enough, outlander. Now, why should we think about aborting the mission?"

"Didn't start until noon. Going to move get back institute by dark."

"Fair comment, outlander Lauren. But Crichton decided, and what Crichton decides gets done."

"Or else what?"

Ellison laughed, his finger rising to touch the scar by his mouth. "Or things can become terminally unpleasant and unpleasantly terminal."

THERE HAD BEEN a serious avalanche ahead of Ryan's group. From the weathering and the plant growth, it had probably happened at least ten or fifteen years earlier. A slab of the hillside, a hundred yards long and fifty yards high, had fallen away, tumbling into a heap of lichen-dappled rocks and scree.

The group now had to detour above it, following what looked like it was some kind of animal trail.

A vicious flurry of snow, peppered with sleet, stung the skin of the face and dropped visibility to a handful of paces.

Ryan called out to the blurred figure, stalking along ahead of him. "Gibson?"

"What is it now?"

"This isn't good weather for hunting a big mutie grizzly and her cub."

"What is it good weather for?"

"Suicide."

She almost laughed. "Direct, aren't you? The fact is that Professor Crichton has ordered this hunt. The repercussions for taking any other course of action are not pleasant, outlander Cawdor. Not pleasant at all."

The blizzard lasted less than ten minutes and for a brief while the skies cleared and, miraculously, they walked along under a golden sun.

"Suicide, Cawdor?"

Ryan hesitated before replying. "If I owned all the jack in Deathlands, whitecoat, I'd stake it that the weather closes down within the hour."

Gibson stared squint-eyed at him, unsmiling. "If you owned all the jack in Deathlands, outlander, then I might just accept your wager."

MILDRED SUDDENLY LAUGHED.

"What is it?" Krysty asked.

"You wouldn't get the joke, honey. Just that most of the hospitals in the old predark days were notorious for keeping people, patients, waiting for hours on uncomfortable benches in long corridors. Here we are, a hundred years or so down the line, in the heart of Deathlands, sitting on an uncomfortable bench in a long corridor, being kept waiting for hours in a hospital. Nothing really changes."

"Guess not," Krysty agreed. "Wonder how the guys are getting on with their hunt? Last time I looked out the window, the snow seemed to be getting worse again."

There was nobody else around. They had been taken down to wait for the examination to begin, but they had already been kept hanging around for well over an hour.

Mildred suddenly stood. "Listen, since there doesn't look to be any whitecoats here and a lot of the sec men have gone off after the grizzly, this could be a good moment to try to do a little scouting on my own."

"Could cause trouble if you get caught."

"I won't. I'll just turn into a stupe woman and say how I'm sorry I got lost. And I was never any good at finding my way around places. Tell them I got a headache and went back to our quarters to lie down. I didn't want anyone to come along and disturb me."

"Sure." Krysty reached out and squeezed her friend's hand. "Take care, now."

"'Course." Mildred started to walk away, then returned. "Remember what I said about this examination. Under no circumstances let them give you an injection. Or take anything to eat or drink while you're down there."

"My mother didn't raise me to take no shit from no whitecoats," Krysty replied, assuming a strong Southern accent.

"Just watch them. That's all. See you later. Bye." Mildred waved her hand and disappeared along the passage, through one of the innumerable pairs of double swing doors.

"YOU SURE WE'RE ON the right track, Professor Gibson?" one of the sec men asked, his voice floating from the thickly falling curtain of snow.

"I have hunted here for many years, thank you, Brunner. I can find my way around this region blindfolded and in the dark. I know precisely where we are. The trail will shortly begin to drop down and then we'll be at Witch Hole Pond. Just concentrate on doing your job, which is to carry the supplies and be ready to open fire if we are attacked."

"Sure thing," he muttered in a sullen voice.

The woman stopped and peered back over her shoulder. "Remember what happened to Ellison," she said quietly. "And also remember, Brunner, that Ellison was one of the lucky ones."

Ryan's prediction had been proved correct. After the falsely smiling half hour of sunny weather, the sky had clamped down once more, like a dark, malevolent god, tipping a blizzard of snow down across that part of Maine, visibility dropping to less than ten paces.

One of the sec men had slipped on a patch of slick ice and nearly gone clear off the trail, falling into the whiteout on the left. Trader had been at his heels and had reacted with lightning speed, stooping and grabbing at the straps of the man's pack, hauling him back from the brink of the ravine, from possible death or probable injury.

Ryan had moved to walk with his old chief, keeping his voice quiet enough so the woman at their head didn't hear him. "I don't feel this track starting to go back down toward any lake, do you?"

"No. Climbing up and up. I reckon that we're starting to move in a half circle, away to the east. Unless the wind's veered, of course."

"Think we should tell the whitecoat lady that we want to go home?"

Trader grinned at him, ice hanging from his eyebrows, frosting the stubble on his chin. He blew his nose into the thick white carpet around his boots. "Why don't you go tell her, good buddy. You're the one got a soft spot in her heart. If beaten brass had a soft spot at all."

"AGREED." Buford had gathered his hunting party around him. They were near the ruins of some kind of shelter, with three walls standing, offering a little protection against the rising wind and driving, blinding snow.

J.B. had insisted that they call an immediate halt, realizing that the way the weather had clamped down meant they were in far more danger from a rogue grizzly than a rogue grizzly was from them.

"It can come at us and be less than fifty feet away and we wouldn't know. We have the blaster power, but not if it charges. Give us less than two seconds to open fire and stop it. Big mutie bear, like they say it is, won't just check and turn tail with a couple of charges of buckshot peppering it. More than likely it'll warm it up some."

After the speech from the Armorer, Buford stamped his walking stick in the snow. "Right," he said. "Turn back right now and head for hot showers and warm food. Rest of them'll probably have already done the same."

ELLISON GRIMACED as some snow slipped down the gap at the back of his collar. "Reckon we've gone far enough here. Haven't heard any shots, so I figure the other two groups have likely turned back to the institute already. Professors aren't known for liking any hardship."

Jak smiled thinly. "Woman whitecoat looks like swallows razor blades for breakfast. Hardship falls off her like water off duck's ass."

The sec boss nodded at the albino teenager. "Reckon that there's something in that, kid."

"Don't call me that, Ellison."

The man weighed him up, finger loose, close to the trigger of the Mossberg. He saw that the slightly built youth was standing, relaxed, the right hand out of sight, somewhere close to the small of his back.

Knife, was what hopped into Ellison's mind. "Sorry about calling you 'kid,' outlander Lauren. You agree about the idea of us turning back now? Or do you want a fine mutie grizzly's head as a trophy for your wall?"

"Go back," Abe said quickly.

Jak moved his hand very slowly away from the taped hilt of one of his hidden leaf-bladed throwing knives. "Yeah," he said. "Go back."

"ALL RIGHT, ALL RIGHT!" The woman scientist banged the butt of the Anschutz Kadett bolt-action rifle on the icy rock beneath her feet.

"Not a question of laying blame," Ryan said urgently. "Fact is we're lost, right?"

"Yes. But only until the snow clears away. Then I shall be able to locate our position."

Trader laughed. "Sure you will, lady. Sure you will. But by then we might all be blank-eyed corpses, frozen stiffer than a coon dog's pecker."

"Shelter," Brunner said. "We got way up high on this trail. Freezing so hard now with dark on the way that it's solid ice behind us. I nearly went over the cliff. Would've if not for the outlander. We got food. Find a cave or something like that."

Thea Gibson glared around, the exposed part of her face as white as bone. "But the snow's so thick, we can't see a cave even if we were nearly inside it."

"We move ahead. Keep close to the cliff on our right. Luck's with us and we find a shelter."

"If we don't?" Trader asked.

"Have to use drifted snow and try to build us a kind of igloo. Snow house. Need to be big for all of us. Wait here, huddled together, until this blows itself out."

"My cheeks are frozen," the professor complained, rubbing at her skin with both hands, trying to restore the circulation. "And my toes."

"Frostbite, Thea," Ryan said, having to raise his voice almost to a shout to counter the howling banshee wind. "Colder it gets, with the chill factor, as well, you got less and less time. Get down around minus fifty and you lose blood flow in about ten minutes to exposed flesh. Frostbite and gangrene in a few hours."

One of the other sec men had wandered a little ahead, returning from the blizzard. "Could be something ahead," he yelled. "Like a cavern."

"That's a miracle," Thea Gibson said, almost weeping in her relief.

"Man who counts chickens before they hatch ends up with a handful of broken shells," Trader said, but only Ryan heard him.

"WE'RE READY TO SEE you now, Miss Wroth," said the shy little scientist. "Sorry to have kept you waiting for so long out here."

"All right."

"Where is your colleague?"

"Mildred had a migraine headache and she's gone back to her room for a lie down."

"Perhaps I could send along someone to—"

Krysty shook her head. "No need. She didn't want to be interrupted. Said so herself. Can we get started?"

"Of course, of course."

THEY STOOD TOGETHER, eight strong, in the arched entrance to the cave, peering into its black, soundless deeps. They were just out of the main force of the snow, though flakes still whirled around them.

"Go inside there and check it out, Brunner," Thea Gibson ordered, pointing into the blackness with her rifle, in case there was any misunderstanding about what the sec man was supposed to be checking out.

"Not on my own."

"Take Moore with you and Cooke. Hold each other's hands in the dark."

"Should've had lights," Brunner complained. "Stinks inside here."

Ryan sniffed. The man was correct. There was a strong musky scent, like rotted meat, overlaid with a more bitter smell that reminded him of urine.

The three sec men disappeared inside, talking quietly to one another for comfort.

Ryan slowly took the Steyr SSG-70 off his shoulder and readied it for action. At his side, unbidden, Trader did the same with his Armalite.

Thea Gibson saw their movements and hesitated. "Think there's trouble in there?"

"Does a bear shit in a cave?" Trader asked.

A deep-throated roar came from the pitch-dark interior, followed instantly by a scream and the thunder of one of the Mossbergs.

"Best give ourselves some room here," Ryan suggested, leading the way quickly out onto the ledge, barely ten feet wide, into the worst of the snowstorm.

There was another shot, and a repeat of the reverberating roar, so deep and angry that it felt as though it shook the marrow of the bones.

Brunner appeared first into the blizzard, sliding and slipping, almost dropping the scattergun. "Quick, after us!" he screamed. "Got Cooke!"

Moore was next, weaponless, his head thrown back, eyes staring, as though he were finishing the hundred-yard dash. His mind wiped by fear, he never even checked his stride, running across the snowy trail and clear over the edge, falling soundlessly into the abyss below him.

"Get ready," Ryan shouted, kneeling and leveling the rifle. Trader and the woman followed his lead, the surviving sec men watching them, frozen by terror.

"Here it comes," Trader warned.

The dark bulk loomed from the cave mouth, and they all opened fire.

Chapter Twenty-Six

Krysty had once seen a brief snippet from an ancient vid, so ancient she thought it might have been in black and white without any color enhancement. A young person had been standing in front of a circle of judges, all perched up at high benches, being interrogated by them.

She felt rather like that as she was shown into a white-walled laboratory by the shy little scientist. A clock on the wall told her that it was already twenty minutes to two. Through a long, narrow window Krysty could see that there was a serious blizzard raging outside, and her thoughts turned to Ryan. She tried to feel how things were, but could only receive a number of confused, jumbled images, mostly overlaid with blurring whiteness. But at least there was no sense of danger.

Crichton, tiny and frail, was sitting in a black leather-and-chrome chair. He waved a clawed hand toward her. "So sorry to have taken so long, my dear. There was some rather extended argument among ourselves about the form that this examination should follow."

Krysty sat in a straight-backed wooden chair with a padded seat and short, stubby arms, facing her inquisitors.

They numbered nine in total, most of them vaguely familiar from the supper.

She noticed banks of computers all around the walls, making the place look like one of the gateway control centers. There were a number of silver headsets, like crash helmets, with long curling wires leading from them.

"Krysty," Crichton said gently. "Please pay attention to what I'm saying."

"Sorry."

"I was telling you that we have agreed to start with an informal question-and-answer session about your earlier life. See if there are any significant environmental factors that should be taken into account." He smiled wearily. "But all this is probably beyond your intellect."

"No."

"No?"

She shook her head, aware that the sentient, flaming hair was curled defensively around her nape, clinging tightly to her skull. "No," she repeated.

"Very well. Please respond as quickly as you can to our questions. Don't bother to try to work out what would be a good or a favored response. You understand that?"

"Of course."

"Very well. Your first memory?"

KRYSTY HAD THOUGHT that a very old woman on the far right of the line of questioners was sleeping. Her eyes had never opened, her hands folded on the desk in front of her, seeming to be oblivious to the interrogation that had been going on for more than an hour without a break.

Then, reacting like a lizard sensing food nearby, her ancient eyes creaked open and the toothless mouth spoke. "How did you lose your cherry, my dear?"

"That falls into the box labeled my own business," Krysty snapped.

"Why?" A long finger pointed at Krysty, who noticed that the nail was so uncared for that it had curled in on itself, like horn, the tip almost piercing the flesh.

Krysty considered the question and decided that there wasn't really a good reason not to answer it. "The blacksmith back at Harmony ville was called Herb Lanning. He had a real good-looking son, Carl. I chose him."

"You selected him? Isn't that contrary to the usual way of doing things?"

"My mother raised me to be different. I know what sex can be like in Deathlands. Good chance I might lose my virginity to violence. I didn't want that. I wanted it to be the way I wanted it. Under my control. Carl was sweet and gentle, and he had a great body. Beautiful muscle definition across chest, shoulders and stomach. Sorry thing was that he only had a brain the size of a horseshoe nail."

"You raped him?" asked a male scientist at the other end of the row.

"Seduced is so much nicer a word." Krysty smiled. "It was good for me, and I think it was like an angel's gift from heaven for him. So, we both got what we desired."

"You never considered marrying him?" The question this time came from Crichton.

Krysty threw her head back and laughed. "Be like marrying a fence post. 'Course not. We never did it again, though he kept asking me. Gaia, but he tried!"

Crichton nodded. "I think that we would like to talk about this mysterious power now."

MILDRED STOOD WATCHING the weather, concerned for the well-being of J.B. and all the others in the hunting party. There had been a very brief snatch of watery sunshine, ten minutes earlier, but that had passed quickly away. Now the dark clouds were so low that she almost felt that she could open the window and reach up to touch them.

The last half hour had been uneventful. She had wanted to try to gain access to the part of the wing where Ryan had seen the faded remains of the sign indicating that there might be a working gateway somewhere inside.

But the sec guards were vigilant, and she'd been lucky not to get caught by them.

Now she was in a narrow corridor that ran along the outside of the building and seemed to be very little used. There were dust bunnies in the corners and spiderwebs across the angles of the windows.

It seemed as though it had been originally utilized by cleaners or service operatives in the old times. Once she slowed her pace, going on tiptoe past an open skylight above a sealed door. Inside she could smell the bitter tang of coffee sub and hear a murmur of conversation.

There were three or four men inside. Mildred gathered that they had just come off a research shift and were about to go and join in the questioning of Krysty.

It was difficult to hear properly, and she could only catch occasional snatches of the conversation. But what she overheard was exceedingly interesting.

"Once it's done, they'll test to try and overcome the personality typing."

"...happened to the Ellisons."

"...growth accelerator...will tell her...ignorant of matter transfer..."

"Crichton reckons this could be the big..."

"I say the others should have been excised from the frame of reference while outside. Could have been handled easily enough out there."

Mildred shifted her weight from one foot to the other, wincing as her boot sole squeaked on the tiles.

"What was that?"

She didn't wait, moving as fast and quietly as she could, ducking into a storage closet and waiting, heart pounding. But nobody came after her.

Mildred stayed in the musty darkness for several minutes, replaying the odd moments of conversation, trying to make some sense out of them.

"No."

Crichton leaned forward, his head trembling, a thin thread of spittle trailing down onto his scrawny chest. "It is such a small request."

"Not small enough, Professor."

"A tiny prick."

Krysty couldn't resist a grin. "I bet you say that to all the girls."

The very old woman at the end of the line scowled at her. "Foulness in the mouth of a female is as to a jagged crack in fine porcelain."

"Thanks for telling me that," Krysty replied. "Would never have known it."

"One injection to relax you?"

"No, Professor Crichton. I will not allow a thief into my blood who might try to rob my mind."

"We all feel that you are holding back from us."

Krysty glanced at the clock. "I've been down here a long time, including the hour and more you kept me waiting. It's kind of tiring. I reckon this is long enough for today."

"Surely another hour? This is only a talk between friends, is it not?"

Krysty shook her head. "Frankly, no, it is not. I want to go and get ready to greet Ryan and the others when they come back from the bear hunt."

At that moment a door opened behind her. She turned to see a youngish sec man, staring at Crichton, waiting for the order to come in. He received it and marched smartly to the dais, lowering his head to whisper into his leader's ear. He paused as Crichton gave a gesture of irritation.

"Louder, boy, louder."

The guard repeated his message, this time getting a dismissive wave of the hand. He walked briskly out past Krysty without even glancing in her direction. She heard the hydraulic hinges hissing shut.

Crichton beamed at her. "I have just heard that the hunters chose to split up into three separate groups. Two out of the three have arrived safely from the heart of a severe snowstorm. The third one has not yet come home."

"Who is in the third party?" Krysty asked.

"Five of our sec men, Professor Dorothea Gibson and the two outlanders named Trader and Cawdor."

"Are they all right, Professor?"

He shook his head. "We don't know. But I suggest we carry on until they get back. Then you can go and welcome them to the institute."

Krysty stood. "I don't think so. I think I'll go and talk to the rest of my friends. Mebbe tomorrow."

Crichton nodded reluctantly. "If that is your final answer. Tomorrow at nine?"

"At nine."

As she walked out of the room, past the pair of sec sentries at the door, Krysty wondered where Mildred was and what she was doing.

THE ANSWER at that precise moment was that she was looking warily around a corner at the very farthest end of the forbidden wing of the complex.

About twenty yards away from her there was a pair of the double swing doors that were so familiar to her from her own work in predark hospitals. Each of the doors had a large circular pane of glass at its center to avoid the danger of people bumping into one another.

One of the doors had been propped open, so that she could see beyond it to where a couple of sec men were sitting at a small table, playing cards.

What was particularly interesting to her was what she could glimpse behind the men—a heavily bolted door, painted pale green, with an iron grille in it.

It wasn't the sort of thing that Mildred had ever seen in any hospital that she'd ever visited. But she had once seen a documentary about the women's prison at

Tehachapi, and there'd been an awful lot of similar barred and bolted doors in that.

Mildred had been concentrating so hard on this peculiar sight that she had failed to pay attention behind her. Suddenly she was aware of the sound of studded boots, marching fast toward her along the corridor.

Her hand dropped to the butt of the ZKR 551 revolver, and she tensed herself for the arrival of the sec man.

Chapter Twenty-Seven

The snow was blinding, but it was just possible to make out the blurred shape of the whirling, snarling, scratching bundle of dark fur that came bounding toward them, out of the heart of the stinking cave.

Ryan opened fire from the hip, working the bolt action on the Steyr, pumping three of the powerful 7.62 mm rounds into the bear. At his side, he heard the distinctive flat snap of Trader's Armalite. A little way over to his right there was the lighter sound of Professor Gibson's .22-caliber Anschutz Kadett rifle.

Out of sight in the blizzard, there was the muffled boom of two of the Mossberg 12-gauges.

Ryan heard a shriek of pain that was so unearthly that it crossed his mind that someone in their party might have been shot in the panicked cross fire.

There was another blast from one of the shotguns and another from the woman's rifle. The wind dropped for a moment, and it was possible to glimpse their prey, lying twitching and scrabbling with its claws at the shattered ice, blood soaking into the smooth dark fur.

"I'll be hung, quartered and dried for the crows!" Trader exclaimed. "It's only a little cub."

Brunner was on his hands and knees at one side of the narrow trail, staring back into the cavern, his eyes wide and staring. "Wasn't the cub that chilled Cooke."

Ryan stood still, trying to see into the opening of the den, but it was blacker than pitch.

"Got to be the mother in there, Trader!" he shouted. "Run or fight?"

"Fight," Trader yelled, down on one knee, reloading the Armalite, his eyes never leaving the cave. "We try and run, and it'll take us out from behind."

"Bullshit! We gotta get out right now." It was one of the unnamed sec men, his silvered Mossberg dangling from his right hand. "Come on!"

Brunner and the third survivor followed him, blundering off into the shroud of white that made rapid progress impossibly dangerous.

Thea Gibson tried to stop her men, but her words of protest were whirled away by the eldritch scream of the wind. She watched the sec guards flee, turning back to face Ryan and Trader, shrugging her shoulders.

"They have lost their nerve," she called.

The dying cub made a last, feeble effort to try to rejoin its mother within the cavern, struggling to its feet for a moment. As it toppled forward on its face, breaking its prominent lower jaw, it gave a final desperate howl of agony.

The response was almost instant.

Ryan dropped flat in the snow, gesturing for Trader and the woman to do the same. After a moment's hesitation they followed his lead.

Just in time.

The earth seemed to shake as the mother grizzly emerged from the dark mouth of the cave, its head turning from side to side. It was difficult to make out any details through the blizzard, but Ryan was sure that the object in the mutie beast's jaw was probably a severed human leg.

The snow obscured the three prone figures and the bear, bigger than any grizzly Ryan had ever seen, failed to pick them up. But the fleeing sec men, trying to run over the treacherous trail, were still yelling and screaming. The monstrous head moved slowly in their direction, and the snarl turned into a deafening roar of terrifying anger.

For a second or two it rose to its hind legs, towering close to twenty feet in height, eyes glowing in the storm like beacons of insensate rage.

Then it dropped to all fours and lumbered down the trail, in pursuit of the humans that were responsible for the slaughter of its cub.

In five seconds it had vanished.

"Now what, Ryan?" Trader asked, standing up and brushing powdery snow from his knees.

"See if we can get down the other side."

"Will it catch the sec men?" Thea Gibson asked, trying to remain calm and thumb more shells into her rifle, her shaking fingers betraying her attempt at coolness.

"Probably," Trader replied. "Big grizzly can outswim and outsprint and outlast any man ever born over any distance you can think of."

The three of them stood close together, waiting and listening in the thick snow.

"There," Ryan said, holding up his left hand. "Hear that scream?"

Trader and the woman shook their heads. "The wind overlays everything," Thea Gibson said. "But if you say—" This time the cry was louder, more desperate. "I hear it now. Nothing we can do?"

Trader shook his head. "Nothing, except go and die along with them."

"It might come back to its dead cub soon as it's finished the butchery," Ryan told them. "Sooner we find an alternative way out of here, the better."

THE PATH WOUND around the side of the cliff, becoming markedly more narrow. As Ryan, in the lead, reached the sharp turn, the wind increased, blowing whiteout snow into his face and eye, blinding him.

Trader was following right at Ryan's heels and bumped into him when he suddenly stopped, knocking him a couple of clumsy steps forward.

His left foot slithered on a patch of ice, his right foot landing on...nothing.

Ryan was aware of the heart-stopping reality of the emptiness of eternity hanging below him. With a violent contortion that nearly pulled muscles in his back and shoulders, he spun on his left foot, the sole of his combat boot whispering on the ice, teetering on the brink, his vision and brain filled with a tumbling, swirling whiteness.

"Got you, buddy...." Trader's voice was in his ear, and he felt a tug on the strap of the Steyr across his shoulder. Pulling him back from the endless fall to the sightless crags below him.

Once he'd recovered, Ryan dropped to his knees and tried to see if there was any way across the divide. But a rock slip had carved a slice out of the granite, clean as a razor cut, taking away the path for as far as he could make out.

"No," he said, straightening. "No chance at all."
He patted Trader on the back. "Thanks."

THEY HAD RETURNED as far as the corpse of the young
grizzly, now dusted with fresh snow, when Ryan
caught the sound of death heading their way.

"Mother's coming," he said.

"Can we hide back along the path?" the professor
asked. "Might not scent us."

Trader had readied his Armalite. "No fuckin' way,
José! It comes after us, we're in a single file. Can't
shoot back. It'd swat us off like flies."

"The cave?" she asked.

Ryan considered the question. The massive mutie
bear was lumbering ever closer and would be on top of
them in a matter of seconds. If only they knew how
big, deep and wide the cavern was, whether it would
give them enough room and options to try to take out
the animal.

His combat mind raced through all of the alternatives, weighing and balancing them all, rejecting most
of them, accepting just the one.

"I'll go in the cave," he yelled. "You each take a
side. Chances it won't spot you when I draw its attention. Soon as it's real close, open up on it with everything you got."

"How about..." the woman began, but Ryan gestured for her to shut up.

"No time." He turned and ran past the dead cub,
into the relative stillness of the cave. The light was very
poor, but he could see enough to realize that he'd
made the right decision. There wasn't enough room

for all three of them to fight the grizzly with any chance of all making it.

At the back he could see a wall of blank rock, water seeping across it, shining in the pale glow from outside. There was a pile of crushed bones in one corner. The urine stench of the animals was overlaid by rotting meat and offal.

Ryan crouched, drawing the SIG-Sauer and laying it on the damp stone, bringing the Steyr to his shoulder, finger settling lightly on the trigger.

Outside, he was conscious only of a wall of unbroken white, which made him realize that there was a fundamental weakness in his plan. From where he was crouching, he couldn't judge the arrival of the giant grizzly, wouldn't be able to distract it and lure it past the guns of the others.

He scooped up the SIG-Sauer in his left hand and darted to the entrance of the cave, peering into the windswept waste. He was just aware of Trader, on his left side, flattened against the rock, Armalite at his shoulder. But the snow was too thick for him to see the woman scientist.

For a moment Ryan couldn't see the grizzly, though he knew it had to be within spitting distance of him.

Then it was there, so huge that it blotted out what light remained. The wind dropped for a moment, and Ryan found himself staring into the bear's small eyes, mesmerized by the blood-clotted muzzle, the great curved teeth that were still gripping the neck, head and shoulders of sec man Brunner. Below the chest there was only strings of muscle and ragged tendons, the flapping of part of the wretched man's lungs and the white of splintered ribs.

Ryan, off balance, snapped a single shot at the creature, left-handed, hearing from the angry roar that the 9 mm round from the handblaster had found its mark somewhere in the flesh of the mutie beast. The bear's breath belched out, steaming as it opened its jaws, dropping the poor raggled remains of the dead man. For a moment the grizzly started to rise onto its back legs, then changed its mind as its attention was caught by the figure of the man, crouched just inside its own den.

Ryan backed away making sure the animal was following him. His feet slipped on a patch of frozen urine, and he nearly went over on his back, but he managed to fight for balance.

"Come on, you bastard!" he yelled, leveling the SIG-Sauer and putting a second bullet into the mutie bear's chest.

The noise of its roar filled the cave, reverberating off the walls, coursing through Ryan's body.

As it began its charge, Ryan opened fire with the Steyr, shooting from the hip, as well as pumping lead from the handblaster. He actually heard the solid thwacking sound of the bullets striking solid muscle and bone.

He also heard the noise of the Armalite and the lighter pecking of the woman's .22.

It was all over in four or five seconds, but the climax of the hunt seemed to last forever.

The charging animal staggered as a burst from the Armalite struck home in its belly, but its vast size and momentum seemed to have made it invulnerable.

The arched roof of the cave was thirty or forty feet high. When, at last, the grizzly reared up on its hind legs, it looked to Ryan as though its head were scraping the raw stone. The front paws flailed at the air, the bellowing ceaseless.

Ryan dropped the SIG-Sauer and instantly leveled the rifle, aiming below the creature's jaw, knowing from the angle that the 7.62 mm full-metal-jacket round should penetrate upward into the brainpan.

As he sighted, a nanosecond before squeezing the trigger, he saw an odd thing. A bullet from one of the others had to have hit the animal from the side and traveled through the upper bones of the skull, bursting the grizzly's left eye as it exited.

He worked the bolt action with a fluid ease, snapping off a second bullet into the same target area of the throat.

Then it was on top of him.

One paw knocked the Steyr spinning from his hands, nearly dislocating his thumb and forefinger. Ryan tried to dodge clear of the toppling giant, but there was simply nowhere to run.

It crashed down from its full height, smothering him, sending him backward, the rear of his head striking a rounded boulder with a sickening thud that plunged Ryan into instant blackness.

WHEN HE BLINKED his good eye open, the only thing that he knew was that he was still alive. There was no sense of passing time. Ryan could have been unconscious for five seconds or for five days.

He was lying inside the cave, his head propped against the corpse of the monstrous mutie grizzly. The air was filled with the foul stink of its passing—blood, urine and fecal matter—as well as the fading scent of discharged blasters.

Trader was kneeling at Ryan's side, rubbing snow over his forehead, while Thea Gibson was sitting cross-legged a yard or so away, her Anschutz Kadett across her lap.

"You all right, bro?" Trader asked.

"Think so." Ryan lifted a hand to touch the back of his head, wincing as his fingers encountered a large raw lump. When he squinted at his hand, he saw a smear of blood.

"That was simply the most terrifying experience of my entire life," the scientist said. "I had no idea that such creatures still roamed the earth."

Trader rested a foot on the body. "Well, I'll tell you one truth, lady. This daughter of a bitch won't be doing no more roaming."

Chapter Twenty-Eight

"You two!"

The voice was so close that Mildred jumped and nearly rattled the barrel of the Czech revolver against the tiled corridor wall.

From where she was standing, it wasn't possible to see down toward what had looked like a prison cell. But she heard the scrape of a chair being pushed back.

"What?"

"Wanted at reception area. Seems the hunt's gone wrong. Two lots came back."

"Who?"

"Buford and one of the Ellisons."

"Which one?"

"Who knows, now one of them's shaved his mustache. Now we just got identical scar-faced bastards."

Mildred heard a bellow of laughter. She inched backward, glancing behind her. Only a part of her mind focused on the talking.

"Might be a search for the Gibson woman, Brunner and Cooke and some of the outlanders. Not sure of all of the details about who's missing."

There was a window with a long white blind that came right to the floor. Holding her breath, Mildred began to edge toward it.

"Go out in this shitting blizzard to look for that wrinkled dike and some outlanders! You gotta be greasin' my wheels."

"No. Order comes right from the top."

A third voice spoke, which Mildred assumed to be the second of the cardplayers. "Tell Crichton that you looked double hard and couldn't find us."

More laughter. "Yeah, he'd love that. Come on. Get the carrot out of your stew and follow me."

The blind was made from thin sheets of plastic slats, made fragile by the passing of time. Mildred lifted one side and began to try to slip behind it. The glass of the window was close to her back, and she caught a glimpse of fading light and whirling flakes of fresh snow.

"All right, all right. We're coming."

In her hiding place, Mildred couldn't catch what was said next, but it seemed to be a joking reference to whoever or whatever lay behind the bolted door.

"What could those sorry bastards do if they ever got loose, anyway?" one of the sec men asked.

"Not a lot."

There was a crack in one of the slats, right at eye-level, and Mildred could see the short stretch of corridor, where she'd been hiding. She drew in a sharp breath as two figures appeared in her line of sight. One of the cardplayers and the messenger sent to fetch them, she figured. They were joined almost immediately by the third sec man.

"Still snowing?"

"Was last time I looked."

"Window there, behind that old blind. Go see what it's like outside."

"You go and look yourself."

Mildred had the revolver cocked in her right hand. She didn't have much doubt that she could probably manage to take out all three sec men.

If she had to.

If she wanted to.

Might be better to just pretend she was frightened and had gotten lost.

But she was becoming increasingly suspicious as to what she and the others had stumbled upon.

"All right, I'll go look myself." One of the men walked toward her.

"No, leave it, Eddie. See when we get back up there. Crichton was getting fired up. Better if we don't keep him waiting any longer."

If Mildred had stuck out her right hand, holding the ZKR 551, the barrel would have touched the white plastic jacket of the nearest sec guard.

He belched noisily, revealing that he had to have eaten some garlic-flavored mush for part of his most recent meal. "Yeah, sure. I just love the idea of goin' out into this shittin' weather in the dark."

He turned and she could hear the sound of the three pairs of boots moving quickly down the corridor toward the institute's central atrium.

Mildred wondered how Krysty was getting on at her interrogation, considering if she ought to start making her own way back to the living quarters. The news about some of the hunters being lost was bad. But she tried to blank any worry about J.B. from her mind.

Behind her she could see that it was still snowing. There was a catch on the window and Mildred tried to open it, wondering whether she might escape from the trap by going around the outside of the institute. But the metal was fragile and the lock snapped in her hand, leaving the window a little ajar. A freezing wind blew a few flakes of white in around her feet, melting as soon as they touched the floor.

She eased herself from behind the blind, wincing as it rattled back into place. A careful look around the corner of the passage showed it to be completely deserted. When Mildred glanced the other way, the sight of the bolted iron door was too tempting to ignore.

Moving quickly and quietly, she passed the table where the two guards had been playing cards. For a few moments she stood quite still, listening, hearing nothing. It was as though she had been locked into an underground tomb, away from all sight and sound.

Mildred turned and looked at the pale green door. Then she placed her hand on the cold metal of the closed grille, slid it open and looked through.

There was a short passage that appeared to end in a blank wall, with half a dozen green painted doors on either side. By pressing her face to the metal, Mildred could see that they were all bolted on the outside. She was just able to hear the faintest murmur of conversation.

"Nothing ventured, nothing gained," she whispered, quoting one of her father's favorite sayings.

The large bolt moved easily. There was a keyhole for a security lock, but the door, unlocked, swung open.

The revolver steady in her right hand, she moved into the corridor.

KRYSTY WAS LYING on her bed when the bulk of the hunting party returned to the living quarters.

All of them looked cold and tired, melting ice dripping from faces, hair and clothes.

J.B. went straight to her room, dropping his blaster on the spare bed. "Ryan's missing," he said.

"I heard. And Trader."

"Yeah. Blowing up a real blizzard out there." He took off his fedora and shook water from its crown. "They went toward the east. Five sec men and the woman whitecoat."

Krysty sat up as the others drifted in from their own rooms.

"How went your inquisition?" Doc asked. "I trust you resisted bravely."

"I guess so. The first thing they—"

J.B. interrupted her. "Wait a minute, Krysty. Where's Mildred?"

"Went off on a recce on her own."

"What?" The eyes behind the misted glasses were bright with anger.

"We were kept waiting a long while. We realized that the sec forces were seriously depleted with the hunt going on. She's been double curious about what was going on in that locked-off part of the wing."

"Dark night!" J.B. turned away from her and stared at the blank wall. In all the time that Krysty had known the Armorer, she had rarely seen him so upset.

"She'll be all right. Worst that can happen is that they catch her and she explains she got lost. And they'll just bring her back here."

"You think so, do you, Krysty? Your mutie powers of seeing tell you that, do they?"

"Hey, back off, J.B.," she said, feeling her own anger rise, covering her anxiety about Ryan.

"Back off!" He threw the hat against the door. "She shouldn't have been so triple stupe as to go off and do that, and you—" he pointed accusingly at Krysty "—should've had more sense than to let her go."

Jak had been standing by the window. "Cool out," he said. "Shouldn't have done it. Shouldn't come to harm. No reason think danger."

"I just hope you're right, Jak. Rad blast it, but I hope you're right."

A WHITE CARD WAS FITTED into a slot outside each of the cells. *Cells.* There was no way that Mildred could avoid that word in her mind. There was a long string of coded letters and numbers on each card, presumably giving information about each of the inhabitants.

Mildred reached up her left hand, swallowing hard and taking a long, slow breath, and slid open the first of the rectangular ob slits. She looked in, closed her eyes, then looked again.

The cell was about eight feet square with a toilet facility in one corner, along with a small basin and faucet. There was a fold-down table on the left-hand wall, clipped upright. A white steel bed covered in a white plasticized mattress was against the far wall. There was no window in the cell, just a small vent slit high above the bed.

The overhead light was relentlessly bright, revealing the naked figure that lay on the mattress.

At first sight Mildred thought it was a hermaphrodite, until she saw that it had no sexual organs at all. There was simply smooth skin at the junction of the thighs. No body hair was visible, and none grew on top of the rounded skull. As though it sensed her presence, the thing turned its face toward her. The eyes were covered with a caul of lacelike skin, the nose was missing and the mouth was a lipless circle of dribbling flesh.

The arms were absent, but Mildred could see that there was a line of individual, dwarfish fingers, running from the shoulder, along the side of the body, almost to the hip. They moved in a strange, hypnotic rippling rhythm, like the cilia in the respiratory tract.

Very slowly, Mildred closed the grille and moved to the next door.

The second cell was empty.

The third one wasn't.

It was a tiny person, no more than one quarter of normal size. As far as Mildred could see, through the slotted grille, it was male, as there was some dark curly hair around the mouth. Like the thing in the first cell, this one also lacked eyes.

At the faint sound of the inspection vent opening, it turned its little face toward the door. The mouth opened, and a long forked tongue slid out, seeming to taste the air.

For a moment it stayed frozen, then it hurled itself at the door with a fearsome ferocity. Mildred recoiled instinctively, though there was no way the creature could reach her through a half inch of tempered steel. From the soft thud, she guessed that the guards were aware of the habits of their prisoner and had padded the inside of the door.

She could hear it leaping up and down, its small hands clawing at the grille, a birdlike chirruping coming from the toothless mouth.

With a shudder of horror, Mildred slid the grille shut and moved to the last cell on that side.

Lying on the mattress was half a woman, naked, fast asleep. But it wasn't that she'd simply lost her legs. It was as if a giant guillotine had dropped on her with unimaginable force, cutting her diagonally, from just below her left armpit through her groin to the top of her right thigh.

What made the sight even more bizarre was that the flesh seemed to have sealed and healed itself. There was no stitching or scarring. Just the dreadful clean cut.

Mildred gently closed that grille and moved to the other side of the small passage. Tears were gathering at the corners of her eyes. She was barely winning the battle to keep herself from puking on the floor, dreading what awful abomination of nature she might stumble on next.

The sound of conversation was a little louder, seeming to come from the last cell in line.

The first cell was empty, though the floor was covered in a strange, translucent coating of gelatinous slime. Mildred stared at it, trying to convince herself that it wasn't moving.

The grille on the next cell showed a large man sitting on the toilet in the corner. His body was covered in hair, and both hands were gone, replaced by brutish paws with yellow claws.

He had only eye, set close to the center of his fore-head.

The movement of the grille attracted his attention, and he stood, revealing grotesquely large genitalia that hung almost to his bowed knees.

To add to Mildred's horror and shock, the creature spoke, in a deep, melodious voice.

"Hello."

She cleared her throat. "Hello."

"Yes. Hello."

"Hello."

It had moved to stand close by the door, head to one side, smiling at the woman. "Hello, yes."

Mildred looked into the deep-set brown eyes and realized that nobody was home. Whatever had been done to the man had totally robbed him of his intelligence.

"Hello, yes, hello, yes, hello."

Mildred managed a smile as she closed the grille. The person inside immediately fell silent.

One more door.

Now the conversation was louder, as though an argument were taking place. The voices were female, and Mildred wondered why two women had been locked up in the same cell, when one of the others was vacant.

The grille showed her the unbelievable, unspeakable answer.

There was a naked woman sitting on the bed. Her body seemed fairly normal, though the right arm and leg looked to be better developed, as though she had played some strange sport that favored just the one side.

But it wasn't the woman's body that drew Mildred's appalled attention.

It was her head.

Both of her heads.

One was set on an ordinary neck, slightly to the right of the shoulders. It had cropped blond hair, rosy cheeks and bright blue eyes.

The other head was visibly a little smaller, its neck sprouting off to the left side. The hair was lanker and longer, colored like wet straw. The eyes were of a duller shade of blue, and the complexion was noticeably more pale.

The two heads were having a conversation and seemed oblivious to the eyes watching them through the grille.

"Patience is the great virtue," insisted the larger, more dominant head.

"We have waited an eternity too long already." Even the voice of the smaller head was quieter and weaker.

"As long as I have the strength, you will never be able to take our life."

"When you sleep I can strangle us."

"You tried and it woke me, and it was all empty and pointless." A bitter laugh.

"Our dreary existence is empty and pointless."

"The whitecoats have promised to try and reverse what they did to us in their laboratory."

The smaller head shook from side to side. "And you believe the lies of the whitecoats."

"There is nothing else to believe."

"After the horrors they perform on us and others? After their endless failures?"

This time the larger head shook. "No. They tell us they are close to success. The copying is working better every time."

"It could not work worse even—" The rheumy eyes suddenly widened as they spotted Mildred's face peering through the grille in the cell door. "A watcher," it said.

Now both heads were staring at Mildred. The body rose and walked toward the door, with a slight sway and limp that favored the right, dominant side.

"Hello," Mildred said.

"Hello," came the reply, simultaneously from both of the woman's heads.

"Who are you?" asked the larger head.

"And why is your face so black? Are you a failed experiment like the rest of us?"

"No. I'm an outlander. Just visiting the institute with my friends."

The chorus of laughter was perfectly synchronized. "Visiting? We were all visitors here, you know."

The small head tried to push in front of its larger twin. "If you can run, then run as far and fast as ever you can. And your friends. This is a bad place of wicked, wicked godless evil."

Mildred suddenly felt a hand grip her shoulder, the muzzle of a blaster dig into her ribs and heard a man's voice, whispering in her ear.

"Well, well, admiring our freak show, lady?"

Chapter Twenty-Nine

"Don't work so hard," Ryan said, patiently cutting with his cleaver at the fifteen-foot-high wall of drifted snow. "Take it easy."

"But it's nearly dark and the temperature's dropping. We'll all die." Professor Dorothea Gibson was on the ragged edge of mental and physical exhaustion. Using her bare hands, she worked alongside Ryan and Trader.

"I'm not going to fucking die, just because of a little snap of cold and dark." Trader laughed. "Fact is, lady, I'm not ever intending to catch that last train to the coast. No, not ever."

Ryan paused and straightened. "If you work too hard, you get in a sweat. You get in a sweat and your clothes'll get wet. Make you colder when you settle for the night. So just go slow and easy, all right?"

They had been working on making a snow hole for the past half hour.

Trader had gone to collect some fallen branches from a nearby grove of spruces, spreading them across the snow to form a binding layer for the roof of their shelter.

Now there was a hollow about six feet across and four feet deep, floored with some more green branches that Ryan had hacked down.

"Help to insulate us," he said. "Cold can get you from all directions. When you crawl in, try to avoid getting loose snow on your clothes. It could easy turn to ice in the night. Keep dry and keep warm."

"What about a fire?"

Ryan looked at the scientist. "Still snowing hard. If we had some pyrotabs we could mebbe get something going hot enough to stand against the weather. But we don't. Everything's soaking wet and frozen."

Professor Gibson looked mistrustfully at the crude hole in the snow, squinting sideways at him. "You think it'll save our lives, Ryan?"

"Yeah, Thea, I do."

"WHOEVER THAT IS, keep your hands to yourself."

In the total darkness, nobody spoke for a moment until Trader sniggered. "Sorry, lady."

"Now, how did I guess that it was you?"

"Because I'm the only real, red-blooded man here. Ryan always preferred sheep and young men."

Ryan didn't rise to the teasing bait. He'd managed to snatch a few minutes of comforting sleep, secure in the certain knowledge that their snow shelter would keep all of them alive until the morning, when they could set off again on the trail back to the institute.

They had left a small hole clear, about three inches in diameter, at the front of the snow wall, for ventilation. With the three of them bundled so tightly together, they generated enough heat to keep the temperature inside the hole only a degree or two below freezing.

"What about frostbite?" Thea Gibson asked.

Trader laughed. "No danger of that. We're all warm enough. Fact is, we'd be even warmer if we all took off our clothes and got busy."

"Is that right, Trader? Sexual congress is the last thing on my mind."

"You sure? How about if I wriggled around a bit and you sat on my face?"

She laughed. "I suppose that it would, at the least, shut you up for a while."

Some time around two in the morning, Ryan slipped out of sleep to find a hand reaching under his clothes, trying to get his fly open. He kept very still, guessing that conditions were too cramped. In a few minutes the effort stopped and everyone got back to sleep.

TRADER GOT UP very early in the morning to relieve himself, breaking through the frozen crust of snow, letting in the first filtered light of the false dawn. Ryan woke immediately but Thea Gibson sighed and pressed her face harder into his shoulder, staying locked into sleep.

"That lady could be banged," Trader said, as he returned. "If we had more time, I'd have her falling into my hand like a fine ripe peach."

"We getting up?"

The older man stamped his feet, kicking up splinters of powdery ice. "Might as well. Snow's stopped. Cold as a baron's charity, but we could get moving. Soon warm up."

Ryan nodded. "Agreed." He nudged the woman next to him. "Wake up, Thea."

"Turn on the enzyme coolant," she muttered fuzzily. Ryan pushed her harder. "What's the—" She seemed alarmed. "Has the grizzly returned?"

"No. Just time to get up and moving. Nearly dawn. Sooner we start the better."

"Snow stopped?"

"Yeah."

She sat up. "I can't believe that we're all still alive after the bear and the cold."

"Not all alive," Trader said, breathing on the Armalite to get ice off the side of the butt. "There's five of your men back up there won't be eating breakfast today."

"Yes, you're right." The scientist managed to get to her feet, nearly slipping on the packed snow. "I owe you both my life for butchering the grizzly and for preventing me from freezing to death last night."

Trader shuffled his feet. "Shucks, ma'am, it weren't nothin' at all."

"You may turn it into a joke, but I mean it. I would most certainly be back there with Brunner, Cooke and the others if it weren't for you. I owe you everything."

Ryan was also on his feet, doing a few exercises to try to restore circulation. "Well, we always try and help each other out when we can."

Her cold blue eyes turned to him. The left eye did; the right one was looking out across the snow-masked valley. "I am placed in an impossible situation. One that you can't possibly understand, a dreadful dilemma that woke me several times in the night and which I can't solve."

"What is it?"

She shook her head. The tight knot of iron gray hair had come unpinned during the night and now it tumbled down over her shoulders, reaching almost to her waist.

Trader whistled. "Hey, lovely bunch of hair you got there, lady."

She ignored him, concentrating on Ryan. "There are things happening at the institute...research of nearly a hundred years coming toward fruition. And the culmination happens to involve you and your party. Particularly..." She shook her head. "No. I'm not ready to betray everything that I have been raised to hold dear. But there is danger."

Ryan held her arm, considering whether it would be a good idea to spend some time on persuading her to speak, but rejecting the idea for the time being. "What is it?"

"No. May the institute forgive me, but I can't tell you. Not yet. I need to think more. The debt is so heavy and I can't bear to carry it."

"Is THERE ANOTHER WAY to the institute," Ryan asked, "save going past the sec barrier?"

They had been slogging through the deep snow for three quarters of an hour, stopping every ten minutes or so to recover, their breaths pluming out into the air around them.

Thea leaned her hand against the slick trunk of a silver birch. "Why do you ask that, Ryan? Why do you want to go around the barrier?"

"Just curiosity, I guess."

The truth was, all his instincts were on red alert after her strange, muddled speech. It was clear as crystal that something was wrong at the institute, and it involved them, possibly involved Krysty. So he thought it might be worth a try to get back in without being seen.

"There is a narrow hunting trail," she admitted. "We're more or less on course for it here. But the Professor doesn't like anyone to do that."

"We won't tell him. There's no reason for him to check us past the sec barrier, is there?"

"Perhaps not." She thought about it for several seconds. "I have said how much I owe you. This can be a small part of that debt between us. We can always say, if questioned, that the main track back over the highway was blocked by snow. It's a very small untruth."

THERE WAS A BRIEF MOMENT as they crossed a steep ridge, where they were visible to the men who guarded the barrier across the blacktop into the valley.

Trader went first, crouched low to keep his skyline silhouette to a minimum. Thea Gibson went second, stumbling over some loose shards of granite. Ryan was last, running with knees bent, holding the rifle in his right hand.

As soon as they were all safe he crawled back and peered carefully around a spur of rock, looking down from the steep hillside at the group of sec guards to check if there was any sign that they'd been spotted.

Ryan counted eleven of them, most grouped together, staring down the track toward the outside world. Even at that distance he could read the nervousness among them, and it all added fuel to his own growing worry.

TRADER WAS IN THE LEAD, walking with the woman, talking constantly to her in a low undertone. Occasionally he turned back to Ryan and gave him a wink. Twice it was a grin and a cautious thumbs-up. Ryan doubted whether his old chief would succeed in his obvious aim of seducing the starchy woman scientist.

Even so, Trader's ceaseless efforts made Ryan smile as they picked their way along the back entry to the institute.

Because there seemed no reason to expect any trouble at that point, it appeared unexpectedly around the next corner of the narrow snow-filled trail—three sec men, hooded and goggled against the cold and the risk of snow-blindness, all carrying Mossbergs, literally bumping into Trader, who was too busy leering at Thea Gibson.

There was a moment of intense confusion when startled fingers could easily have found triggers, and blood could have been steaming on the ice.

"Don't shoot," the woman yelled, her voice carrying the crack of command.

Everyone edged off a little, kicking up a veil of powdery white, behind which Ryan drew the SIG-Sauer, transferring the Steyr rifle to his left hand. He held the 9 mm blaster behind his back.

"It's you, Professor Gibson," said the tallest of the three sec men.

"Who were you expecting? Santa Claus? Of course it's me. And there are outlanders Cawdor and Trader. What are you doing on this trail?"

"Could ask you the same. Not supposed to go around the sec barrier, Professor."

"I am aware of that." Her voice was at its most glacial. "We got into serious trouble and the main route back to the institute was snow-blocked."

"Where's Brunner and the rest?" one of the other men asked. "Everyone else is back safe."

"Chilled."

"They found the grizzly?"

Ryan answered the man. "It found them."

Professor Gibson looked at the patrol. "Why are you here? You never answered that."

The scatterguns were all held in a ready position. Ryan had been in more firefights than he could remember, and he recognized the nerves that were showing, knew that Trader would recognize it, as well. The sec men were bracing themselves, ready to make a move against them. He didn't know what it would be, but he could tell that it would be specifically directed against Trader and himself, and it was coming close and fast.

"Trouble at the institute."

"Who with?"

The eyes flicked to Ryan and Trader. "With the outlanders, Professor."

"Have they learned more than they should know? Well, have they?"

"Yeah, sort of."

"Is it under control?"

"Oh, sure. Yeah, everything's handled, Professor."

Thea turned slowly around and caught Ryan's eye. She was trying to send him a message with her whole tense body language, but he couldn't work out what it was.

"Handled," she said, turning back to face the trio of armed guards. "Good." She hunched her shoulders, and the Anschutz Kadett fell off. The woman grabbed it, clumsily, only making it worse, knocking the bolt-action .22 onto the stony trail, where it landed with a tremendous clatter.

It attracted the attention of the sec men for a vital, precious second or two.

That was all it took.

Ryan leveled the powerful automatic, squeezing off the first shot with great care and precision, putting the 9 mm round through the middle of the nearest man's face. The bullet drilled through the center of the right lens of the snow goggles, starring the plas-glass. Blood welled out, flooding over the white thermal jacket.

Ryan didn't waste any time in watching the sec guard dying.

The next round lay under the hammer.

Just before he fired again, Ryan was aware of the waspish crack of the Armalite, seeing a gout of blood fountain from the second guard's ribs, patterning the crisp snow. But the sound was drowned by the boom of the SIG-Sauer. The shock of the 9 mm round jarred his wrist, the force running clear up to his shoulder.

The last of the trio was just beginning to react to the horrific danger, lifting the Mossberg toward Trader. Ryan's bullet glanced off the butt of the scattergun, angling upward, through the sec man's right wrist, shattering both radius and ulna, exiting through the elbow joint.

The gun dropped and the man began to scream, reaching for the shattered limb with his left hand.

Ryan calmly shot him through his open mouth. The bullet sliced his tongue neatly in two, plowing a furrow through the soft palate and driving its lethal path out through the back of the neck, just beneath where the skull was set on the spine. The blood-slick, distorted bullet buried itself in a snowbank.

In less than two beats of the heart, all three of the sec men were down and dying, kicking and thrashing in the crimsoned snow, puking up more blood, moaning and gasping.

"Think anyone heard?" Trader asked, stepping quickly to check that all three were finished.

"Doubt it. Wind's against it and we're in a valley here. Snow'll muffle the sound even more."

Thea Gibson had only just finished picking up her fallen blaster and was standing, stricken, at the slaughter about her. "You didn't—"

"Yeah, we did," Ryan interrupted. "And thanks for distracting them."

"I didn't mean you to murder them."

Trader laughed and slapped her on the backside. "Thought we'd make them lay down their guns while we tied them up, gagged them and told them to count to one hundred before they tried to escape?"

"Something like that."

Ryan shook his head, reloading the three spent rounds. "Not the way it works, lady. This isn't fiction. This is living and dying. Us or them."

"But what do we do now? The Professor'll find out and what will he say?"

She was almost in tears.

"He's going to be very seriously pissed at us," Trader told her, "and at you. No more extra helpings of soup for you, Thea. Early to bed for a week with a red ass."

"It's not a joke, you cretin!" she screamed. "We're all chilled by this."

"Simmer down," Ryan said. "The only people dead are these three. Way I saw it, and I think you saw it, too, they were planning to take us back to your bastard institute. And they didn't care much whether we were still breathing or not."

Trader gripped the woman's chin in his steely fingers. "What do you say to that, Thea?"

"I can't tell you. I owed you my life. I've settled that debt here, and I'll never forgive myself for being the innocent agent of these men's deaths."

Trader glanced at Ryan, and there was an unmistakable question in his eyes. But Ryan shook his head. "No," he said quietly. "Not yet and not here."

"Sure?"

"Sure, Trader. We got some talking to do first, and the lady is going to help us find a good way into the institute without flags waving and a band playing."

"I've done all I will."

Ryan stepped in close, staring at her. "One more pays all, Thea. A back way in. Then we leave you. We won't let on you helped us, if the leaves fall against us. You'll be safe, and we can plan what we need to do. That a fair, square deal." He offered his hand.

After a moment's hesitation, the scientist shook it. "Deal," she agreed.

Chapter Thirty

"We walked into that like blind children into the jaws of a panther." J.B. banged his fist against a wall of their room, hard enough to chip plaster.

"No reason to think danger," Jak said, lying flat on his back on one of the beds, staring up at the ceiling. "Spilled blood can't go back in body."

Doc sighed. "An unusual variant on a famous old saying, Jak, my dear friend. The question now must be how do we get out of here?"

"I wish I knew the answer to two questions." Mildred stood next to the Armorer. "When they picked me up I heard that Ryan and Trader's party is missing. Love to know where they are now."

"That's only one question," Abe said.

"Second is where's Krysty? She should have been brought back to us by now."

J.B. nodded his agreement. "We all set off at noon, yesterday. Now it's around ten in the morning. After they disarmed us they kept us separated before bringing us back to this wing. Where's Krysty been all this time?"

KRYSTY HAD BEEN LOCKED UP in a small side ward at the far end of the top floor of the secret wing of the institute. After the relatively gentle interrogation, she had expected to be returned to the rest of the group.

But Crichton had other ideas.

"There is so much more we want to talk to you about," he'd said in that desiccated, croaky voice. "We do not wish you to be tainted by discussing this afternoon with your colleagues. It will render our research soiled and impure."

"You mean you're making me a prisoner instead of just, like, a guest?"

The lizard head had trembled, the hooded eyes blinking rapidly at her. "Prisoner? Was that the word I heard you use, my dear? Not so. After tomorrow, or the following day at the latest, you can go back to the rest of the outlanders."

"And we can go?"

"Oh, yes. Then you can all go."

The men with the scatterguns had escorted her, having taken the elementary precaution of removing the 640 Smith & Wesson from its holster.

It had all been very polite and calmly efficient. There had been four sec men, including Ellison, and they hadn't taken any chances. Two stood off on each side, covering her as she walked along the brightly lighted corridor.

"Dead lock on the door," the sec boss said. "Two men outside. This was used for restraining patients who'd got themselves sort of crazed after experiments. That's why there's also bars on the window. So, save your strength." He laughed, making the deep scar by his mouth curl up even more. "Though the white-coats'll sure like to see you use that mutie power you got. That's what interests them more than anything."

SHE HAD SLEPT WELL, quieting herself with the meditative techniques taught to her by her mother Sonja. It had been a calm, dreamless night, and she woke at dawn feeling refreshed.

There had been a change of guards since the previous evening, and Ellison greeted her when he unlocked the door. "Have a good night?"

"Not bad."

"You notice the walls and ceiling are kind of padded in this part of the institute?"

"Yeah."

"That's because this end of the wing was used for crazies when the old-time scientists' predark experiments went wrong." He grinned at her so that the livid scar twitched as though it had a life of its own.

"You told me that last night."

"I did?"

"Yeah, you did."

He sniffed. "You say so. Anyway, they want you bright and early for the next round."

"Sure. Can't wait. Listen, is there any news about the rest of my friends?"

Ellison looked suddenly suspicious. "Why? What've you heard? Someone flapped his mouth?"

Krysty shook her head, aware of how tightly curled her flaming hair was, a sure sign of a threatening situation. "No. I heard that the hunting party had gotten separated. Most got back. Just Ryan and Trader out there."

Ellison nodded noncommittally. "I heard that."

"Will I see the others at breakfast? Hear the latest news from them?"

"No."

"Why not? The scientists want me to cooperate with them. If they don't help me, then I won't help them. You can tell them that."

"Wouldn't think that's a good idea, lady. They'll easy make you do what they want. Don't matter to the whitecoats whether you want to help or not. I should know."

"Why? Why should you know?"

Ellison backed off. "I didn't say...didn't mean nothing. But you don't get to see the others."

"Until I've been a really good girl with the whitecoats. Is that it?"

"Sure."

"What about Ryan and Trader? They must have come back during the night."

"No news." He hesitated. "Sorry, lady. Weather's been triple cold and snowy. Chances can't be that good for anyone stuck out there all night. Not with that giant grizzly on the loose."

Krysty nodded. "Bear's not born that could take out Ryan Cawdor and Trader."

CRICHTON WAS WAITING for her, with Ladrow Buford hopping nervously about at his side. There were eight or nine of the other scientists gathered around him, and half a dozen sec men. Krysty was immediately aware of a barely suppressed air of intense excitement.

The old man greeted Krysty with a warm smile. "Sleep well, child?" he asked.

"Sure. Can we get one thing straight right away?"

"Of course?"

"I don't like being held a prisoner. Don't like being cut off from my friends. I guess they're prisoners, as well. And I want to know what's been done to send out search parties to look for Ryan and Trader."

Crichton's smile disappeared like a rabbit down a hole. "What you don't like doesn't matter. I've had enough of your outlander arrogance. This is the Crichton Institute, founded by my grandmother." A thread of white frothy spittle sprayed from his lips. "We have been playing Mr. Nice Guy with you peasants far too long."

"Peasants! Just—"

"I will have you beaten unconscious by the sec men if I have to. Whatever it takes to shut you up. Your friends are our prisoners. We shall find uses for them. The albino boy might be interesting, and the black woman."

Krysty felt a wave of anger swelling inside her. Despite her efforts to use the Gaia power to calm herself, she was aware that the rage was in danger of running the red arrow and getting beyond her control.

Buford was watching her closely, and he tugged at Crichton's sleeve, whispering something urgently in his ear.

"You think she..." Crichton muttered. "Not with all these guns around her, surely. If we could try the experiment while she is in such a vein it would be..." Krysty couldn't catch the rest of what was said.

Ellison caught her eye and winked at her. It helped Krysty break the vicious spiral of rising anger that had trapped her, and she felt her breathing slowing, control fighting its way back into her mind.

Crichton turned to her. "We have wasted enough time. For your information, we believe your companions—the middle-aged man and the one with an eye missing—are probably dead. We have sent out search parties. If they are found, they will be dealt with out in the field. Neither are of any value to us here." He wiped his hands together. "Now, we will attempt what my colleagues call 'the big one.' The excitement is nearly too much to bear." His face had become flushed, and Krysty noticed he was rubbing his left arm with his right hand. "Perhaps, Ladrow, you would give me one of my green pills. It would be a sad irony if I was to miss my date with destiny."

Buford had reached into the pocket of his lab coat and fished out a small black box. He opened it and offered a tablet to his boss, who laid it beneath his tongue.

"Thank you," he said. "Now, let us to it. This is the day that we have been working toward for a hundred years."

"FEAR IS A BEAST that can be small and easily beaten, or it can grow and swell until it could swallow the world. The decision is yours alone."

That was what Krysty's mother had said in one of her lectures on life and living.

It came back to Krysty as she was marched, under escort, into the largest laboratory she had yet seen. It was divided in two by a huge powered door, and she couldn't yet see what lay in that distant half.

There were a number of cubicles of different sizes, scattered around the part of the room where she stood. Most of them had walls of clear glass, though one or two were heavily smoked. The rest of the lab looked like sets for predark science-fiction vids, with bubbling retorts, whirring computers and flashing lights. None of it made the least sense to Krysty.

"Sit over there," Buford directed her. "Professor Crichton has to go and rest a little. His health is far from excellent. But he has delegated to me the responsibility for continuing. And—" he paused for effect, throwing out his chest like a pouter pigeon "—he has allowed me the honor of telling you of the work we have done here. The work which is now near to its conclusion."

"So, tell me."

It took the better part of an hour, with his narrative constantly being interrupted by Krysty's questions.

At the end, she sat back, fighting to mask her emotions, trying to recount what she'd learned.

"You have nearly mastered the skill of duplicating living creatures while removing or controlling their worse aspects? Is that it?"

Buford nodded, his glasses glinting, his bald skull shining under the harsh overhead lights. "That really is a massive oversimplification, but yes. It will mean a Deathlands free from genetic mutations. As we copy, so we improve. That was the maxim of our beloved founder. Simple genetic engineering that will rearrange the DNA of our specimens. Any kinks in the chain can be removed and tweaked sideways." He demonstrated with a delicate gesture of his hands.

"A cleaner world." Krysty rubbed the side of her nose. "Uncle Tyas McCann, back when I was a girl, had plenty of old books. There was one from the Nazi times. Talked about something called eugenics. Racial cleansing. Rid the world of undesirables. Stop any kind of physical or social deviation from the norm.'' She paused. ''They called it their 'final solution,' back then.''

''Yes, yes!'' He clapped his bony hands together. ''You see, don't you? Oh, Krysty, I am *so* glad you do both see and understand.''

''I understand real well. Though I'm not sure I believe it. I heard it took years and years to try to reproduce even the simplest organism.''

''Not now.'' He looked around, then limped over to a cage of silvered wire on a bench, leaning heavily on his cane. ''This rat, for instance.''

It was white, with a pattern of black spots and patches, including one that looked amazingly like a spoon with a curved handle. Its eyes were pink, and its nostrils twitched as it peered out of its prison.

''You see its markings, Krysty?''

''Yeah.''

''The bit here, like a ladle? Good. Now, I shall take it beyond the doors and return with it in less than five minutes. Sit quiet and wait.''

THE SEC MEN STARED at her with a studied indifference, except for Ellison, who came and stood by her. ''Having fun, Red?'' he asked. ''Better than watching paint dry, ain't it?''

''You can say that,'' she replied, ''but you can't really expect me to comment, can you?''

''They tell you about their twinning?''

''Ah.'' She sighed, nodding, suddenly making the connection in her mind. ''Of course. The hounds that

went missing. They were identical, weren't they?"
Krysty thought of the dying man they'd encountered
who had been cruelly subjected to hideous medical
experimentation, but decided it was wiser not to let on
that she had seen him.

Ellison wiped his nose on his sleeve. "Sure were.
Like as two peas in the pod, Red."

Buford appeared from a small door set in the side
of the large door.

In each hand he held a cage, and in each cage there
crouched a rat, each a perfect copy of the other, down
to the last detail of their complex markings.

"There. Now do you believe?"

Krysty sniffed. "I've seen better tricks done by a
medicine-show conjurer with a rabbit."

"Trick? Trick!" His face flushed, and he nearly
dropped the cages in his temper. "It's not a trick, you
mutie triple-stupe bitch!"

"I'm not stupid. There isn't any growth accelerator
in the history of the world that could copy like that.
Has to be a chautauqua trick."

"Right." He handed the rats to Ellison.

Raising his voice, he commanded, "Open the main
doors."

A sec guard pressed a recessed button to the right of
the room, and Krysty heard a faint grinding of ma-
chinery, a sound almost identical to the opening of the
heavy sec doors in a gateway. The lab door began to
lift.

The other half of the room was slightly smaller and
less cluttered. But Krysty's eyes were drawn instantly
to two pieces of equipment. She remembered what
Ryan had said about the faded sign.

Though they were much smaller than the mat-trans chambers she had seen in a number of buried redoubts, Krysty didn't have the least doubt what she was looking at—hexagonal, made from armaglass, with small metal disks in floor and ceiling. They stood about fifty feet apart.

Then she knew.

Chapter Thirty-One

"It's an amazing stroke of luck finding a window open like this," Thea Gibson hissed. "Normally it's locked tight as a fortress."

Ryan carefully rearranged the slatted blind so that it looked secure to a casual passerby. "If it hadn't already been open, we'd have broken a rotten latch like that in all of six seconds."

The three of them had approached the institute in a looping way, following a narrow trail that the wind had scoured clear of snow. It had taken them hard against the sheer wall of rock to the west, through a screen of pines, close by the research wing of the institute.

Ryan drew the SIG-Sauer, leading the way along the small side passage to the corner of one of the main corridors. He glanced around the angle of the white-painted walls, seeing that it was empty to the right. A series of closed doors led toward the central atrium of the complex.

To the left there was a small sec door, partly closed. Beyond it Ryan could just make out what looked like a barred prison cell. The faint murmur of conversation came from behind the first door.

Ryan retreated to rejoin the other two. "Could be guards, to the left. There's a half-open door. Like a cell beyond it."

He turned to the scientist. "What's there?"

"Experimental failures. They have to be kept locked away for their own safety." It was clearly a touchy subject, and Ryan had the distinct feeling that the woman was hiding far more than she was telling.

"Sec men?" Trader asked.

"Normally a pair of them. But it looks like the institute is on alert with extra parties outside. So, there might only be one man there."

Ryan shook his head. "No. Heard talking."

Trader went to look for himself, then returned. "The way up to the right's clear and open. But we don't know what's behind that door to the left. Anyone could open it at any time and we'd be cold-cocked."

Ryan nodded. "Yeah."

Thea Gibson looked from one face to the other. Her severe squint made it difficult to work out just which of them she was actually addressing. "You intend to creep along and murder those men!"

Trader smiled thinly at her. "You got it in one, lady. Guess that's why you're a whitecoat and I'm not."

She swallowed hard. "You saved my life. I know that. I'll never possibly forget that debt. But you are still enemies of what we do here. If you see the unsuccessful experiments, then you will hate me and hate all of us."

"Why should that be?" Ryan whispered.

"Because there have to be sacrifices. For science to progress, there will be those who fall by the wayside.

Melissa Crichton left us that firm, unshakable belief.''

''Can't make an omelet without breaking a few eggs,'' Ryan said. ''That your belief?''

She looked puzzled, not familiar with the saying. Then its meaning penetrated and she nodded. ''I guess so. We are more important than anyone outside the valley. The research matters. It's so close. Any day now.'' She smiled with a touch of smugness. ''Any hour now.''

Ryan's deep unease about why the whitecoats wanted to get their hands on Krysty became worse.

''You want to wait here while we go and do the business with the sec men?'' Trader asked.

''Better we go the other way,'' she said. ''You truly wouldn't like to see the failed experiments in those rooms beyond the barred door. Trust me, please.''

''We do trust you,'' Ryan said, catching the expression on Trader's face. The older man had moved to stand directly behind the woman.

''I know how much I owe you, but—''

Trader shut off her words by clamping his hard left hand over her open mouth. His right hand gripped the hilt of his hunting knife, which he drove into Thea's back, just to the left of the spine, a hand's span down from the shoulder.

Ryan was just in front of her and he saw the shock in her face, the walleyes widening, rolling toward the ceiling. The force of the blow nearly lifted the scientist off her feet. There was a rictus of pain as Trader twisted the knife while pulling it out, then driving it in again, with a ruthless force.

"Best thing, Ryan, old friend," Trader said, panting with the effort of holding the doomed woman, stopping her from screaming out a warning. She was struggling frantically, trying to claw at his left hand, kicking out at Ryan.

"Yeah."

He stabbed her a third time. "It was when she said that 'but,' you know."

Ryan turned away and checked the corridor, but nobody had heard the slight scuffle. He looked back, seeing that Trader was lowering the corpse to the floor, a little blood seeping from the mouth. More crimson daubed on Trader's knife and hands.

"I heard the 'but,' as well," he said to his old chief. "Meant she was readying herself to betray us. If you hadn't taken her out, I would've done it."

Trader wiped the blade on her coat. He looked at the woman's Anschutz Kadett rifle, considering whether to take it, straightening. "No. Stick with the good old Armalite," he muttered.

"Best see to the sec men," Ryan said.

"Why not?"

THERE WERE TWO OF THEM, totally occupied in playing cards at a little table. As Ryan pushed the door open, using the barrel of the SIG-Sauer, Trader right at his elbow, they didn't even look up at first.

"Pair of fours takes one. Close the door behind—"

"Quiet," Ryan ordered. "Keep real quiet and it'll all be fine. Keep your cards in your hands, and your hands flat on the table there."

"You're the two missing outlanders," said one of the guards, a young man with a stocky build and curly blond hair. "The two they went out to—"

"To what, son?" Trader asked, pushing the muzzle of the Armalite under the sec man's chin, the foresight cutting the soft skin, a worm of blood crawling down toward his collar. "They went out to do what?"

The older man, older with hollow cheeks, answered. "They said to chill you."

"Why?" Ryan asked. "What's going on here?"

The young man swallowed hard. "Redhead is someone special. Mutie but not gross. They've got the rest of your party locked up. Once they're finished with the woman, they'll chill them all. That's what they told me." A note of panic ran ragged in his voice. "Let us go."

Ryan heeled the heavy door closed behind him, hearing the lock click, shutting them off from the rest of the institute. "Tell me what they want the woman for."

"Going to..."

The older man suddenly lost his nerve and kicked out, sending the table spinning over. Trader pulled the trigger of the Armalite, the 9 mm round taking off most of the top of the young sec guard's skull, spraying blood and brains across the wall and ceiling.

Though Ryan was very much on the alert, he was still taken by surprise at the older sec man's attempt to escape. The man had rolled away from the threat of the SIG-Sauer, his hand groping desperately toward the silvered Mossberg that stood in one corner of the little room.

Ryan shot at him, but the tumbling, flailing body of the other dying guard got in the way, the bullet striking it through the left shoulder, blowing the joint apart.

"Fireblast!" He shot a second time, moving sideways, off balance, seeing chunks of bloody flesh erupt from the older man's forearm, the 9 mm round almost severing the wrist, the hand dangling by shreds of torn sinew.

The attempt for the shotgun was instantly aborted and he rolled into the corner, huddling in a ball, the fingers of the shattered hand leaking blood in five pathetic trails across the clean plastic tiles of the floor.

"Please?"

Ryan took careful aim and shot him neatly through the bridge of the nose. The head bounced against the wall, leaving a long smear of brains and blood, decorated with bright splinters of white bone.

The body slumped slowly down to the tiles, exhaling a long murmuring breath as the spirit left it.

"Stupe," Trader said. "Why'd he think he could get away with something as stupe as that?"

"The door'll muffle the noise of the shooting." Ryan looked at the bolted door beyond. "You hear someone talking through there?" he asked.

"Yeah. More guards?"

"No." Ryan laid a hand on the cold iron of the sec bolt. "You wouldn't keep your sec men behind a locked door. No. Must be those experimental failures that Thea told us about, ones she sort of hinted about."

"We going to take a look?"

"Might as well. Check the corridor first."

Trader hesitated. "You telling me or asking me, Ryan?"

"Why? Does it make a difference?"

"Might do."

"I'm telling you."

"What if I don't think that's a good idea?"

Ryan gave him a thin, angry smile. "Then you don't do it. I go and do it. Think we're going to fall to blasters over who checks the fucking corridor?"

Trader favored him with his best, most wolfishly dangerous smile. "Tell you what, bro. Why don't I go and check out the corridor?"

"Yeah. Why don't you?"

Trader opened the outer door and peered around it. "No sight, no sound," he reported.

"Then we'll check out what's behind the bolted door. Best be quick. Won't be forever until someone finds the woman's body. Or the dead patrol."

"WHAT'S WRITTEN on these cards?" Trader asked, pointing to the white slips stuck in slots outside each of the cells. "Names of prisoners?"

"Codes letters and numbers. Probably refer to the experiments they've been part of."

"We going to take us a look?"

"Why not?" Ryan slid back the grille on the first room on the right side of the short dead-end passage. He and Trader peeked in together.

It seemed to Ryan that a very long time passed as they stared in silence at the hideously freakish occupant of the eight-foot-square room—the lack of any sexual equipment, the ghastly parody of a face, the armless shoulders and the rows of tiny fingers that performed their silent rhythmic dance.

The time was probably no longer than half a minute, though it seemed endless and infinite.

It was Trader who reached up and swiftly closed the slatted grille in the door.

"I don't think I care all that much to look in on the other rooms, Ryan," he said, unable to quite control the tremor in his voice.

"While we're here..."

Ryan was overcome with the blinding horror that one of the cells might contain his dearest love—or whatever remained of her after the sick-brained whitecoats had finished their blasphemous games with her.

The next room was empty.

The third wasn't.

Despite his obvious shock and revulsion, Trader couldn't hold back from joining Ryan in staring through the grille. Both of them stared back as the diminutive creature with the forked tongue hurled itself blindly at the door, its tiny claws scrabbling at the sec steel as if it would have died to reach them and rend their flesh.

"By oak and ash!" Trader exclaimed. "Come on, friend. Let's go chill us some whitecoats and then flee from here on our burning feet of fire."

Ryan waved a hand at him for silence. "Might as well check the others," he insisted.

In the last cell on that side he saw a naked woman, with half of her body missing. Her eyes flicked open at the sound of the grille opening. The lips parted, but the only sound that came out was a dreadful, inarticulate gobbling noise.

The first of the small cells on the other side of the corridor was empty. Ryan checked again, tricked into thinking he had seen a sort of translucent slime, throbbing gently in the corner of the room by the toilet. But when he looked for the second time there was nothing moving.

"Hello." The booming voice greeted him as he slid open the narrow grille in the next door along.

"Who the fuck was that?" Trader asked. "That someone a bit closer to human?"

Ryan swallowed hard. "Yeah. Sort of."

"Yes, hello," said the huge shaggy man, standing by the door of the cell.

"Let him out. Any ally's better than none, is what I say."

Ryan tugged at the bolt and opened the door. The massively naked figure stood still in the doorway, clapping its taloned paws together. The oversize genitalia showed all too clearly its state of excitement.

"Hello, yes, hello, yes," it repeated tonelessly.

"Close the door again," Trader said calmly. "Quick as you can."

"Hello, yes," Ryan replied, getting a toothless leer of appreciation from the mutated freak. Very slowly he brought his hand to the bolt of the door, pushing it hard and slamming the sec lock across to hold it secure.

There was no response from the thing inside, just further muted repetitions of its two words of conversation.

"Don't reckon he would have added very much to our small force," Trader stated, laughing nervously. "Did you see the size of his—"

"Yeah. But it's not the biggest bullet does the most damage."

"Not sure that's true. Anyway, let's at least take a look in the last cell and then we can get moving into the heart of this evil place."

There was the sound of two people talking, louder as the grille slid open.

"I'll be damned," Trader mumbled before his voice failed him.

"Are you new sec men?" the larger of the heads asked, turning to peer toward the door.

"They don't look like sec men," the second head stated.

"What would you know?"

"I know from the way they look at me, admiring my breasts and my thighs."

The larger head laughed, mockingly. "*Your* breasts and thighs! I think you mean *my* breasts and thighs, don't you?"

"One dark night I shall place my hands around your fat neck and squeeze and squeeze."

"You know what would happen to you, as well, if I died, sister dear?"

The lank-haired subsidiary head nodded slowly. "But the price might be worth the paying, sister dear."

Trader moved away, tapping Ryan on the shoulder. "Leave them be," he said.

"Not yet." He spoke through the grille. "Would you like to be released from here?" he asked.

"Released?" the two voices asked in perfect harmony. "Set free from here? Where would we go?"

"Come with us."

"Where, outlander?"

"To rescue our friends before the whitecoats experiment on them. You can have a blaster. We've chilled both the sec men guarding you."

"And would we kill some of the whitecoats?" the larger head asked.

"That would be so pleasant, sister. I think we should accept the offer from the outlander."

"You said that we have waited an eternity too long already. And you spoke the truth."

"I know I did."

"I said you did."

"I know you said I did."

Ryan turned to Trader. "Why not?"

"Your decision. But I give you a fair warning, bro. One wrong step from it…her…and I'll blow off both of their fucking heads."

Ryan slid back the bolt on the cell door. "Take clothes from one of the dead men," he said, "and pick up a Mossberg for yourself. Yourselves."

THERE HAD EVEN BEEN an argument about the name of the two-headed mutie woman. The dominant voice claimed to be called Evangelina while the drab said that they were really called Edna. They agreed that the naked giant along the passage had once been called Todd, who had been a local hunter.

"Before the whitecoats changed him, as well," they chorused. "And him and us are among their better successes. Oh, yes, oh, yes we are."

The right hand had taken charge of the silvered Mossberg 12-gauge and now flourished it. The woman had picked the more bloodstained and ragged uniform to cover her nakedness, and now stood facing Ryan and Trader.

"Can we go and start the repaying and the punishing?"

"Sure. Follow us," Ryan said.

Chapter Thirty-Two

"You don't stop their endless chattering, O'Mara, then I'll fucking stop it myself."

"O'Mara, Trader? He was a machine gunner on War Wag One, wasn't he?"

"So?"

"So, my name's Ryan Cawdor, not O'Mara."

Trader rubbed his forehead hard, with the back of his left hand. "'Course it is, Ryan. I don't know what happens sometimes. It's like my brain makes a malfunction connection and the wrong word slips out of my mouth. It's not that I really think you were O'Mara, you know?"

"Sure. I understand."

"Anyway, it doesn't make a spit of difference to what I said. Shut up this two-headed freak or I'll shut them . . . I mean her permanent."

Ryan wasn't in the mood to argue. Edna-Evangelina hadn't stopped talking and arguing with each other since the moment that they let her out of the cell. He'd hoped that the "failed experiment" might be able to give them information about what the whitecoats planned to do with Krysty, but they were totally ignorant, not even seeming to have much idea of what had really happened to them.

They had, unknowingly, chosen the same route—in reverse—that Mildred had taken on her ill-fated recce, walking along the little-used side corridor that paralleled the main central passage of the wing.

But the two combatative heads kept up a ceaseless running commentary, taking every opportunity to try to score points off each other.

"Never been down here."

"I have."

"I'd like to know how you came down here without me."

"Easy. It was when I was me and you were you and before we became us."

Ryan had taken up the point skirmish position, leaving Trader to act as rearguard, covering them against a sudden sneak attack from behind.

The woman limped behind them, occasionally aiming the long Mossberg at doors as they passed them, both making synchronized shooting sounds.

"Bang, you're dead, whitecoat! Bang, take that whitecoats! Eat lead, whitecoats."

Ryan turned around, making the two heads shrink from him, the two pairs of eyes blinking anxiously. "Not a sound more," he hissed. "There's more whitecoats around us now than there are wasps in a nest. If they hear us, then you'll go back to the laboratories for lots and lots more experiments. And they'll try to chill us, as well. Understand?"

"Yes," was said with a single voice.

Ryan dropped his voice still lower, so that the twin heads leaned toward him to catch what he was saying. "One more single sound and I'll cut the throat of which of you makes that sound. And the other one'll have complete, total control."

The reaction was what he'd expected. The dominant head strained to look at its weaker twin, grinning triumphantly. "It won't be me who loses, sister."

"And it won't be me, either," retorted the other head. "Count on that."

"MUST BE CLOSE to the main atrium now," Trader whispered, as Ryan stopped at an intersection of the corridors. "Been lucky to get this far."

"Yeah, I know." Edna-Evangelina waited patiently and silently behind them. "Trouble is, we don't know where Krysty is. Or where the others are being kept."

"Probably in our rooms in the other wing," Trader suggested. "That'd make sense."

"And Krysty?"

Trader shrugged his shoulders. "More likely to be in this wing, I guess. What we could do with is a whitecoat prisoner. Make 'em talk to us."

Ryan looked around them, listening. "There's someone coming," he said. "Might get us a prisoner real soon."

"Or get to be a prisoner, partner." Trader patted him on the shoulder. "Like the good old days, isn't it?"

There wasn't time to answer.

Just to their left was a set of double doors. Ryan could hear nothing from behind them so he pushed them boldly open, letting the gaping muzzle of the SIG-Sauer precede him into the room. If there had been anyone in there, and he'd tried to inch the doors open, they would have had plenty of warning.

Trader always used to say that if you were going in, then you went in all the way.

The room was empty. It had a row of basins and faucets along one side, with hooks for clothes on the wall. Other than that it was completely bare. Ryan beckoned the others in, moving quickly to the far end where a wide single door stood half open.

It was an operating theater, fully equipped with tables, lights and several sets of instruments glinting hygienically from racks on the wall.

Ryan figured another set of double doors at the far end of the room had to open onto the busy main corridor of the wing. It took him only a moment to check that those doors were locked.

"Wait in here," he said. "I'll go back and recce who's coming this way."

Trader stepped inside, whistling at the stark cleanliness of the place. "Looks like it hasn't been touched in a hundred years."

Edna-Evangelina followed him, the heads swiveling separately, trying to take in what it was seeing.

"Been here before," the dominant head said, fear making the voice ragged.

"Yes. Remember lights in the air and the pretty knives on the wall."

"Sharp pretty knives," the first head agreed.

"Quiet," Ryan warned. "Whitecoats and sec men behind that other door."

He went through the room with the washbasins and flattened himself against the wall by the entrance. He reached out with his left hand and very slowly turned the white plastic doorknob, squinting through the narrow gap into the corridor.

The sound of feet was much closer, with a strange tapping sound that reminded Ryan of the ferrule of

Doc's sword stick. But he couldn't recognize the voices.

Then they suddenly came into sight, the slight figure of Ladrow Buford, limping on his cane, cloak hunched around his shoulders. With him were two of the sec men.

"In here, Buford," Ryan whispered urgently.

He closed the door and moved to stand behind it. It was flung open and the two guards charged in, Buford at their heels. Neither of them spotted Ryan hidden by the open door. Keeping all three men covered with the automatic blaster, he heeled it shut, the noise making them turn.

"Morning," Ryan said. He gestured with the SIG-Sauer as he saw one of the sec men make a threatening move with the Mossberg that he held. "Best put those big shiny blasters down on the floor, slow and careful. Good."

"Cawdor! It's really you." Buford's glasses nearly fell off his narrow, beaky nose, he was shaking so much. "How can you be alive?"

"Easy. Live a good clean life, go to bed early and get up with the sun."

"But, is Thea with you?"

"No. Thea met with an accident."

"The rest of the patrol?"

"Trader's with me. Rest of the sec men sort of headed for the exit, pursued by a bear."

Buford swallowed, his prominent Adam's apple nearly choking him. "We didn't know."

"Sure." Ryan grinned. "How's everyone?"

"They're fine." A glint of hope shone in the scientist's watery eyes. "No need for the blaster, Cawdor.

You come along with us, and you can meet your friends."

"Sounds good." Ryan waved the blaster at the sec men. "Stand still awhile. Movement makes me nervous, and when I get nervous my fingers become sort of tense."

Ladrow Buford was sweating so much that Ryan could see clear beads trickling down the inside of the smeared lenses of his glasses. "Is there just you and Trader here? You haven't met with anyone else?"

Ryan could almost taste the whitecoat's fear. "We met a patrol. Tried to take us in. We chilled them all."

"Oh, no!"

"And then we broke in and met two more of your guards."

"Where?"

Trader had appeared unseen in the doorway behind the three men. "By your freaks' prison."

Buford spun. "Freaks! Prison! What in the name of science are you talking about?"

"Go through into the operating room," Ryan said, "and we'll talk a little more."

One of the sec men spoke for the first time. "What happened to the two guards by the—" he hesitated for a long moment "—by the quarters for the unsuccessful experiments? You bastards chill them also?"

Trader smiled at him. "You can bet mother's tits to a crock of shit that we did."

Buford turned to babble desperately to Ryan. "I don't know what you heard or saw, but it's all a total lie. We never did anyone no harm."

"Any harm," Ryan corrected.

"Right. Not never any harm. And we wouldn't have hurt you or your companions. Never hurt a fly."

"Liar, liar, pants on fire." Once again, in perfect unison, the words floated from both Edna and Evangelina.

Buford sagged at the unexpected sight of the two-headed mutated woman, dropped his stick and would have slumped straight to the floor if one of the sec men hadn't grabbed him by an arm and held him upright.

The guard looked at Trader. "You in charge?" He didn't wait for the answer. "This isn't anything to do with the ville's security forces. The scientists do all the experiments." He made the last word sound like something you found at the bottom of your boot. "Don't blame us."

Edna-Evangelina stood by the wall, hands behind her. Both heads had hectic spots of angry color at the cheekbones, staring intently at the semiconscious Buford.

"Lay him on that operating table and fix the straps to his ankles and wrists," Ryan ordered, ignoring the sec man's plea. "Good and tight. Then buckle that inflatable gag in place. Don't want him making a load of noise."

When they'd finished, Trader checking their work, the second of the guards, who'd been totally silent, suddenly spoke to Ryan. "Listen, One-eye."

"What?"

"Beyond that outer door there's all the whole powerful world of the institute going on. Must be at least twenty or thirty of our friends within calling distance. You don't dare squeeze the trigger on either of your blasters. Be signing your own death warrants if you do."

"So?" Ryan moved a little closer to the speaker. "We might die tomorrow, but you'll die right here and now. Is that a good deal?"

The man laughed contemptuously. "I know you dumb fucks from the outlands. You value your own skins too much. I'm walking out right now."

He turned to his comrade. "Come on, Jerry."

Ryan had already holstered the SIG-Sauer, and now drew the eighteen-inch panga. Trader was in the act of dropping the Armalite to the tiles, reaching for his own slim-bladed knife. But both of them were way, way too slow.

There was the lightning flash of the bright overhead lights on tempered steel as the perfectly honed scalpel swung toward the throat of the leading sec man, held in the strong right hand of Edna-Evangelina.

"Give it him, sister!" cried the weaker head, pale eyes open wide with delighted excitement.

"We will, sister."

The man staggered away, blood pulsing from the opened artery, spraying ceiling-high, the fountain weakening as the crimson flood slowed. He dropped to his knees, then slid onto his face, the gash leaking the last drops of blood.

"Bitchin' freakin' bitch!"

The surviving guard had drawn his own knife, which looked like an old military bayonet. Turning, he stabbed upward at the neck of the exultant woman, catching the dominant head squarely under the chin, driving the blade home before Ryan or Trader could do anything to stop him.

Trader was a half step nearer and he stabbed the sec man through the heart from behind, cutting off what might have been a desperate cry for assistance. The guard moaned once, his own blade clattering to the blood-sodden floor, then fell alongside his dead colleague.

"Too slow to save, in time to avenge," Trader said, kneeling to check his victim was truly dead. He wiped his knife clean on the man's pants.

Ryan, seeing that the chilling was over, had stepped immediately to the side of the wounded woman, aware at a first glance that all was done for her.

For them.

The knife had done its work too well, and there was no possibility of checking the flow of blood. Ryan helped her to lie down, away from the lake of crimson at the center of the floor that was already seeping into a network of strategically placed drains.

The eyes were closing on the dominant head, the mouth open, a tiny thread of blood inching between the parted lips. The other head was turning frantically from side to side, trying to see its sister.

"You all right? We did it. Did it!"

"I'm real sorry," Ryan said quietly, "but I don't think she's goin' to make it."

The tongue came out to moisten the dry lips on the wounded head. "Don't cry for me, sister," it said feebly.

"I'm not, truly." Tears were bubbling from the weak eyes, down the cheeks.

"I'll wait for you."

"Around the next turning, sister?"

"Yes."

Trader stood by Ryan's shoulder, silently watching. Buford had recovered consciousness and was making muffled grunting noises through the gag.

The eyes on the dominant head became still, fixed on the bright lights above. But the other head didn't seem to have noticed what had happened.

"Sister? We paid them back some. For what they did to us. Didn't we?"

"She's gone," Trader said.

Ryan nodded. "I know."

Now they could see that the wound was mortal for both Edna and Evangelina. The blood still seeped out, more slowly, but the life was fast draining away from the surviving head. The cheeks had grown even more pale, the eyes losing focus.

"Can't feel you anymore, sister."

The fingers were opening and closing, the legs, in their borrowed uniform, not moving.

"Sorry fought so...sister...loved you...loved..."

The room was quiet.

Even the helpless Ladrow Buford had stopped his futile struggling, aware of the moment of death for the poor, bedeviled creature that he and his colleagues had given such a tormented and distorted life.

Ryan lowered both heads to the tiles very gently, then straightened. "Know what I hope, partner?" he said to Trader. "I hope that little fuck on the operating table refuses to tell us what's happening so we can work on him awhile. I swear that I would like that."

But Ryan was disappointed.

Trader held his knife to the throbbing artery beneath the little scientist's ear, while Ryan carefully removed the inflatable gag.

"Just d-don't h-hurt me," Buford stuttered. "I'll tell you anything and every single thing you need to know. Just don't hurt me, I beg you."

Chapter Thirty-Three

"If Ryan's dead, then we have no choice. If he's alive, out in the snow, we still have to make our own break."

"What about Krysty, John?" Mildred asked. "I'm seriously frightened for her. For what those so-called scientist bastards might be doing to her."

Jak nodded. "Agree. Morning's much gone. Time get out of this place."

Dean had been crying in a corner of the room where they were all imprisoned. But everyone had been tactful about it and pretended not to notice. Now, red-eyed and sniffling, he'd rejoined the council of war.

"I reckon Dad'll try and break into this shitter's hole as soon as he gets through the snow," he said. "He and Trader'll need help. We can give it."

Abe nodded. "Ace on the fucking line, young'un," he declared. "Anything we can do'll help."

Doc cleared his throat portentously. "If I may express my opinion?" he began.

"Sure you can, Doc," Mildred told him. "Just so long as you keep it short."

"I was merely proposing that if Ryan were here with us he could carefully formulate a proper plan, taking in true military fashion the enemy dispositions as well as calculating our own strengths or weaknesses. He would not be the man to simply leap, winking, into the great unknown. If it is to be done, then it will be well if it can be done quickly. As the justly famous bard of Avon so succinctly put it.''

"Doc!" Mildred protested. "By the time you get to the end of this, we'll all have passed away of old age. And I hope and pray you'll be the first to go."

"Temper, temper, my dearest lady." Doc waved a reproving finger at the woman. "Hope, charity and patience, there abideth these three, Dr. Wyeth. And the greatest of all of these is patience."

"So, get on with what you have to say, you pompous old fart."

He beamed at Mildred, showing his fine set of perfect teeth. "Then I shall..." Doubt clouded his eyes. "If it were not for the sad fact that I have momentarily disremembered what it was. If you allow me a moment or two?"

J.B. shook his head. "Enough wooly talk, Doc. Time for a combat plan. I've been thinking about it since they locked us up in here. They got our blasters, but some of us still have weapons. Your sword stick, Doc. Your throwing knives, Jak. So, here's what I suggest we do..."

THE SEC FORCES at the institute had all been well trained, skilled at patrolling the perimeter, scouring the isolated valley in the heart of Acadia National Park, picking off any stragglers who had wandered there, though the numbers had decreased over the years.

But they had never come across any group of outlanders like Ryan Cawdor and his companions.

It had been easy taking the guns away. They were large and easily spotted. Dean's turquoise-hilted knife had been sheathed at his belt, and the guards had removed that. J.B. had surrendered his own blade to them, as had Abe.

But they had totally overlooked Doc's Toledo rapier, concealed within the ebony case, and a quick patdown had missed all of Jak Lauren's hidden throwing knives.

Ellison, the sec boss, had been keeping a close personal eye on them, swaggering in, proudly wearing Doc's beloved Le Mat in his belt. The twisted scar at the corner of his mouth curling in derision every time he visited the prisoners.

Now, not long before noon, he came into their prison ward, past the two men with their scatterguns who were on watch in the passage outside.

"Snow's stopped," he said. "Sure you don't want to break the window and jump out to join your dead friends? One-eye and the old-timer?"

Though he didn't know it, that had been one of the options that they'd been discussing only a few minutes earlier, rejecting it mainly on account of the noise it would entail. The glass was very thick, and it would take enormous force to splinter it. Then you had to clear away the loose shards or you'd cut yourself to ribbons going through. A rope of sheets might've reached the ground, but it would have taken at least five minutes for all of them to have gotten away down the face of the building, past the windows of the busily occupied first floor.

The chances of being caught were too great.

So, they'd selected what seemed to be the best of the alternatives. Or what J.B. had called, quoting Trader, "The least worst option."

"We'd like to see Krysty," Mildred said, standing by the window, as far away as possible from the door, gazing mournfully out at the bleak landscape.

"Sure you would, lady."

"When can we?"

It was said so quietly that the sec boss took a couple of steps across the room toward her.

"What?"

Mildred looked away from him, muttering something in an undertone.

Ellison was aggrieved. "Can't you fucking outlanders speak up?" He walked to stand right by her, grabbing her by the shoulder. "Can't you do anything properly?"

Jak stood in the center of the room. "Do chilling properly," he stated.

As Ellison turned, the albino hurled the leaf-bladed, weighted knife from his right hand, with a crisp snap of the wrist. At a range of less than twelve feet, with a stationary target, he couldn't miss.

Jak's target had been the red-veined right eye of the senior sec man, bulging in instant shock as he saw his death slicing toward him.

The honed steel thudded wetly home, bursting the right eye open in a flourish of clear liquid, followed instantly by a wave of bright blood. The taped hilt of the thrown knife protruded from the ruptured socket like some obscene ornament, the ultimate in facial decoration.

Ellison gasped in pain, letting go of the Mossberg. Dean was right at his side, prepared for that, and grabbed the blaster before it could clatter to the tiles. As the sec man's mouth opened, ready to scream,

Mildred moved from behind him and clamped both hands over his mouth, shutting off the cry.

The point of the knife had searched out the front part of Ellison's brain, and he was dying.

As his strength failed, Mildred and Abe supported him, laying him gently on the floor. One foot was jerking, beating out a rhythmic tattoo for several seconds, before Jak himself knelt down and held the leg still.

"Done," J.B. said.

"One of them down, and only five or six dozen more to go," Doc added, stooping to pluck his Le Mat from the dead man's belt. "Mine, I think."

The scarred mouth was twisted in a rictus of horror, the one good eye staring blankly at the ceiling.

"The end of friend Ellison." Mildred looked down at him. "Ugly son of a bitch, wasn't he?"

Precisely at that moment the door of their room was flung open and in strode the sec boss, Ellison. He slammed the door shut behind him and walked toward the group of friends, their bodies hiding the corpse on the floor from him.

"What're you..." he began, the great curved cicatrix that disfigured the corner of his mouth tugging the lips into a parody of a smile.

"Dark night!" J.B. breathed, for once knocked completely off balance.

There was Ellison, stone dead at their feet, Jak's knife still rammed into the weeping eye socket.

And there was Ellison, alive as could be, standing less than six feet away from his own corpse.

The only one of them who reacted to the bizarre situation with any sense was Doc. He walked quickly from his place in the circle and stepped right up to Ellison, the Le Mat concealed behind his back.

Ellison stopped and stared suspiciously at him. "What the fuck do you want, you old goat?"

"I want only to speed you along to meet the dark ferryman, Charon of the Styx."

He pressed the .63-caliber, gold-embossed shotgun barrel of the revolver into the sec man's midriff as hard as he could and squeezed the gold-plated trigger.

Ellison's body absorbed much of the noise of the blaster, muffling it. The charge ripped through the man's belly, tearing his intestines to bloody rags of sinew, pulverized a section of his spine, completely blowing away four vertebrae into tiny white shards of bone. The spent slugs scattered bloodily into the wall behind Ellison, spraying it with dappled crimson.

Doc stepped quickly back, tutting as blood gushed over the toes of his cracked knee boots. He allowed the body of the sec man to stagger three broken steps backward, before dropping to the floor.

"His twin?" Abe suggested.

Mildred shook her head. "No. Dean, remember you thought you heard that dying man whisper a word? Said it sounded like 'coning' to you?"

"Sure."

"It wasn't 'coning,' Dean. It was 'cloning.' I know it. The twin dogs. That's what the sick bastards are doing here. They're cloning, copying people. One of these would be the original Ellison, and the other is a copy of him, perfect in virtually every detail. Probably genetically engineered and matched from a DNA sample." She took a deep breath. "My God, friends.

We should find Krysty and all get out of here as fast as we can. There's true evil here."

THE SOUND OF THE SHOT hadn't penetrated through the soundproof door to the guards in the corridor.

J.B. had taken one of the pair of matched silver Mossberg scatterguns, tossing the second one to Abe. Jak had retrieved his knife from the eye of the first Ellison, replacing it in its hidden sheath.

Doc reloaded the spent .63-caliber shell from one of his deep pockets. Mildred and Dean each took a knife from the bodies.

"Right," the Armorer said. "Take the sec men from outside now, as quick and quiet as we can. Bring them in here like we talked about."

"Chill them." Jak's voice didn't leave room for very much discussion.

"Yeah," J.B. agreed. "We chill them."

Mildred looked at him. "Can't we tie them and leave them here, John?"

"If this was an old predark fic vid, then sure we could, easily. But this is real life, Mildred. Real Deathlands living and dying. Only takes one to get loose or someone to come by while we're wasting all that time and..." He drew his index finger across his throat.

She nodded. "Then we try to find a way across the top of the atrium at this level. Into the research wing and look for Krysty. Then out and run for it. Hope Ryan and Trader eventually link up with us?"

"That is indeed the plan, Dr. Wyeth," Doc said. "You sound just a tad dubious about the possibilities of its success. Of course, if you have invented a better option, then I am sure we would all be delighted to hear it.''

"Fuck you, Doc. The least worst option, isn't it? And so far, so good. Let's carry on the killing."

Jak went to the door and opened it a little way, calling out for the guards to come inside the room.

J.B. DISCONNECTED a sec alarm that would have closed off the aerial walkway that spidered high over the central atrium. Then they were all able to pick their way, in single file, over what had obviously once been a maintenance catwalk, with ventilation ducts and electrical conduits opening off it.

Far below they could see the white of the scientists' coats, and the bustling sec men.

Once they were all safely over, Dean commented that the scene below looked like a nest of snow ants, disturbed by a hungry bear.

J.B. agreed with the boy. "Something's got up their asses, that's for sure."

They had to work their way through a maze of narrow passages, then descend through a trapdoor into a deserted service corridor. J.B. led them along the hall and down an iron staircase onto the first floor.

Mildred took over the job of guiding them, using the experience of her previous recce.

"The operating rooms and main research labs are down here," she informed them, "but we need to sneak across toward the outer passage that runs behind the rooms."

That was easier said than done with the whole institute buzzing. Twice they had to cut into side rooms, luckily finding them empty, while sec patrols jogged by.

They were nearing the farther end of the wing, where Mildred had spotted the poor ruined victims of the scientists' crazed research, when they all heard the sound of clicking heels approaching from a side corridor.

"One person," Jak said.

"Take him quietly," J.B. warned.

The last two side doors had been locked and bolted, so there was nowhere to run and hide. The only option was to stand and fight.

"Take him with one of your knives, Jak," the Armorer ordered, "first moment he appears."

The noise of the feet was growing louder, closer, echoing and distorted.

Jak reached behind his back, under the ragged jacket, feeling for his concealed blade. Beneath the stark overhead lighting his white hair seemed like a veil of blazing magnesium, his eyes glinting like tiny rubies. He gripped the hilt tight between finger and thumb.

Doc whispered to the Armorer. "Might it not be a risk worth the taking to try to capture this person alive? Then we can question him concerning the whereabouts of our three missing companions."

J.B. shook his head. "No, Doc. Too risky. Just a quick clean chill."

Now the sound of boots was almost on top of them, right around the nearest corner.

The moment the figure appeared, Jak sent his knife spinning through the air, aimed toward the throat of his intended victim—Krysty Wroth!

Chapter Thirty-Four

The woman's reflexes were so miraculously fast that it was almost as if she had known that the thrown knife was driving toward her throat.

She already seemed to be ducking against the needle-sharp point, moving sideways with the grace and power of a ballet dancer, dropping almost into a full crouch, so that the steel whispered through the tight fiery curls, snipping off a shredded lock that tumbled in slow motion to the white tiles, lying there like a tiny dead flame spider.

The knife hit the wall, angling off in a shower of snowy plaster, hitting the opposite wall, lower down, before losing its momentum farther down the passage, sliding along the immaculate floor.

"Gaia! That's a good greeting from my oldest friends."

"Sorry. You all right?" Jak asked, running quickly toward her, touching her shoulder lightly with a hand as he passed her. He stooped to pick up and sheathe his knife, first checking the point to make sure it hadn't been damaged by the miss.

"Fine," she replied, straightening, touching her head where the knife had sliced by.

Mildred put her arms around the taller woman, hugging her. "Thank God you're all right, honey. They didn't hurt you with their experiments?"

Krysty shook her head. "No. I think they mean well. Just asked me a lot of questions." She hesitated a moment. "Then they let me go again."

J.B. patted her on the shoulder. "We've found out what they're doing here, Krysty."

"What?"

"Cloning," Doc replied. "They are replicating animals and humans, and we believe that they don't 'mean well,' as you put it."

"Really?" Krysty looked genuinely surprised. "Why?"

"We're not sure." Mildred glanced behind her, wondering if she'd detected a sound. "Seems that it's what they've been working toward for all this time. Want to create a sort of cleansed master race. Doc's right, Krysty. They don't mean well, any more than the Nazis meant well when they created Dachau, Auschwitz and Belsen. Don't let them kid you."

"What are you going to do?" Krysty asked, her bright green eyes fixed on Mildred.

"First thing was to find you. We've done that. Now we're going to try to get away from here. Look for Ryan and Trader outside. There's still no word of them."

Doc tapped on the floor with his sword stick. "I am personally very strongly in favor of seeking out the throbbing, infected heart of this complex and lancing the pestilence."

"What?" Dean asked, puzzled.

J.B. answered the boy. "Doc means blow the place apart before we leave."

"Sounds good to me," Abe said enthusiastically. "Let's go light the fire."

"I'm not at all sure," Krysty said doubtfully, shaking her head.

Mildred noticed in passing that the bright sentient hair of her friend was much more tightly curled than usual, in its most defensive mode.

"Have you heard anything from Dad, or any word about him?" Dean asked.

"Dad? Ryan? No. They didn't tell me anything at all. Just that he was lost in the snow with Trader."

"You sure you're all right, Krysty?" J.B. asked. "Only you seem sort of... distant."

"Fine. Just that I'm worried about Ryan. I need to see him real triple bad. I *have* to see him as soon as possible."

"But we don't know for sure that he's still alive, Krysty. The storm was terrible and there's supposed to be that mutie grizzly out there, as well."

"Oh, he's alive all right. I know that."

"Mean can feel it?" asked Jak, who had always been fascinated by Krysty's unique mutie talent for sensing what was going on around her.

"Feel?" she repeated, sounding doubtful.

"Sure. Feeling Ryan's alive. You know."

She stared at the albino, her brow furrowed, as if she were trying to work out a complex geometric theorem.

The odd moment was broken by J.B. "Someone's coming this way. Let's move."

BUFORD WAS LEADING Ryan and Trader through a maze of narrow corridors, past research labs and operating rooms, storerooms and a vast area that was filled with comp disks.

"This is all the work that's gone on," the little scientist told them. "Our past. Our records."

"You taking us to Krysty?" Ryan grabbed him, fingers biting like steel pincers, making the whitecoat wince and squeak in pain. "You don't, then you're dead meat, Buford."

"I told you. She's almost certainly in with Professor Crichton at the moment. He has his own private suite at the back of the laboratory where the mat-trans units are kept. All your blasters will be there, as well. So you can get away quickly and not hurt anyone."

"And the rest of our friends are in their rooms?"

"Sure, Trader, sure."

"But there'll be sec men there?" Ryan had the SIG-Sauer cocked and ready in his right hand.

"'Course. Crichton always has guards around. But I'll help you take them by surprise and chill them easily."

Trader squeezed the cheek of the sallow scientist. "Regular prince among men, Buford, aren't you?"

"Survival is what matters. If I die, then the last few steps of our marathon of research might be damaged and seriously held back for years."

"That so?" Ryan nodded, interested. "Then we'll have to be real sure we take good care of you, Ladrow."

KRYSTY HAD STOPPED, bringing everyone to a halt. "If Ryan's in the institute, then he'll probably make for the heart and soul, won't he?"

Mildred answered. "Could do. But we don't know what the heart is, or where it is." She grinned bleakly. "And I don't believe there's anything in here that anyone could call a soul."

"I would not be too surprised to learn that Professor Crichton himself might be found at the core of this wicked place." Doc rubbed his hands together. "Rather like some vast Shelob of a spider, waiting with infinite patience for its victims to enmesh themselves in its web."

Krysty nodded. "Doc's right. Crichton is where Ryan'll go. That's where I have to go, too." She paused a heartbeat. "Where all of us must go."

"Don't suppose you know the way?" J.B. asked. "Did the bastards take you there during their experiments on you?"

"Yeah, they did. Follow me."

RYAN AND TRADER had stopped to hold a brief council of war. Buford had brought them within a door and a corridor of Crichton's quarters, which were situated close to the end of the research wing where the botched experiment victims had been held.

"Been lucky so far." Trader rested the butt of the Armalite on the floor.

"Yeah." Ryan couldn't have disagreed. There was a feeling of movement and hustle all about them. Twice they'd been nearly picked off by fast-moving sec patrols, finding empty rooms to hide in at the last moment.

Trader moved closer to him, dropping his voice. "When do we chill the little fuck?" He gestured toward Buford, who was leaning on his stick, looking tense and exhausted.

Ryan considered the question. "When we have to," he finally replied. "Not before."

"Could take him out right now. He's brought us where we want to be."

"No."

"Like I've said, Ryan, you've gotten soft with being away from me."

"You can say that, Trader, but you can't really expect me to comment."

The older man shrugged. "All right. But I'll watch the whitecoat like a hawk after a rabbit. One wrong step and he's off the mountain."

"Sure."

Ryan turned to Buford. "Sure Crichton's in there?"

"Sure, at this time of day. His chamber is next to the main lab. And after all the alarms that have been going on in the last couple of hours, he'll be resting in there. His health is far from excellent."

Ryan nodded. "Right. We'll pay him the call right now. You go in ahead of us, Buford, and take the edge off any sec men in there. We'll be right at your heels."

Krysty was angry.

"I tell you this is the best way to do it. Head for Crichton's quarters. If Ryan and Trader are anywhere around, then that's where they'll be. And I have to see Ryan quickly."

"'Course you do." Mildred managed a smile. "We all want to see him again."

J.B. wasn't happy. "Are you really sure that this is the way to get to the headman's place? How come you know the back ways in this warren?"

"I was brought and taken back in different ways, and they also showed me around a lot. Through here."

They went into a narrow room, with doors at either end, cutting a corner off two corridors. There was a box on one of the shelves that brought the Armorer up short.

"Hey, hold on!"

"What?" Krysty stamped her booted foot. "You trying to fuck me around here? We have to get on."

"Simmer down," Abe said.

J.B. reached up and took down the heavy box. On the end facing them, in neat stenciled lettering, was the single word *Grens*.

"Now these could be useful." He pried off the lid, his face showing his disappointment. "Most are blank training grens." He brightened. "But there's a couple of burners. One blue-and-scarlet implode with a loose fuse. Two delays and a couple of frags. Here, Jak, you take the delays. Abe, you carry the frags. I'll pocket the burners."

"You don't need those," Krysty said abruptly. "You got blasters enough."

"Better to have weapons and not need them than to need them and not have them," Abe said. "Trader used to say that. Guess he still does."

"Right," J.B. agreed. "There, Krysty, that didn't take long. Lead on."

BUFORD WAS PUSHED into the big room, stumbling and nearly falling, only saving himself with his stick. Ryan and Trader were right behind him.

It was furnished like a bedroom, with a large mattress laid on the floor at one side, covered in a pale green duvet. There, his head resting on pillows, was Crichton. He looked pale, eyes closed, hands folded on his chest.

Ryan was more concerned with the three sec men who'd been standing around a table, picking at some cold meats and bowls of varicolored mush. They had turned around as soon as the door opened, then relaxed when they saw it was Professor Buford.

By the time they saw the two outlanders, it was too late and they were too slow. The edge was gone.

"Blasters on the floor, then move over away from the table and lie down," Trader snapped. As the men hesitated a moment, he added, "One chance of living. Do like you're told, or you all get to be dead right here and now."

The cold wolfish smile on the carved granite face told the sec guards that Trader was a man who meant what he said. They all obeyed him.

By now, Crichton had awakened and was sitting up in his bed, hand reaching out toward a bellpull that hung from the ceiling. He froze as Ryan turned the SIG-Sauer toward him.

"Look," Trader said, pointing toward a smaller table. On it lay, in a jumbled pile, a Smith & Wesson M-4000 scattergun, an Uzi, a Smith & Wesson double-action 640, a .357 Magnum, a Czech revolver and a couple of other big handblasters.

"Useful." Ryan turned to Crichton. "What have you done with our friends?"

"Where is Professor Gibson? Have you murdered her like you've murdered many of our men?" Crichton was trying to put on a brave face, but his head was trembling like someone with an ague. "Tell me."

Ryan felt the familiar surge of anger, the deep scar that ran from his right eye to the corner of his mouth starting to pulse.

"We haven't even started the chilling yet," he snarled. "Wait till we get into our stride. Then you'll see something worth the seeing."

"Can I go now?" Buford whispered.

"No. I want you right here at my side. Just in case any traps start springing closed."

Trader stood over the trio of huddled sec men, the Armalite ready.

Crichton had a violent coughing fit, his face turning a bizarre shade of purple for a few moments before slipping back to its normal ivory hue. "Just what do you want? I suppose you expect me to surrender the institute to you?"

Trader answered before Ryan could speak. "No, shit-for-brains, we expect you to die."

Ryan sniffed. "We want Krysty Wroth back, safe and untouched. And all our friends—" he pointed to the table "—with their weapons. Safe passage through the sec barrier on the blacktop out of here. No pursuit. That's all."

"All?" Despite the threat of the guns, Crichton was still defiant. "You are at the heart of our complex, with literally dozens of armed men within call, and you try to set terms to me?"

Buford had been standing nervously, shuffling his weight from foot to foot. "They aren't like any of the other outlanders we've taken over the years, Dave. They've got this far. Who's to say they can't go further?"

The question was destined to remain forever unanswered.

A small door, partly hidden by a geometric Amish quilt, swung open and in came Krysty, followed by the rest of the group of friends.

"Hi, Dad," Dean chirped. "You all right?"

"Fine. Questions and answers come later." Ryan smiled at Krysty. "Hello, lover."

She walked toward him with that familiar stride, her green gaze fixed to his face, ignoring Buford who was standing close to Ryan, between them.

It was the little crippled scientist who broke the sudden silence. "No, Krysty," he yelped in alarm. "Don't do it. Negative conditioning instruction."

"What?" Ryan started.

Krysty ignored the whitecoat, ignored everyone else in the room, all of her attention focused on Ryan.

When she was only five paces away she reached inside her dark blue jacket and pulled out a black-hilted knife with a ten-inch steel blade.

"You dirty bastard, Ryan Cawdor," she hissed, and lunged at his face with the knife.

Chapter Thirty-Five

It was a waking nightmare for Ryan.

The one person in his entire life that he had truly loved, the woman that he'd given his heart to, was coming at him, spitting abuse, thrusting toward him with a carving blade in her right hand. Her mouth was curled in psychotic hatred, her beautiful eyes narrowed in vicious rage, her whole face distorted by murderous madness.

He had the SIG-Sauer in his hand, and it would have been the work of a moment to level it at Krysty and blow her head from her shoulders.

But his finger froze on the trigger, paralyzed by total blind disbelief.

He even tried to call out to her, but his tongue cleaved to the roof of his mouth and he couldn't make a sound.

Ryan had always known since he was a young boy that death comes calling for all men.

Now it had come for him.

Ladrow Buford made his move.

With Krysty right on top of him, he thrust out his hand in front of her, like a predark traffic cop.

"No!" he roared, his voice suddenly sounding amazingly deep and powerful.

He might as well have tried to pick a sec lock with a piece of wet string.

Thwarted by finding the little middle-aged man in her way, Krysty stabbed at him. The point of the knife struck him in the center of his right cheek, slicing down, hacking off a neat section of his face, exposing the pearly whiteness of teeth in the gum beneath, until the silent wave of crimson came washing down to obscure them.

Buford's crystal-shattering scream was the catalyst that sparked chaos.

Krysty stabbed again and again, cutting the whitecoat's face apart, ripping flesh away, carving the end off his nose, lunging and popping one eye neatly out of its socket. Buford was unrecognizable, his features ripped apart like a ruined carnival mask, sodden in spurting, gouting blood.

She was now shrieking at the top of her voice, like an enraged harpy. "You next, Ryan, you dead-meat bastard!'

And still he wasn't able to pull the trigger on the SIG- Sauer, wasn't able to blow the madwoman away.

Buford had sunk to his knees, his cries for help and mercy drowned in his own blood.

But the chaos didn't end there with the savage butchery of the scientist.

It began there.

The three sec men, lying prone under the threat of Trader's Armalite, noticed that the red-haired woman's attack on the whitecoat had distracted everyone. Even Trader, the survivor of a thousand firefights, had been taken aback by Krysty's insane behavior and lost his combat concentration.

So they made their play.

The large room was a bedlam of screaming. Crichton had taken his own chance to ring the emergency bellpull, summoning more sec men to help. Dean shouted to his father to run away from Krysty. Mildred yelled at her friend to stop the slaughter. Jak had spotted the blasters on the table and was moving to regain his own Colt Python, J.B. at his heels. Doc stood with his Le Mat in his hand, eyes staring in disbelief at what was happening. Abe had been walking toward Trader when Krysty had started her crazed attack, and now he was frozen, halfway across the floor.

There was the sickening sound of the knife still hacking away at the dying whitecoat, the point grating on the planes of bone around the eyes, cutting the lips to ragged tatters of crimson flesh. Buford's hands were also destroyed as he'd tried to fend off the merciless strokes of the gleaming knife, two of his fingers completely severed.

Ryan had backed away several steps, the SIG-Sauer pointing uselessly at his woman.

The three sec men were all up on their hands and knees, one of them clutching at Trader, trying to bring him down and grab his blaster.

It seemed to break the spell.

Ryan spun and fired quickly, seeing one of the guards go down, clutching at his chest. Trader had wrenched away his Armalite, using the butt to batter the second man to the floor. Jak had thrown one of his knives, miraculously backhanded, into the third sec man's neck, knocking him onto the bloodied floor.

Buford was finally down, death bringing him its dubious, delayed mercy. And nothing stood between Krysty and Ryan. The point of the knife in her hand was snapped off, broken against the scientist's jaw or teeth, but it was still a terminally lethal weapon.

"Shoot her, Trader," Dean screamed in a fragile, piping voice. "Shoot Krysty!"

"No," Ryan protested, but his voice was so quiet that nobody heard it—except Krysty, who leered at him.

"That's right, lover," she whispered. "Just you and me."

At that moment the doors at either end of the room burst open.

Through the far door came eight or ten sec men, all holding Mossbergs, nearly falling over one another as they took in the scene of dying and death.

Ryan half turned to the figure who had come in through the entrance just behind him, blinking his eye in disbelief.

It was Krysty Wroth.

"Hi, lover," she said. "Get out of the way so me and that phony bitch can get to it."

"Chill slut, Ryan," whispered the Krysty who stood facing him.

Ryan hesitated, deciding for a moment that he had totally lost his mind. The two women were identical except for the fact that one had a homicidal grin pasted on her lips and was holding a bloodied blade in her hand.

His attention was distracted by the beginning of a short, brutal firefight. He remembered the comment about how the sec men at the Melissa Crichton Institute were efficient enough, as far as they went, but they'd never come up against murderous fighting machines like Jak, Trader and J.B., and they were hopelessly outclassed by them.

One of the Mossbergs roared, the charge starring out across the room, the pellets narrowly missing Abe, galvanizing him into rapid motion. He dived at the table where the others had helped themselves to their weapons, snatching up his own stainless steel Colt Python, distinguished from Jak's blaster by its four-inch barrel against the albino's six-inch barrel.

There followed a devastating assault by Ryan's friends, led by the vicious crack of the Armalite, overlaid by the snarling Uzi and the boom of the Le Mat, with the other handblasters all playing their part in the abattoir symphony.

The sec men were overwhelmed.

Apart from that single round from one of their Mossbergs, they never fired a shot in retaliation, being cut down where they stood, their bodies dancing and whirling as the bullets tore them apart in fountains of thick blood.

The stillness was frighteningly loud in the big room, scented with cordite and death.

Ryan had personally taken out two of the hapless guards with his SIG-Sauer, but now he turned back to face the twin figures of Krysty Wroth, one vengeful, one avenging.

"Don't anyone shoot her," called the Krysty who stood close to the nearer door into the bedroom.

The Krysty who was much nearer to Ryan hadn't moved since the shooting began, as if the noise and dying had somehow disorientated her.

Now she shuddered as though an invisible life force had been injected into her. Her green eyes came back into focus, staring this time past Ryan, past him at the doppelgänger standing a few steps beyond.

"Yes. That's right, that's right. Chill the twin, first among equals."

"Move your ass, lover," said the other Krysty. "Rest of you cover the doors in case we get more company."

Ryan took a few cautious paces to his left, toward where Trader was already hurriedly levering more 9 mm shells into the Armalite. He had only the barest idea of what was going on, but logic told him that one of the two women had to be the real Krysty and the other was some kind of genetically engineered false copy.

Common sense said that the murderous Krysty had to be the imitation.

Everyone was watching the bizarre duel, including Professor Crichton, who was sitting up on his bed, hands to his chest, breathing hard, having miraculously avoided being hit by any of the hail of full-metal-jacketed death.

The first Krysty, with the knife, had backed away a little, glancing down at the lake of blood that lay across half the floor, careful not to slip in it.

The second Krysty, unarmed, was advancing, smiling, arms out wide, like a wrestler.

Dean had sidled around to stand by his father, reaching up to take his hand for reassurance. "Which one's the real Krysty, Dad?" he breathed.

"Don't know. Don't know what's going on at all."

Doc was near them, and he whispered a quick explanation of what they'd already found out—about the two Ellisons, the identical dogs and the failed experiments resulting from altering DNA.

"No good ever came from tampering with Nature and trying to emulate the Almighty," he said. "I think that the notorious Dr. Robert Oppenheimer—the destroyer of worlds—would be the first to confirm that. Were he still alive.''

Ryan had never heard of the man, but he nodded anyway, his gaze fixed to the fight.

"Come on, Krysty," Mildred called encouragingly.

Both the redheaded, green-eyed women turned toward her, smiling.

They closed on each other, and the unarmed Krysty grabbed at the wrist of the armed double, keeping the knife away from herself. But, from then on, the fight was seriously weird. Every move one would make, the other would instantly counter, like a pair of mirror images locked in identical combat.

It was as if each knew precisely what was in the other's mind and was preparing to counter it before the initial action had even begun.

For several seconds they stood locked together, straining like statues. The Krysty with the knife spit at her twin, but the other woman turned her face away and the saliva pattered harmlessly into the lake of blood.

Ryan realized that the twin had all of Krysty's memories and thoughts typed into its own brain, so that it knew everything that its original had ever done and was tuned in to anything that she might attempt.

"Help me, Ryan, lover," called the first of the Krystys—or was it the second one? They'd been spinning and staggering around, boots sliding in the blood, so that it wasn't possible to figure which was which. "Cut the slut's throat, lover."

Ryan knew that Krysty almost never used bad language.

He drew his panga and started to move in, ready to slit open the neck of the speaker.

But the other Krysty called for him to stop. "I told you, she's mine!"

There was a convulsive jerk as the two women wrestled close together, a gasp of pain and shock, and then they parted.

One had the knife buried in her chest up to the hilt, blood trickling down from the cut in the white shirt.

The other stepped back, panting with the effort of the fight, watching her rival, her other self, drop to her knees, dying.

"Krysty?" Ryan said doubtfully. "You all right?"

"Sure, lover. I worked it out. Wasn't a stalemate like it looked. They used a mat-trans unit to clone me instantly. But this poor bitch was only a kind of first-generation copy of me. They programmed her by tweaking molecules or neurons or something to make her hate you. It was the last test. She could only react to what she thought I was doing. So, I positively decided to pull at the knife, then I pushed it instead. She just wasn't quite quick enough to react."

The twin rolled onto her side, hair matted in the coagulating crimson pool. Her eyes closed and she died, silently.

"Sorry for her," Krysty said, "in a way."

"How did you escape?" Mildred asked.

"Easy. Big alarm about some killing going on. Left me with only one sec man. I kicked him in the groin and sent his balls into the back of his throat. Came here."

Ryan moved to hug her, feeling the tension in her body as he clasped her tight. "Good to have you back safe, lover," he said.

"You, too. Reckon we should get our asses in gear, out of this place. Wish we had some plas-ex to blow the heart out of it. Seriously evil things going on."

J.B. grinned, holding up two grens. "Got these babies and four more beside. Enough to start some real damage."

"Lab's next door," Mildred said.

"Look, Dad," Dean called from the side of the king-size bed.

Professor David Crichton, grandson of the founder, the mastermind behind everything that had gone on in the institute, was dead.

The last few minutes of violence and savage slaughter had been too much for his weak heart and he had simply fallen back on his pillows, lips pulled back off his yellow teeth, eyes staring into infinity.

"Don't weep for him," Krysty said.

"Wasn't going to." Jak grinned.

THE REST WAS MAINLY downhill and easy.

With all of the friends together and all fully armed, it was simple to split their force, with J.B. taking Abe and Jak into the vast laboratory next door, with their six grenades. They picked the main targets, including the pair of mat-trans chambers, using the delays to give themselves time to get out and close the doors, avoiding any danger.

Ryan spread out the others into a tight perimeter, covering themselves against any putative sec man attack from any direction.

But there was no direct threat.

Ryan was watching along a main passage that ended up in the central concourse. Twice he saw guards appear in the distance, then vanish quickly. There was no way they could know that their chief was dead, along with Buford and a dozen of their fellows. But it looked like fear alone was enough to keep them well away from the cold-blooded outlanders.

He heard movement and glanced around, seeing Jak moving toward him. The albino crouched, giving a thumbs-up signal. J.B. was at his shoulder, showing Ryan the two-minute warning for the grens.

When the explosion came it was surprisingly muted, but it still blew out windows and doors all through that section of the research wing.

Ryan could smell the fire from the burners, seeing thick black chemical smoke already starting to billow out into the rest of the complex.

"Let's go, people!" he shouted.

THEY ESCAPED through the damaged window near the cells, out into a cold, gray day. The snow lay packed and deep, but it had a frozen crust and walking wasn't difficult.

It took them less than twenty unchallenged minutes to make their way around the outside of the institute and up toward the guarded sec barrier on the hillside at the neck of the valley. Ryan had anticipated trouble there, but the five or six sec men came out, hands high, weaponless.

"We saw what happened down there," said the oldest of them, pointing to the pall of smoke that hung over the white-walled building. Flames were already glowing through the roof, and a number of figures could be seen filing out of the destruction. "We got no quarrel no more with you."

"That's good," Ryan said. "You best go and join the others."

As soon as the sec men were on their way, he led the friends down the far side of the steep blacktop, on their way toward the redoubt.

Doc HAD BEEN in high spirits as they picked their path through the wintry landscape toward the redoubt, singing snatches from old half-remembered Christmas carols. Now that they were about to make the next jump, his good nature had abandoned him once more.

"I wish that we could simply make our way around this blighted country as God intended. We have seen in the last few days the sorry results of man setting himself over Nature. By the three Kennedys, but I would be a happier man if these matter transmitters had never been invented and Overproject Whisper had died along with the malignant brains that invented it."

"Come on, Doc," Krysty said. "Think of the excitement of never knowing where you're going to end up."

He patted her on the shoulder. "Better to travel hopefully, than to arrive, my dearest lady? We shall see."

They all eventually walked through the control room and into the gateway chamber itself, with its dark gray armaglass walls. Krysty shuddered as she sat between Dean and Mildred, leaving a space beside her for Ryan to occupy, after he'd closed the outer door and triggered the jump mechanism.

"Hope we don't all end up getting cloned," she said.

Mildred laughed, easing the tension. "I'm with you on that. Even one Doc Tanner's one too many."

Before the old man could reply, Ryan was with them, the door firmly shut.

He sat, feeling the familiar swirling in his brain, like feathery, exploring fingers. The disks in floor and ceiling began to glow, and the white mist appeared in the chamber.

He reached and clasped Krysty's hand in his, feeling the warmth and reassurance of her touch.

Ryan closed his eye and entered the darkness.

Take
4 explosive books
plus a
mystery bonus
FREE

Mail to: Gold Eagle Reader Service
3010 Walden Ave.
P.O. Box 1394
Buffalo, NY 14240-1394

YEAH! Rush me 4 FREE Gold Eagle novels and my FREE mystery gift.
Then send me 4 brand-new novels every other month as they come off
the presses. Bill me at the low price of just $14.80* for each shipment—
a saving of 12% off the cover prices for all four books! There is NO extra
charge for postage and handling! There is no minimum number of books I
must buy. I can always cancel at any time simply by returning a shipment
at your cost or by returning any shipping statement marked "cancel." Even
if I never buy another book from Gold Eagle, the 4 free books and surprise
gift are mine to keep forever.

164 BPM ANQY

Name _____ (PLEASE PRINT) _____

Address _____ Apt. No. _____

City _____ State _____ Zip _____

Signature (if under 18, parent or guardian must sign)

* Terms and prices subject to change without notice. Sales tax applicable in
  NY. This offer is limited to one order per household and not valid to
  present subscribers. Offer not available in Canada.

AC-94

In June, don't miss the second
fast-paced installment of

D. A. HODGMAN

STAKEOUT SQUAD

MIAMI HEAT

Miami's controversial crack police unit draws fire from all
directions—from city predators, local politicians and a
hostile media. In MIAMI HEAT, a gruesome wave of cult
murders has hit Miami, and Stakeout Squad is assigned
to guard potential victims. As panic grips the city, Stakeout
Squad is forced to go undercover...and dance with the
devil.

Don't miss MIAMI HEAT, the second installment of Gold
Eagle's newest action-packed series, STAKEOUT SQUAD!

Look for it in June, wherever Gold Eagle books are sold.